UNCLE
STORIES

J. P. Martin

Illustrated by Quentin Blake

RED
FOX

A Red Fox Book

Published by Random House Children's Books
20 Vauxhall Bridge Road, London SW1V 2SA
A division of The Random House Group Ltd

London Melbourne Sydney Auckland
Johannesburg and agencies throughout the world

Uncle first published in Great Britain by Jonathan Cape Ltd 1964
Copyright © text J.P. Martin 1964
Copyright © illustrations Quentin Blake 1964

Uncle Cleans Up first published in Great Britain by Jonathan Cape Ltd 1965
Copyright © text J.P. Martin 1965
Copyright © illustrations Quentin Blake 1965

3 5 7 9 10 8 6 4 2

This Red Fox edition 2000

Printed and bound in Great Britain by
Cox & Wyman Ltd, Reading, Berkshire

Papers used by The Random House Group Ltd are natural, recyclable
products made from wood grown in sustainable forests. The manufacturing
processes conform to the environmental regulations of the country of origin.

THE RANDOM HOUSE GROUP Limited Reg. No. 954009

www.randomhouse.co.uk

ISBN 0 09 941141 5

CONTENTS

UNCLE CLEANS UP

SOME OF THE CHARACTERS

Uncle's Followers ─────────────────────────

Rudolph
Auntie
The Companion
The Old Monkey
The Muncle
The One-Armed Badger
Butterskin Mute
Gubbins
Don Guzman
Dr Lyre
Noddy Ninety
The Maestro
The Little Lion
Mig
Whitebeard
Captain Walrus
The Old Man
Eva
Lilac Stamper
The Respectable Horses
Dr Bunker
Titus Wiley

Samuel Hardbake
Cheapman
Dearman
The King of the Badgers
The Marquis of Wolftown
Badgers
Wolves
leopards
Goodman
Cloutman
Cowgill
Noddy Ninety
Oldeboy
Whitebeard
Wizard Blenkinsop
Will Shudder
Mr Benskin
Joseph Cadcoon
Wisdom Sage
Needler
etc. etc.

The Badfort Crowd

Beaver Hateman
Nailrod Hateman (Sen.)
Nailrod Hateman (Jun.)
Filljug Hateman
Sigismund Hateman
Flabskin
Hitmouse
Mud-Dog
Oily Joe
Skinns
Crackbone
Hootman
Jellytussle
Abdullah the Clothes-Peg merchant
Toothie
The Wooden-Legged Donkey
The Bookman
Ghosts
Etc., etc.

Hated by Both Sides

Old Whitebeard

UNCLE

To
James, Andrew,
Alice, Judith, Matthew

1

A RIDE ROUND

Uncle is an elephant. He's immensely rich, and he's a B.A. He dresses well, generally in a purple dressing-gown, and often rides about on a traction engine, which he prefers to a car.

He lives in a house called Homeward, which is hard to describe, but try to think of about a hundred skyscrapers all joined together and surrounded by a moat with a drawbridge over it, and you'll get some idea of it. The towers are of many colours, and there are bathing pools and gardens among them, also switchback railways running from tower to tower, and water-chutes from top to bottom.

Many dwarfs live in the top storeys. They pay rent to Uncle every Saturday. It's only a farthing a week, but it mounts up when there are thousands of dwarfs.

There is one mysterious block in the middle called Lion Tower, which hardly anybody has been into. People have tried, but they get lost.

Exploring in Uncle's house is a tricky business, but there's one comfort, you are sure to come across something to eat, even if you have lost your way.

On the morning when this story starts, Uncle was waking in his room which looked out on to the moat.

His big bed was hung with red silk curtains, and they looked very grand in the morning sunlight.

In came the Old Monkey with a bucket of cocoa. He looks after Uncle very well because Uncle once saved him from a mean old stepfather who tried to sell him for sixpence. There are lots of other people who work for Uncle, but the Old Monkey is the chief one. They get on splendidly.,

"Good morning," said Uncle. "Anything happening over at Badfort?"

He drew the cocoa up with his trunk, and squirted it down his throat, never spilling a drop.

"Everything seems quiet, sir," said the Old Monkey, drawing the window curtains and picking up a telescope which lay on the sill. He focused it on a large ramshackle building about a mile away and reported: "Beaver Hateman is just setting off for a ride on the Wooden-Legged Donkey, and Hitmouse is washing up."

"Washing up, eh! They are peaceful," said Uncle. "It might be a good day for a ride round."

"Oh yes, sir, let's go, sir," said the Old Monkey,

enthusiastically. There is nothing he likes so much as a ride round.

"Perhaps they're turning over a new leaf at Badfort," said Uncle, the bed groaning and creaking as he got out of it.

The Old Monkey said nothing. He knew from past experience that this wasn't likely, but he put down the telescope.

"I'll go and get the ham ready, sir," he said.

Uncle picked up the telescope as soon as the Old Monkey had gone and had a look at Badfort himself. It's rather hard when you have a splendid house yourself that the chief view from your windows should be that of your enemy's dingy fortress, but this had to be endured, and it's quite useless to pretend that Uncle wasn't interested in the huge sprawl of

Badfort, and the unseemly Badfort crowd who inhabited it.

Since Uncle became rich the people who live at Badfort have been his chief critics. They are jealous of him, and are delighted when they discover anything against him. For instance, he used, when he was young, to find it difficult to tell the truth always, but he wasn't a very clever liar, because he couldn't help blowing softly through his trunk when he was telling a lie, and people got to know of this. Also he once borrowed a bicycle without permission when he was at the University, and, being rather heavy, broke it. People have long memories for such deeds in a great person.

It is hard to say who is the head of Badfort. Beaver Hateman is the most active person there, and he has two brothers called Nailrod and Filljug. Then there's a cousin called Sigismund Hateman. One of the most objectionable characters is Jellytussle. He is covered with shaking jelly of a bluish colour, and whenever he is about Uncle looks out for trouble. But perhaps it is safe to say that Hootman is the master spirit. Many people think he is a kind of ghost. Certainly he keeps in the background, but he works out many successful plots against Uncle.

Uncle looked with disapproval along the whole rickety length of Badfort, noting that there were more windows than ever stuffed with sacking. He changed the focus a little to look at the small Nissen hut outside the gate of Badfort. Yes, it was just as the Old Monkey had said. Hitmouse was washing up. Hitmouse, a little coward, who carried skewers as weapons, and who hated anybody else to be prosperous, lived a very untidy life. He had hundreds of cups and saucers, and he kept on using them till he had only a small place to sleep in near the door. When the muddle became unbearable he began to clean up.

"It may be a sign of trouble," said Uncle thoughtfully.

Then he got on with his dressing.

There are no stairs from Uncle's room. Instead he takes a big slide which lands him in the hall. When he wants to go up there's a moving rope at the side. He can get hold of this with his trunk and it draws him up very quickly.

The Old Monkey was soon hard at work supplying him with hams. The Young Monkey came stumbling in with a net full of cabbage, but he is no good as a waiter. He stutters and shuffles about. When Uncle blows through his trunk he shakes like a jelly.

"Well," said Uncle, "what's in the post this morning?"

"Just this," said the Old Monkey. He handed Uncle a cheque for £1,000 for the sale of maize, and a gold elephant's trunk ring weighing three pounds.

"Ring up Cowgill," said Uncle, "and tell him to get the traction engine ready."

Cowgill, the engineer, was once an enemy of Uncle's. He used to make splendid mechanical traps in the ground, and powerful steel catapults to discharge bags of ashes at him – a thing Uncle hated, for the ashes got up his trunk and spoilt his grandeur. However, that was a long time ago, and now all Cowgill's skill is at Uncle's disposal.

The traction engine was kept by him in first-class condition at his works, which are part of Uncle's house. It is painted red, but the big fly-wheel is polished brass. In front of the engine is a small brass elephant as a mascot. This is kept very bright, but someone from Badfort often succeeds in throwing mud over it. This makes Uncle furious, for he can't bear to see a spot on it. Uncle has a gilded armchair set among the coal, and there is a steam trumpet which makes a noise like an elephant. It's most thrilling to hear it.

Uncle, the Old Monkey and Cowgill set out.

"We'll call on Butterskin Mute on the way," said Uncle.

Mute is the best farmer in the neighbourhood, and he supplies Uncle with fresh vegetables. He's a little, smiling man, and he sometimes wears spade boots. These boots have short spades attached to them for digging.

"What's the matter, Mute?" asked Uncle, thinking the little man looked low-spirited today.

"Beaver Hateman and some of the others have been over in the night and stolen my largest pumpkins," said Butterskin Mute sadly. "Including one – a very big one – I was saving for you."

"Those miscreants shall not go unpunished," said Uncle. "Meanwhile, here is a bag of sugar, and a bag of coal from the traction engine to cheer you up. Now we must hurry on to Badgertown. We're lunching at Cheapman's today."

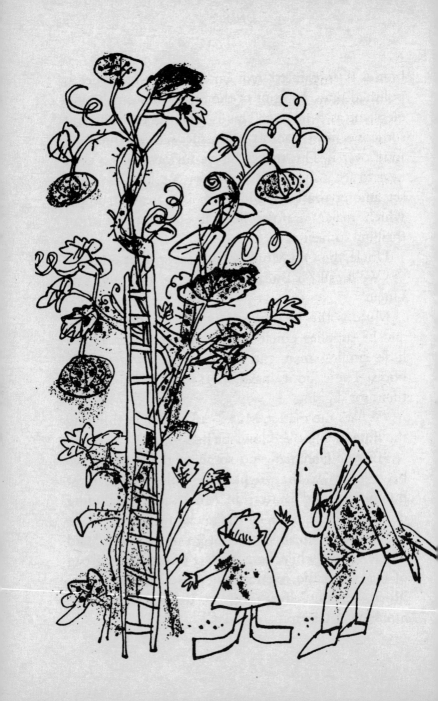

An old man called Alonzo S. Whitebeard has the farm next to Mute's. He has long white whiskers down to his feet, and he is a great miser. He has a silver sixpence as big as a millstone. It's two feet thick, and almost six feet high, and therefore almost impossible, even for the Badfort crowd, to steal. At night he sits and looks at it, and as they went past now they thought they caught sight of it through a window.

They neared the dark hulk of Badfort. On the way they passed Gaby's Marsh. The mud there is intensely sticky and infested by small savagely-biting fish called scobs. They are awful to eat.

"Beaver Hateman was catching scobs yesterday," said the Old Monkey.

"They must be getting hard up for food," said Uncle.

Everything seemed quiet at Badfort today. Nobody was sitting on the broken chairs outside the door, but as they got near, Beaver Hateman slid down the strong wire which is stretched from the door of Badfort to the door of Oily Joe's where they mostly do their shopping.

"He must have quarrelled with the Wooden-Leg," said Uncle.

Beaver Hateman and the Wooden-Legged Donkey are always together, and always quarrelling, but today the Wooden-Leg had remained behind. Perhaps it was he who put on a comic gramophone record as they passed a broken window — 'Uncle Goes Fishing'. There was a yell of laughter, but Cowgill put on speed, and also blew the steam trumpet, and they got past without further incident,

Badgertown is a large flat place inhabited by badgers of the most simple and credulous nature. In the middle of the town there is a huge building known as Cheapman's Store. It's really a delightful place. You can get things there for next to nothing. Nearly all the badgers shop there,

Of course there are other shops, but they have a struggle. They get what customers they can by weeping at their doors and entreating people to come in. Of course they can buy their own provisions at Cheapman's, but that naturally goes against the grain.

"What's the special line at Cheapman's today?" asked Uncle.

"Motor-bikes only a halfpenny each, and flour at four sacks a penny," said the Old Monkey with delight.

They went in, and Uncle ordered a halfpenny

lunch for himself, the Old Monkey and Cowgill.

"There are twenty-five courses, sir," said the Old Monkey, "and it will take about three hours to get through it."

"Oh well," said Uncle, "we might as well have it; we haven't got a lot on today."

At Cheapman's, instead of your tipping the waiter, *he* gives you a present. Today the waiter handed Uncle a parcel containing a sewing machine, seven pounds of chocolate and a very good brass trumpet.

"You can have the sewing machine," said Uncle to the Old Monkey. "It's a mystery to me how Cheapman makes his profits."

But make them he did. Cheapman is almost as rich as Uncle, and far richer than the King of the Badgers, who lives in a tumbledown palace on the edge of the town, and frequently has to arrange for loans from Uncle to tide him over difficulties.

They returned home a different way, a pleasant route through a deep lane with high hedges, but Uncle does not like it much, because it's a noted place for what he calls treachery.

"Run through the lane and keep the hooter going!" he said to Cowgill.

The latter replied by putting on all steam and raising a deafening roar from the steam trumpet.

As they brushed through some thick bushes Uncle filled his trunk from one of the buckets he always keeps filled on the traction engine, just in case.

But nothing happened. They came out into the open unmolested.

"What's happened to the Badfort crowd?" asked Uncle testily. "Are they losing their spirit or what? They've done nothing today!"

"Perhaps it's because you are going to give out bathing tickets this afternoon," suggested the Old Monkey. "Even the Badfort crowd like to go to the baths, sir."

"Glad you reminded me," said Uncle, feeling in the pocket of his dressing-gown for the bundle of tickets. "I'd almost forgotten."

Homeward looked magnificent as they rode towards it, the sun shining on its pink and green and blue towers. At the base of one, a train was unloading six thousand cases of oranges. They stopped to watch. This train backed out, and an equally long one came up loaded with pineapples. This had only just disappeared when another came whistling up loaded with sacks of raisins. Each sack was put into a kind of catapult and shot into a hatchway three storeys up. It was a very pretty sight.

When the Old Monkey blew a trumpet Uncle heard a shout from Beaver Hateman: "Bathing tickets for tomorrow!" – and turned to see a strange crowd assembled.

All the Badfort crowd were there behaving very

quietly for once. Whitebeard and his detestable step-father were in the front. Flabskin was there positively blubbering for a ticket, Beaver Hateman was holding out his hand in a lordly way, and the Wooden-Legged Donkey held out his leg which has a small receptacle at the end for cash, tickets, etc.

"Do you think they ought to be allowed to go to the baths?" asked the Old Monkey anxiously.

"Oh, I think they might for once," said Uncle, who was in a good humour after watching the fruit unloading. "They've been almost polite today."

Back at Badfort Beaver Hateman congratulated his followers on their good behaviour.

"We must plan for tomorrow," he said. "Some can be filling the waterpolo ball with glue and ink and tin-tacks, and remember to rub it thin in one place just before you throw it at the Old Monkey. Others can be putting drawing-pins in their bathing suits. The rest can get lunch ready."

"Wait until we get into those baths!" muttered Hitmouse. He began to foam at the mouth with a kind of green froth, a sure sign that he is getting jealous of Uncle.

2

UNCLE'S BATHS

You will want to hear more about these wonderful baths that aroused such interest even among the hardened inhabitants of Badfort. They are situated right in the midst of a group of towers. It is impossible to find them without a guide; even Uncle does not know the way there. When he wants to go, he rings up on the telephone:

WASH–HOUSES 39485765764756

He has it written on a card because it's not very easy to remember. But the moment after he gets through, a strong dwarf called Titus Wiley appears, carrying a bunch of keys in a leather wallet. The bath passage is at the side of the front door. It's handy, but mysterious. There's just a small keyhole, and the door is opened with an ordinary-looking key. But try to open it without that dwarf, and you will find your mistake.

Nailrod Hateman has spent hours working at the lock, and the Old Monkey has had many a go out of curiosity, but it's no good. They have to wait for Titus Wiley.

When Uncle came out to go to the baths, a motley crew were lined up along the moat. Beaver Hateman was at the front, of course, and Whitebeard at the rear, nearly out of sight at the end of a string of badgers. He was occupying his time while they waited in trying to catch some fishes in the moat.

"Are you all ready to go?" said Uncle.

"Yes, we are, and hurry up!" said Beaver Hateman snappishly. Uncle looked at him sternly, and then said:

"Well, you can all turn round, and march round the tower keeping exact order; then the first to arrive at the other side will lead the way. And, mind you, no pushing! When the party arrives at the other side Alonzo S. Whitebeard will be in front and Beaver Hateman last!"

Beaver Hateman bubbled with rage, but he was so anxious to get into the baths that he curbed his temper, merely pinching Nailrod, who was next to him.

Then Titus Wiley unlocked the door, and the march began. The passage was badly lit, and there seemed to be some rough work going on, for every now and then you could hear a yell from the badgers who marched in front and chunks of limestone could be seen hurtling through the air. However, they progressed fairly well. All at once they came to a place where the passage began to show holes at the side. Then it doubled back on itself, and you could see through these holes that the front of the procession had turned and was now moving in the opposite direction.

Uncle stopped the march for a moment.

"Last time when we reached this stage on our journey," he said, "we had considerable uproar, owing to some miscreants throwing things through the holes at their advancing friends. Let this happen again, and the rear part of the procession will be headed round, and you'll all be marched out."

This threat had a good effect, and the march continued in peace, except that Hitmouse tried to singe Whitebeard's whiskers as they blew through an opening.

Then, all at once, they drew up in a lofty vestibule. Over a wooden door were some words written on a card:

ENTRANCE TO BATH HOUSE

And, underneath, in small, neat handwriting:

Any person objectionable in his conduct will be refused entrance.

Uncle pointed to these words with his trunk, and said: "You will perhaps understand my hesitation in bringing you, when you read that!"

"Oh, shut up!" said Sigismund Hateman in a gentlemanly voice. "Really, I shall begin to wonder if it's worth while coming to your old baths, if you preach so much!"

This speech, however, was drowned in a chorus of howling. Everybody was anxious to get in. And here comes another mystery. These baths were of huge extent, and yet, judging by the way they had marched, they must be in the base of a small tower, next to Uncle's dining-room. They have all puzzled over this, but it's no use asking Titus Wiley. He simply grins, and says:

"There's a many things about baths, as people doesn't understand, as isn't employed there."

All the same, it's a bit irritating to consider that this vast expanse of water is so placed that, humanly speaking, it can't be there.

At last Titus Wiley turned the key in the door, and they marched in, and for the moment all strife was over.

They emerged into a building so colossal that the end of it was only a dim shadow. At their feet was the bath, the water of a pinkish colour and very clear.

The first thing to be seen was a gigantic human face carved out of stone, and about the size of a house. The mouth constantly ejected a stream of water ten feet broad. A good swimmer can swim up against the stream, and get inside the skull, where

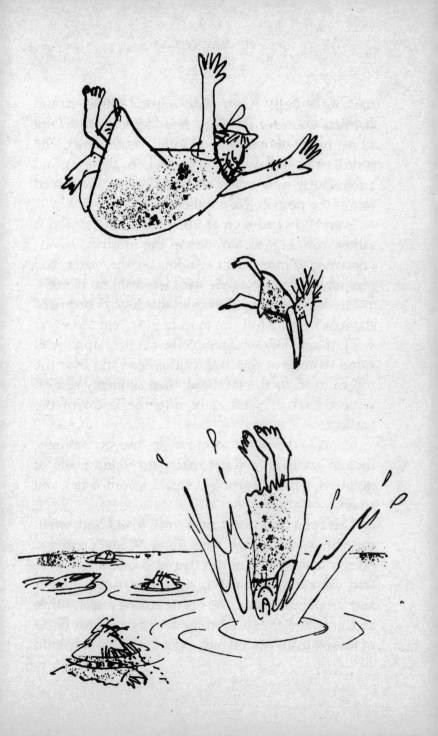

there is a large room with a path round it and swirling water for the floor. A ladder leads to a long stone room above with a water-chute down the nostrils. You just walk in at the side of the eyes, and are instantly caught by a stream of water, and forced out of the nostrils like a bullet.

Everybody had a go at this except Uncle, who is rather too big to go down the nostrils, so he contented himself with standing in the water, and playfully squirting people with jets from his trunk.

He did one thing, however, that always surprised them. When the fun was at its highest, and the water was just bubbling with people, he climbed up a broad stone staircase at the back of the head and over the top of it on to the forehead, then suddenly slid off with a terrific splash right into the midst of the bathers.

He gave the signal to move on, and, accordingly, they all swam to a water merry-go-round made of dolphins, whales, porpoises, sharks, sword-fishes, and so on.

This roundabout was on a small island, and, when the thing was going well, Titus Wiley pressed a button, and all the animals began to submerge.

It was a most fascinating sight. The pace got faster and faster. Everybody was nearly buried under water, and, at last, nothing was to be seen but a great circle of hissing foam from which came every possible kind of yell and scream from the trumpeting of Uncle to the thin piping voice of Alonzo S. Whitebeard.

After about ten minutes of this, the merry-go-round stopped and everybody was ready for the water-chutes. These were very fine. The biggest of them went up to such a height that the top was hidden in steamy mist.

By the side of the chute there was a kind of piston just projecting out of the water. People who sat on it were suddenly shot up towards the roof. When they got above the chute top they hovered and came gently to rest on the platform.

After the chute they had a go at the 'Skimmer', a thing like a sling that skimmed people over the surface of the water, just in the same way as a stone is skimmed. The Old Monkey won, making thirty-one dips.

By this time they were all ready for lunch, and Titus Wiley shouted:

"This way for the dining raft!"

This is a gigantic raft which goes round the baths while they have lunch. It's the only way to see the whole of the baths. It takes fully an hour to go round, and it does not move very slowly either.

On the raft was a huge pile of food: roast oxen, hams, dried goats' flesh, cart-loads of bananas, casks of lemonade, as well as ginger-beer and other liquids. A great loaf of hay as big as a haystack stands in the middle, and a huge cake built like a castle with a passage through it. You walk through the cake, and cut slices with your knife.

When they had all eaten as much as they wanted, and the Badfort crowd had positively stuffed themselves, Uncle looked at his watch, and said:

"Time's up. Everyone must clear out!"

"Do you think we're going to leave this bath now?" said Beaver Hateman, going menacingly up to Uncle.

"Yes, I do!"

"Well, you're jolly well wrong! I'm going to stay here all night, if I want to!"

Uncle was about to reply when Titus Wiley pulled his sleeve, and began to whisper in his ear.

Uncle smiled and nodded, and immediately motioned to the Old Monkey to call out that it was time to go home. Most of them were soon on the bank, but the Hateman crowd were still in the water, and were beginning to produce bladders of vinegar and other objectionable weapons.

Uncle said nothing, but just as the Badfort crowd floated together for a moment to discuss tactics, Titus Wiley pressed a button, and immediately a very strong current rushed out of the bath wall, and began to drive them all before it.

In vain they struggled. They were carried, a shouting mass, to the other side of the bath. There a door yawned for them, and they were instantly washed down a culvert, and hurled, a yelling, gibbering horde, into the moat.

"That's got rid of them," said Uncle gravely, and then, turning to Wiley: "That's a splendid idea of yours!"

"Well, I've thought it out on many a long summer afternoon," replied Wiley. "I call it the 'Whirlpool Chucker Out', and I think I can say as it's effective!"

3

THE CHALLENGE

At about eleven o'clock next morning, Uncle was aroused from the perusal of a very interesting book on the secret passages of Homeward.

The Old Monkey, who had been anxiously scanning the plain with field-glasses, said:

"Here's Jellytussle coming!"

Uncle grunted and went to the front door.

Sure enough, that very repulsive creature was crawling across the moat bridge. Jellytussle looked nearly as big as Uncle, but this was quite deceptive, as he was mostly jelly. He had small glittering eyes, and a large slippery mouth. He came on, holding in one paw a small tightly-rolled piece of parchment.

When he came near he began to bow in the strangest manner, very slowly, and yet the quivering jelly gave him the appearance of haste.

Uncle looked on contemptuously at this display of false homage, and held out his hand for the parchment.

It was written in blood, and read as follows:

To Uncle, the arch-humbug, impostor, and bully.

Yesterday your worst deeds were out-done. When you got us all spouted into the moat, you thought you had done something clever. Well, you've done yourself in by that foul, atrocious action. We give you three days in which to repent.

If at the end of that time you make your appearance at Badfort, with a bag containing a thousand gold pieces, and with a written apology in your hand, we will pardon you.

Otherwise, we shall attack your miserable old castle, and you yourself will know what it means to be imprisoned and publicly tortured.

We are signing this at midnight in our own blood. Our trusty messenger, Jellytussle, brings this.

We hope that we shall see him again alive, and if we don't, we shan't worry, as he's inclined to be too polite in giving his challenges.

> BEAVER HATEMAN
>
> NAILROD HATEMAN
>
> FILLJUG HATEMAN
>
> SIGISMUND HATEMAN
>
> J. HAWKINS FLABSKIN
>
> ISIDORE HITMOUSE
>
> WILLIAM MUD-DOG
>
> MALLET CRACKBONE

J. MERRYWEATHER OILER (OILY JOE)
H. SLIMEGROVE BINNS
JOSEPH SKINNS

And at the bottom, in thin, shadowy, spidery writing, Uncle could just make out the faint signature:

Firlon Hootman

Uncle said nothing, but he measured Jellytussle with his eye. He was going to kick him up. The Badfort crowd are tough and can stand being kicked, but they all hate being kicked up into the air.

He rushed at Jellytussle. There was a squelching thud and the body of the messenger could be seen rising in the air. He looked like an inflating balloon as strips of loose jelly floated round him. He sent out a thin piercing cry as he rose.

It was really a magnificent kick. Snatching up their field-glasses, Uncle's party saw the revolving body describe a stately arc, and then descend, slowly and majestically, into the very midst of the Badfort crowd who were feasting in front of Badfort.

Uncle was gratified to see that his missile had fallen right on to their plates, scattering their dinner and splashing them with hot gravy. Some ran about, clutching their scalded limbs. Some took out hating tablets and began to write methodically. At last, they

all gathered together, lifted up their hands, and sent forth a fierce yell of defiance in the direction of Homeward.

Uncle smiled.

"Well, whatever happens," he said, "that was a first-class kick. I don't know that I've ever given a better. And now let them come. I know quite well that they won't attack me for some time, because they are out of weapons. They've been selling their crossbows and duck bombs to buy bottles of Black Tom, so we're all right for a bit. However, I will just send a telegram to my brother Rudolph telling him to turn up."

Uncle's brother is a celebrated big-game hunter, and he always comes over to help Uncle when he is in serious trouble with the Badfort people.

He is always glad to come, for fighting the Badfort crowd can be excellent sport, but it takes him some time to come, because he's always abroad.

However, on this occasion, Uncle soon got a wire back:

```
HAVING  UNPRECEDENTED  SPORT  IN  WOLFLAND,
BAGGED  NINETEEN  MUSK-OXEN  AND  THIRTY-
NINE  GRIZZLIES.  COMING  AT  ONCE.  DO NOT
MEET  ME  AT  BADGERTOWN.          RUDOLPH
```

"Ah, he's coming to one of the other stations," said Uncle. "Now, we have a day or two before he comes. I've told Cowgill to prepare some vinegar squirts. Have the windows been well rubbed with Babble Trout Oil?"

Babble Trout Oil is a special preparation made from the babble trout, a small fish, difficult to catch. It renders glass tough, so that it is impervious to crossbow bolts and other missiles. Uncle often has his lower windows rubbed with it when trouble is threatening.

"And now," said Uncle, "I think we may as well do a little visiting in the towers. I think we'll call on the Old Man and Eva, and then go right up to the top of Lion Tower to call on Captain Walrus."

The Old Man and Eva live at the top of Homeward Tower. They make medicines for a living.

Only Uncle and the Old Monkey went on this trip, and they took nothing with them but sandwiches. They got into an express lift at the end of the hall, and were soon whizzed up the two hundred storeys.

There was a big field at the top, and some gardens. In the middle of the field was a small house, with a sign which completely covered one side of it:

THOMAS CLATWORTHY SPENCER LIBERTAS
SWEETWATER CLANJOHN BREWAGE
TEMPLETONJOYCE GLEAMHOUND

His real name is Mr Gleamhound, but he is nearly always called 'the Old Man'.

On the other side of the house was another sign:

PURVEYOR OF DRUGS. PROPRIETOR OF GLEAMHOUND'S
HEADACHE MIXTURE, GLEAMHOUND'S HEADACHE PRO-
DUCER (FOR ENEMIES), GLEAMHOUND'S HAIR TONIC,
GLEAMHOUND'S HAIR REMOVER, GLEAMHOUND'S FAT

REDUCER, GLEAMHOUND'S FATTENING MIXTURE FOR
THE THIN, GLEAMHOUND'S STOMACH JOY, ETC. ETC.

They are all very good, but they act the wrong way. For instance, his Headache Mixture gives you a frightful headache, his Jumbo Bunion Destroyer is well calculated to rouse bunions on a perfectly healthy foot. His Jacob's Well Eye Salve can put your eyes out of action for weeks, whereas his Punishment Eyesight Irritant (for enemies) will often cure people who have had to wear glasses for years.

Sitting in the house was Mr Gleamhound. He was perfectly bald, and wore immensely strong glasses over his inflamed eyes. He had been using his own hair restorer and eye salve for years.

Sitting on a low chair at his feet was Eva. Nobody seems to know her other names. She has always been with the Old Man, and he seems quite dependent on her.

"How are you getting on, Gleamhound?" said Uncle, carelessly seating himself on a bench.

"Oh, very well, very well indeed! After two thousand five hundred and eighty experiments, I have at last succeeded in making a nail-biting cure that is satisfactory."

He glanced back as he spoke into his laboratory. It was large; in fact it seemed to take up almost the whole of the house.

On a blackboard, they could see chalked:

EXPERIMENT 2978
  Mix mortar with arrowroot, and boil with gum
mastic.

                    (Unsuccessful)

EXPERIMENT 2979
  Boil shavings of parrot's bill with chopped hair
and peroxide.

                    (Unsuccessful)

EXPERIMENT 2980
  Boil Arnica and Lime in equal parts for the third
of a day; thoroughly souse with rinsings from an old
nitre vat, then pour in one oz. peppermint, reduce to
a jelly, and with great speed whirl in a hot
aluminium pan, taking care to avoid direct sunbeams.

Then, lightly rub in flaked rice, ginger, rhubarb, and orris root, in the proportions of 6 — 313/8 — 9 and 271/8, at the same time shaking in equal portions of boiled candy and lemon curd.

Repeat thirty-one times.

(Successful!!!)

Uncle congratulated him and bought a bottle of Indigestion Producer (for enemies) and also a bottle of Stomach Joy, which was supposed to cure all forms of indigestion.

Then he took his leave, depositing, as he did so, five shillings on the table.

The Old Man's weary eyes gleamed, and he immediately shut up the laboratory for the day, and departed with Eva to Cheapman's Store, where they had a famous lunch, and departed at closing time with a well-filled truck of provisions and with threepence of the five shillings gone for ever.

Meanwhile, Uncle was proceeding to the very top of Lion Tower. He paused on the way to the elevator, and looked in at a small Post Office, from where he dispatched the bottle of Stomach Joy to Beaver Hateman.

"That'll give him something to think about," he said, "and, as I've been feeling a little groggy, I'll just take a spoonful of the Indigestion Producer (for enemies) now." He did so, and gave one to the Old

Monkey, and they both felt warm and braced.

Then they got into the elevator and after about ten minutes they got out at Summit Station.

Summit Station is at the very top of Lion Tower. It is so high that the whole tower bends in the wind. However, Captain Walrus lives at the top of a still smaller tower called Walrus Tower, which stands like a pencil at the edge of Lion Tower, and, if Lion Tower bends in the wind, Walrus Tower positively seems to flap to and fro when there is a gale. But this does not worry Captain Walrus. He actually lives in the top storey of a very slender lighthouse at the top of Walrus Tower, and, rough old sea-dog that he is, he seems really to enjoy the sensation of constant swaying.

He is a staunch friend of Uncle's, and when he heard that there was likely to be trouble with the Hateman crowd, he cheerfully rubbed his hands.

"It's high time those swabs had a lesson!" he said. "I thought something might be in the wind, so I've been getting ready a few extra marlinspikes. Call upon me when you want me, and in the meantime I'll keep a close watch on them through the glasses."

Uncle thanked him for his help, and after a short talk they went back, because the lighthouse swayed so very much that they were in danger of being sick, in spite of the strengthening tonic they had taken on the way.

4

THE MUNCLE

Uncle always gets a lot of letters, but the Old Monkey does not often have one. However, next day he got one that filled him with joy.

"Oh, sir," he said, "my uncle is coming to see me!"

The Old Monkey's uncle is called the Muncle and he's a very nice person, but seems to live for footwear. Uncle likes him, but thinks he is a bit too fussy about shoes.

However, he told the Old Monkey that the Muncle would be welcome, and, about half an hour later, just as he had settled down to his paper, the Muncle arrived. He was wearing an enormous pair of travelling boots. These have electric motors in their soles so that they can run along with him, and they come up so high that he can lean on the top edges. He always keeps a lot of stuff in them, including several pairs of smaller boots and shoes.

He came scooting over the drawbridge with an anxious expression, then drew up with a joyous shout. "Not a spot of mud on them!"

He is always terribly afraid, when he comes to visit Uncle, that Beaver Hateman, the leader of the Badfort crowd, may splash his boots with mud. Beaver Hateman always tries to. But today he had seen nothing of him.

He sat down by the open window with a smiling face.

"So glad to see you, sir, and also my nephew. He looks well, though I am sorry to see his shoes are dusty. Nephew, open the right-side compartment in my travelling boots and you'll find a pair of dove-coloured visiting shoes. Ah, that's a relief. My travelling boots are rather heavy."

Then he looked keenly at Uncle and said: "Excuse my saying so, sir, but your shoes are somewhat shabby. I wonder if you'd gratify me by putting on a really nice pair?"

Uncle said to the Old Monkey:

"Just look in my number eight shoe saloon, and on the fourth shelf to the left you'll find a pair of red ones; I rather think it's the sixty-ninth pair from the door. Bring them here."

The Muncle seemed deeply impressed by this speech. He had never imagined that even Uncle possessed such a vast stock. He was still more deeply moved when the Old Monkey appeared with an exquisitely shaped pair of elephant's morning shoes of a deep red colour.

"Oh, those look very well, sir!" he cried, in a rather envious voice. He was thinking hard how he might regain his lost ground as a shoe expert.

Then his face brightened, and he drew some papers from his pocket.

"These verses," he said, "were written by our local poet, and I thought so highly of them that I had a hundred copies printed. There's one for each of you, and perhaps my nephew wouldn't mind reading the poem aloud. I know you are fond of poetry, sir."

As a matter of fact Uncle is not very fond of poetry, as he is everlastingly having it spouted at him by friend and enemy alike, but he resigned himself to the hearing.

The Old Monkey began to read in a low, well-modulated voice:

THE FOOT-LOVER
or
A Well-Spent Day

When in the morn he waketh
His *shoes* are all his care;
Heheedeth not his jacket
on them he doth stare.

Down the deep stairs he falleth;
For pain he does not care,
For on his *back* he landeth,
His *shoes* are in the air!

He hath a pleasant breakfast,
His well-brushed *shoes* are there;
His bacon tastes like nectar
As on them he doth stare.

At last he starts for business,
His eyes are on his *feet*,
Then the wrong bus he catcheth,
And reacheth the wrong street.

It went on verse after verse, all about shoes.

When the poem was finished, Uncle sat still for a long time.

"Well, what do you think of it ?" said the Muncle

eagerly.

"I think as a poem it's moderately good," replied Uncle, "but I also think you are going too far in your craze for shoes. Shoes are good things, but we should not make them the sole object of life."

Here he was interrupted, as a shadow fell upon them from the window.

Standing there was a great hulking man wearing a suit made of a sack with holes in it for arms and legs.

One look was enough.

It was Beaver Hateman.

"How do, Uncle!" he said. "I see you've got the Muncle here. I nearly got him on the way. He just slipped past in time, or I'd have splashed his precious boots for him all right. However . . ."

He gave a loud whistle, and two of his friends who had been concealed in the ivy around the window suddenly rushed out with buckets of mud and threw them like lightning over the shoes of Uncle and his visitor.

"After them!" shouted Uncle, filling his trunk with water from a jug on the sideboard.

Uncle thundered over the drawbridge.

"Watch the bank!" he shouted.

Would you believe it, the miscreant came into view just at Uncle's feet, where he least expected him, and dashed into the bushes at such a rate that it was impossible to overtake him.

"We might as well give it up, sir," said the Old Monkey. He was secretly laughing because Uncle had fallen over a tree trunk, and one tusk was fast in the ground. He got it out after a while, and with much trumpeting and blowing made his way back to the house.

"All right, Mr Hateman," he muttered, "I will remember this, and your punishment shall be swift and sure!"

They found the Muncle in very low spirits. "My visiting boots are ruined!" he said in a sad voice.

"That's all right," replied Uncle. "Give him a new pair from the store," he told the Old Monkey. "And now, to take my mind off this disgraceful episode, I'll just look through the second mail, which I see has come."

Uncle began to comfort himself by counting over the cash that had come in that morning. There was only a cheque for £2,570 for the sale of maize. He looked at it rather gloomily, and said to the Old

Monkey:

"Not much cash in this morning. What are the expenses for the day?"

The Old Monkey is really very quick. He had it all written out on a small wooden board that he keeps by his chair.

Foodstuffs	£150
Ironmongery	15
Laundry	12
Wages of Staff	1
Total	£178

"That's too much!" said Uncle quickly. "You must cut something down."

However, he gave the Old Monkey £178 0s. 0½d. The halfpenny was a present and he thankfully pocketed it.

You'll think that Uncle's wage bill was small, but you must remember that everyone gets presents as well. Uncle pays very few people more than a halfpenny a week, but still it's a very good thing to work for him. He thinks nothing of giving every one of his staff a hundredweight of butter or twenty hams. They are all pretty well off, and the Old Monkey is positively rich. Besides his stores of tinned foods he has whole boxes full of clothes and books, and about twenty gramophones.

5

A JOURNEY TO THE OIL TANKS

Uncle looked at his watch after breakfast next day, and then consulted a great red calendar that hangs on the wall over the fireplace.

"It's about time I went to see the oil lake again," he said. "I'd like to fit in a visit before anything happens at Badfort."

The Old Monkey's eyes brightened. He likes this expedition very much, because it's rather out of the ordinary.

So they soon gathered up their things, and started off. They only took the One-Armed Badger with them this time, because it's a dangerous place, and they don't want any people with them who are likely to fool about and cause trouble. The One-Armed Badger is an excellent worker, everlastingly scrubbing things. He is trustworthy and good at carrying blankets, baskets of buttered biscuits, bottles of meat extract, etc.

You pass through a little doorway in Uncle's kitchen when you want to go to the oil lake.

The kitchen is huge, partly underground, and all in charge of the little dwarf, Mig. There's a great roasting fire on one side, which lights up the whole place, but most of the cooking is done on the oxy-acetylene gas stove. This oxy-acetylene burner is so hot that it can melt iron like butter. The consequence is that Mig can boil a kettleful of water in a second. He stands on the gas stove to work and wears dark glasses, or else the glare would ruin his eyes.

The way to the oil lake is just behind the stove. The stove runs out from the wall on rails, and behind it you see the opening of a passage.

But, when you're in, you are still confronted with difficulties.

There are seven steel doors to unlock, each one with a very complicated set of keys, and between each door is a short passage paved with very slippery round stones.

When you have passed through the last door, however, it's pretty easy. You just slide down a well-oiled slope to the lake.

Uncle likes to do this very quietly, because then he can see what the man who looks after the lake is doing. They slid down very gently, and glided along the margin. The lake is huge in size and very

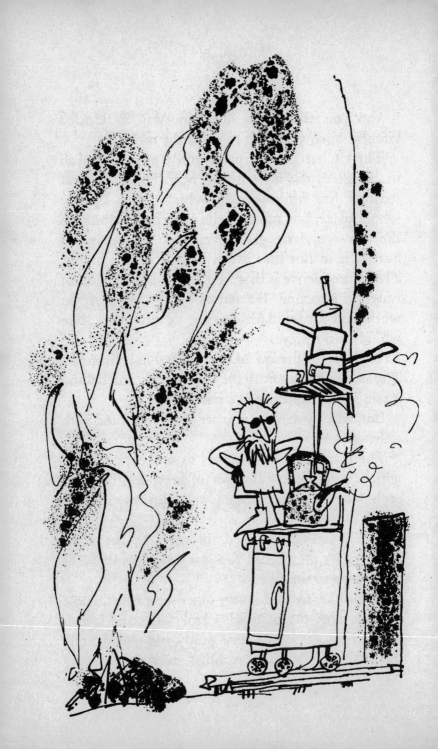

charming to look at, although it's underground, because it's lit up by thousands of electric bulbs of all colours.

Uncle knows just where the man who watches the lake can be found.

"That's the place," he said. "Round that craggy corner."

When they got near the corner, Uncle crept forward and peeped round the cliff. Then he motioned to the Old Monkey to come to his side.

This is what they saw.

In front of them a barge was moored in the lake. Sitting in it, smoking a large cigar, was a little dark oily man. By his side there was a basket of fruit and nuts. He was reading an evening paper.

"Smoking!" hissed Uncle to the Old Monkey in a tense whisper. Just as he spoke, the little man, finding that the cigar had gone out, lit it again with a match, and actually threw the match into the oil lake.

That was enough for Uncle. With a loud trumpet of rage, he turned the corner, and charged down towards the lake. The moment the little man heard him he thrust the cigar out of sight like lightning. At the same time he hid the fruit, and commenced to pull very hard on a rope, calling out as he did so the words of a heaving song:

AH, EETCHA, EETCHA, E E T C H A A–H!" With every 'eetcha' he gave a tug at the rope.

Uncle, however, was not deceived by this display of energy.

He called out to him loudly:

"Guzman, bring that barge into shore at once!"

Guzman is the name of the man; he claims to be a Don, or Spanish gentleman, from Andalusia. He says he lost all his money by speculating in silver foxes; and he's working for Uncle till he gets enough money to retire. He speaks English with rather a rough accent, as he learned it at a sailors' lodging house near the docks when he landed penniless in England many years ago.

The Don sulkily pulled the barge to shore.

"You were smoking," said Uncle testily.

Uncle is very much against smoking on the oil lake, because it's extremely likely that one day the whole place will catch fire. Now Guzman is a thoroughly good oil watcher in every other way, and looks after the lake well, but he will smoke, and this makes Uncle very doubtful about keeping him.

"Good morning, sir," said the Don respectfully.

"You were smoking on the barge!" said Uncle sternly. "I saw the cigar!"

"Cigar!" replied Guzman incredulously. "You must be wrong. It's a reflection on the oil! I often sits watchin' the oil, and when there's a bit of a eddy, it takes all shapes, looks like a barrel or a jug, but specially like a cigar. Often I've said to myself, as I've watched 'em, 'That's a cigar!' and then I've seen it melt away and vanish in the stream."

"Liar!" said Uncle fiercely, and then, pointing to the oil: "Look at all those dead matches! Why, you madman, you've actually been throwing matches into the oil!"

The Don looked staggered. At last he said: "Well, I don't see the harm of an occasional smoke, sir. It gets a bit dull down 'ere continually watchin' the oil. Now, when I was at home in Andalusia, I 'ad my man ter waken me in the morning just as you 'ave, and 'e used ter sing a song as 'e 'ad made. It went like this:

"*Don Guzman, Don Guzman, I call you to the meal;*
Don Guzman, Don Guzman, the price is but one real;
There's hot baconario, and bread and buttario,
Besides a cupario of tea,
So get up your couragio, eat up your poragio,
And feast in the estancia with me!

"Now, I think you'll admit, sir, that after a life of that kind, I need some little solace here!"

Uncle began to relent. It's always the same with the Don – he talks Uncle round.

Soon they were quite friendly again.

The Don talks about his hardships, but after all he doesn't have a bad time. If ever he wants to get away from the lake, he has only to press a button in the wall on the opposite bank, and he finds himself in a cool green meadow at the foot of some gigantic tower.

After a while the Don looked at his watch and said: "I vote we 'ave breakfast; it's half past two!"

It's a funny thing about the Don, he always breakfasts at this time.

As they went in Guzman said: "Now, I've got a old custom as I 'ope you won't mind observin'. I pays for my own meals, and any guests as comes usually doesn't mind dubbin' up a real or so."

He looked up doubtfully as he said this, but Uncle nodded carelessly, so he was reassured.

After a bit, his servant Gaberonez began to sing in the dining-room. It was the song that Guzman had recited to them; he had not mentioned that he still had a servant when speaking of his hardships.

They all walked into the dining-room.

On the table was a large money-box, labelled:

FUND FOR RETIREMENT TO ANDALUSIA.

Uncle dropped in a pound note, and a shilling each for the Old Monkey and the One-Armed Badger, while Guzman himself contributed a real.

The breakfast was a capital one, except for the porridge which was lumpy and sour, but the Don insisted that they should have some, as that was how people liked it in Andalusia. After that, the meal was faultless. The bacon was crisp and plentiful, and so was the toast.

As they sat down in the lounge, nourished and refreshed, Uncle said: "I say, old chap, that money-box seems pretty full; I should think you have nearly enough to retire to Andalusia."

"Oh, some day, some day," replied the Don carelessly. "It's not so bad here, and you must admit that I do the job well. I watch the tank from mornin' to night, and it takes some watchin'. Take them dwarfs now! They're always gettin' in through a place where there's a crack in the wall. They carries jugs with 'em, and tries to sneak the fluid. But I comes up softly, and bangs their jugs on their little bald 'eads.

That settles 'em for the time."

Uncle applauded this display of zeal, and then the Don said:

"'Ow would yer like to go for a pull on the lake?"

"Very much indeed," said Uncle.

They got into the barge, which was pulled across the lake by a rope. Uncle noticed Gaberonez did all the pulling while the Don sat dreamily in the stern chanting an old Spanish work song which he interpreted as meaning:

> Pull slaves pull!
> Our souls are in the rope!
> One day we shall pull, pull, pull,
> Till the rope breaks.

They reached the other side and got out.

After the somewhat stuffy atmosphere of the oil lake they all felt the need of a little fresh air, so they said goodbye to Don Guzman and looked round for a new way home.

They were wondering which direction to take when the Old Monkey found a kind of fire-escape, stretching both up and down the outside of a tower as far as they could see.

Uncle tossed a penny for choice of route. It fell down the ladder, and was immediately snatched by a dwarf who was looking out of a window.

"That means we go up," said Uncle.

After going up about twenty flights of massive iron stairs, they came out on the top of an immense lonely tower. It had a perfectly flat top, without a rail of any kind, and looked very wind-swept and unsafe. At the very edge a huge fire was burning, and beside this lounged a couple of leopards. One of them was resting so carelessly that part of his body was actually hanging over the abyss. It looked awful, for down below you could see rows and rows of windows getting smaller and smaller, and at the very bottom a railway train that looked like a toy. The two leopards were cooking a large joint of pork over the flame. A little of the gravy kept running down the wall, to be licked up by a dwarf leaning out of a window below.

Uncle asked them the price of a share.

They consulted together for a bit, and then one of them came up touching his cap.

"Two bob a slice, sir," he said.

"Two bob!" said Uncle, blowing through his trunk. "I'll give you a penny, and no more!"

They were about to refuse, but the Old Monkey whispered to them for a moment.

"Well, sir," one of them said, "it's rather hard on poor blokes like us, but you shall have it for a penny ... and if you feel like making us a little present ..."

Uncle smiled, and he gave them two large baskets of buttered biscuits, a coil of rope, seven bottles of meat extract, and a tin of Magic Ointment. They were specially glad to have this, because one of them had a sore paw, and the other one had a sick wife who had injured herself by falling off a tower.

By this time the sun was setting, and Uncle wanted to get back. Before they went they walked to the other side of the tower and looked over. Far below they saw Homeward Tower looking very small. Then came the moat and some fields and then the vast bulk of Badfort.

Uncle got out his telescope and looked through it.

"I can see Beaver Hateman, Nailrod Hateman, Sigismund Hateman, Flabskin, and the Wooden-Legged Donkey, all sitting in a circle and drinking Black Tom," he muttered.

"Can I have a look, sir?" asked the Old Monkey.

"No," said Uncle severely, without taking the telescope from his eye. "You don't want to look at those disgraceful hounds! Let's go home another way," he added. "I'm not going to climb down all those ladders again."

"Begging your pardon, sir," said one of the leopards, "if you want to get to Homeward, the best way is to use the iron dive."

"What's that?"

"Come here, sir."

He led them to another side of the tower.

"You just jump off here one at a time, and you fall

on an iron platform that springs."

"But are you sure that it's safe?"

"Sure? . . . Why I'm going that way home myself, so I'll make the first dive. It's balanced on hair-springs at the top, then bigger springs, then bigger ones still. You bounce a bit, but it soon settles. I'll show you. Just make a bundle of my share of the pig and buttered biscuit, and throw it after me," he added to his companion.

He took the dive, turning over and over in the air. After he had fallen about a hundred storeys he struck the platform, which gave way and then sprang back. He bounced for a bit, and then they heard a faint roar from below which showed that he was all right. His goods were flung after him. He gathered them together and slunk off the platform, so they concluded that it would be safe to try the dive.

"You'd like to go first, sir?" said the Old Monkey.

"No, you can go."

The Old Monkey took the jump, and seemed to take a long time to fall. However, he signalled that he was all right.

Then Uncle took the plunge. He hit the platform with a great clanging noise, bumped heavily, and then came to rest.

"I say," he said to the Old Monkey, "we must do this again; it's grand. We'll come here another day soon."

They all agreed that it was a splendid sensation. There was a useful little railway at the foot of the tower on which they ran home in about ten minutes.

That evening Uncle was in such good spirits that he treated everyone to roast turkey and sausage, and he also gave them all good presents. They had six tins of fruit each for one thing, and Uncle also gave the Old Monkey a good suit of clothes and a handbag.

So they all went cheerfully to bed.

6

MISS MAIDY AND DR LYRE

There were two more things Uncle wanted to do before Rudolf arrived. One was to inspect Dr Augustus Lyre's school of which he is a Governor, and the other was to visit an Aunt of his who lives near the top of the highest tower, called Afghan Flats,.Her name is Miss Evelyn Maidy, but she is always called Auntie.

So he set out, taking a few presents with him: a sack of tinned tongues, and a box of oranges. They were carried very willingly by the One-Armed Badger, who also insisted on stacking a suitcase on the top of them, with bandages, ointment, lamps, and spare rations, and some socks for Uncle, in case his feet got tired.

The Old Monkey was there, of course, and the little kitchen dwarf Mig and the Muncle.

"What time shall we get to Dr Lyre's school?" asked the Old Monkey eagerly. "I want to see if that old man Noddy Ninety who works on the tube trains is really there. He dresses up as a boy, sir, and goes to school for fun."

"We'll have a cup of tea with Auntie and go straight afterwards," Uncle promised.

They went up in the spiral lift. This is rather like an ordinary lift, but it keeps going round and round. It's very handy for going up a high tower. It never stops, but it slows down when it reaches the storey you want, and you just step off.

Afghan Flats is not in a very nice neighbourhood. It's full of thousands of dwarfs of the most cross and irritable disposition. You'll wonder why Auntie lives there. I'll tell you. It's because she loves domineering over the dwarfs, and I really believe they like having her there, though they are always having disputes.

Her lady companion is called Miss Wace. When Uncle reached Auntie's street, he asked a dwarf, who was eating a lemon, if he knew which was her house.

"You're her nephew, are you? You look like her — self-important."

Uncle moved towards him menacingly, but he slipped down a side passage.

After a while they came to a very neatly-painted door. On it was a plate:

```
MISS MAIDY AND COMPANION
```

They knocked, and the Companion opened the door. She seemed weak and helpless.

"Oh, sir," she said, "this is good of you. I'm sorry that Miss Maidy is just lying down; one of those wretched dwarfs upset her just now!"

Just as she said these words, another door opened, and Auntie appeared. She had a big bruise on her forehead, but it was rapidly disappearing under the influence of a tin of Magic Ointment, which she held in her hand.

"So glad to see you, dear!" she said.

Uncle doesn't like to be called 'dear', but he has to put up with it.

Uncle motioned to the door, and the Old Monkey led in the One-Armed Badger, who shuffled clumsily along, almost hidden under the great orange-box and other things that he was carrying.

"A few presents for you," said Uncle.

"Oh, that's very good. I'm always short of fruit, and there isn't a decent shop about here."

"Well, why don't you go to Cheapman's?"

"Oh, Cheapman's is all right, but the trouble is getting there. I suppose I shall have to stick to the wretched little shop at the corner of the street. I've had great trouble with the proprietor, a miserable dwarf called Rugbo."

At that moment, there was a knock at the door, and a shout: "MILK O."

Auntie jumped up, her headache forgotten.

"Excuse me a minute, I've just got to settle with this horrible little man. Last time he put a frog in the milk!"

She clutched her umbrella firmly, and went out. Next minute, they heard the noise of a heavy blow, followed by hissing and screeching.

"Now, that's done it!" said the Companion. "She'll come back streaming with milk, and as weak and nervous as a kitten, and I shall have the job of calming her feelings."

Uncle said nothing. He is used to his Aunt's curious ways, so he settled down comfortably in a chair, and had a look round the room, which is hung with diplomas. Auntie has won many prizes for ju-jitsu and wrestling; though in actual life she appears to do everything with her umbrella.

Just as he was looking at these things, they heard footsteps, and Auntie stepped in, humming a tune.

"Just give me a rub down, Wacy," she said.

"How did you get on?" asked the Companion eagerly.

"Oh, very well, very well indeed. I don't think he'll try his tricks again for a bit. I pushed him into the non-stop lift. It only goes up and down once a day, so he's off for a bit, unless he likes to climb six hundred flights of stairs."

"Well, dear, I've been neglecting you," she said, smiling at Uncle, "and the Old Monkey. He's a dear! I really envy you the Old Monkey. Get the tea, Wacy."

The Companion soon had a very choice meal set out, and Auntie seemed glad to exchange a little news.

"You seem to have all the luck, dear," she said. "We hear about your grand times, your thousands of cartloads of good things and cheques for maize. I don't know how you do it! I'm hard up myself. The wear and tear of things is incredible up here. Six chairs smashed yesterday, and the whole of my larder cleared out again! I'm sure I try to help the dwarfs, but they are so sly and cunning."

They listened to some of Auntie's gramophone

records after tea and then took the switchback to Dr Lyre's school.

Warm and glowing they alighted on a green, and were confronted by a long low set of rooms on the bottom storey of a massive tower. There was a rookery twenty storeys up, and some ravens seemed to have nested on a ledge thirty storeys higher still, while right at the top a pair of majestic eagles were slowly circling. A board was hung at the door.

DR AUGUSTUS LYRE
Select School for Young Gentlemen

Dr Lyre has an unfortunate name. His real name is simply 'Liar'. That's how you spell it, and he can't change it because he has had money left him on that condition. He usually spells it 'Lyre' – only sometimes he forgets, being absent-minded, and signs his letters 'A. Liar', and this amuses the boys very much.

When Uncle's party entered the school house, they found it somewhat dark, but a very pretty place. The lamps, though dim, were pink and orange, and the desks were made of blocks of polished cast iron, and shone with many reflections.

The Doctor was sitting in a large railed-in desk-compartment at one end, and the room was so long that it must have been hard for him to see the boys

in the back rows. But the room was full of underground passages. If a boy wanted to see the Doctor, he dived into a hole by his desk, walked along a passage, and came up a short flight of steps near the Doctor's desk.

The Doctor has a bundle of great canes by his desk, and a thing like a flail, which he slaps down on his desk with a noise like thunder.

He seemed glad to see Uncle, for Uncle is the chairman of his Board of Governors. He called some of the senior boys to read aloud. They are not allowed to do this until they reach the top form, and then they do it all the time and all together.

They were reading a book written by the Doctor himself about the history of Lion Tower; that's the huge tower in the middle of Homeward, which has never been fully explored. According to the Doctor it was built in 1066, and that's one date every boy has to learn, or he can't get his G.C.E. According to Uncle the tower was built by Wizard Blenkinsop only twenty years ago, and some of the boys know this and say that the Doctor's book is all wrong. But when they want to put him in a good temper, they all shout together "1066! 1066!" and that makes the old man purr.

When Uncle visits the school the Doctor turns to a page in the book where it describes the day on which Uncle visited Lion Tower and erected 144 drinking fountains for the dwarfs. That's in the modern history section, on page 11,564, only three pages from the end of the book. It's a big book, and expensive, but you've got to buy a copy or you can't get your G.C.E.

Uncle walked quietly to the back of the school-room, for he wanted to see if Noddy Ninety was there that day.

Yes, there he was. The Old Monkey knew him at once. What a spectacle! Imagine an old man of ninety disguised as a schoolboy of ten. He was wearing a little grey flannel jacket, and had a flaxen wig on his bald head.

Noddy Ninety loves to get into the bottom form and pretend he's a schoolboy. Then he has an easy time, because he knows the work, and also he seems to enjoy making himself a nuisance. He's had ninety years experience of every schoolboy trick imaginable, from putting tacks on seats to throwing ink.

He has more than twenty-five ways of stealing boys' lunches, and as for stealing caps and mufflers, well, they mostly keep them on, or they're gone at the end of the afternoon. He has been expelled from the school time and time again, yet he worms his way in again so cunningly that it's only after several weeks that he is found out.

As a matter of fact, they'd really like to have him in the school if only he'd behave decently, for he knows all the work, and goes up from form to form with amazing rapidity, starting with algebra in the bottom form on Monday, and finishing by reading aloud in the top form on Friday afternoon. He yells "1066! 1066!" when he has nothing else to do, and the Doctor, who is rather deaf, likes to hear him.

Then he is very fond of games. His favourite game is cricket, and he's got a special bat. When he plays he presses a button in the handle, and the bat spreads out more than a foot wide. It's quite impossible to get him out.

The Doctor has a megaphone, and when he uses it you can hear him well all over that vast place.

"We will adjourn for games," he said. "A match will be played against a team of fully grown dwarfs from Tower 117. They call themselves the Roast Chestnuts."

Here Noddy Ninety, who had pushed up to the front, said in his piercing voice, "Put me in last, and all of you get out for ducks."

Everybody laughed at this, and they adjourned to the green outside, to find that the team of dwarfs had already arrived. They had all been lowered by ropes and pulleys from an immense shelf of building some fifty storeys up.

The Doctor escaped to his study, which is on the first storey and overlooks the pitch. He really hates watching games, but now and then he comes to the window and shouts as if he were interested.

They soon started the match. The Roast Chestnuts went in first, and a fine score they made. They actually made 1,027 before they were out. One dwarf, an excitable little chap called Whiffam, hit a hundred fours without a break.

At last he was caught out by Noddy Ninety, who at that moment was not looking at the game, but was holding out his hands for a meat pie which a dwarf was offering him from a second-storey window. The ball hit a wall, and bounced into his hands, so Whiffam was out.

The Roast Chestnuts were very much elated at the score, and promised each other such treats as boiled jelly-fish, ram-marrow tarts, and a kind of sweet called "Coggins" to celebrate. Their spirits rose still higher when Dr Lyre's boys had their innings, for they were all coming out for ducks. Whiffam was a good bowler too, and as stump after stump fell he leaped for joy.

At last Ninety went in, carrying his celebrated bat. At first he pretended to play very badly, and nearly came out.

Whiffam gave an elated cry, and sent down a fast one. Ninety hit this very quickly right on to Whiffam's bald head. It glanced off, and he scored two.

Then he began to hit out. He can hit the ball anywhere he likes. He put one ball through Dr Lyre's study window. It came crashing on to his desk and smashed an ink bottle, and the Doctor, though secretly annoyed, went to the window, and shouted "Well played!"

When Noddy Ninety was tired of hitting sixes, he began to get under the ball and hit up. He sent a ball up with such force that it hit one of the eagles that was floating about near the top of the towers, and the infuriated bird came down and attacked him.

By this time a tremendous crowd of onlookers had gathered. Thousands of windows had opened, but it was somewhat dangerous to look out of them with Noddy batting.

Finally, when only a six was wanted to win, Noddy Ninety got right underneath a slow ball, and really lifted it into the air. They watched it soar up and up until it became a speck, then it gradually curved over the tower and vanished.

There was a resounding cheer, and even the dwarfs, though malicious in disposition, seemed to be pleased at Ninety's wonderful display.

By this time the sun was setting. It soon gets dark amid those vast mountains of stone, and Uncle's party decided to go home.

They went back a different way.

They took a circular staircase to the seventh storey, where they found a man in an oyster stall who directed them to a long broad passage hung with red cloth. It ran downwards, and in the middle a stream of oil flowed rapidly. I think this stream goes to feed the oil lake below, but it's also a very handy means of transport, for on it are floating some small rafts, and you just get on one of these and float along till you come to the end of the passage. There the oil stream runs to the left, under a low arch, and you get off.

Right in front of them, when they stepped off the raft, was a tube train, and, to their surprise, Noddy Ninety was driving it. Uncle asked him how he had got there so quickly and he told them that they had come a long way round.

If they had simply stepped into the first doorway past the school entrance, they would have found a slanting lift, which would have brought them to the tube in less than three minutes.

They had a pleasant ride back, and Uncle rewarded Noddy Ninety for his superb playing with a basket of buttered biscuits, and ninepence in cash.

7

RUDOLPH ARRIVES

It was Saturday. Uncle was taking up his rent from the dwarfs. When they come to pay him, they have a long ride on the circular railway and through many winding passages.

The hall was full of a pushing, yelling mass of the little men. They were packed in so closely that every now and then the Old Monkey would run rapidly over their heads to see Uncle, and then back again.

When they had paid, they all struggled back through the crowd to the green space in front of Homeward, where they found presents waiting for them. There were two thousand six hundred dwarfs, and piled up on the lawn were two thousand six hundred linen bags, containing raisins, bananas, and motoring chocolate.

So, after all, their rent is not excessive, as it includes free electric light and gas for cooking and heating, as well as the presents.

As Uncle was putting the two thousand six hundred farthings into a large bag, the door opened, and Butterskin Mute, the farmer, appeared. He was wearing a smock-frock, and carried a rake. He had brought Uncle a netful of green coconuts, to which he's rather partial, and as he was eating these, Uncle told the Old Monkey to bring Mute a bottle of Sharpener Cordial. Sharpener Cordial is a sort of fizzy drink. You put some pink powder at the bottom of a long glass, then add about a tablespoonful of water; it turns blue and expands till it fills the glass.

Mute put down his glass with a sigh of pleasure.

"I thought I would tell you," he said then, "that I passed Badfort this morning, and Beaver Hateman seemed to be ill. There were two fellows winding ropes round his stomach, while he groaned. Then he lay down flat on a big stone that had been warmed in the fire. As I passed, he shook his fist at me, and shouted:

"'Tell Uncle from me I don't mind poisoning people outright, that's all fair and square; but I've never sunk so low as to send anybody a bottle of poison labelled "Stomach Joy". Once I get rid of this pain he's for it!'"

Uncle laughed.

"I thought that bottle would ginger him up," he said cheerfully, "and I guessed he would drink the lot. I've often heard him say that he swallows a whole bottle of medicine at once . . . All the same, I think we had better strengthen our defences a bit, as he'll be in an ugly temper when he recovers."

Just then the telephone bell rang, and the Old Monkey went to answer it. He soon came back, beaming, and with his eyes sparkling with pleasure.

"It's Mr Rudolph, sir; he told me to tell you that he was getting off at Mother Jones's siding, and that he had his own car in the train, and would ride here."

"That's good," said Uncle. "The Hateman crowd will be watching for him at every station, but they'll never think of Mother Jones's siding!"

As a matter of fact, Mother Jones's siding is on a piece of rusty railway on the other side of the marsh. It's really disused, but you can push a special train along to it very cautiously. Rudolph was actually going to leave the train on the other side of Badfort, and then ride straight to his brother's in a small portable car that he was bringing with him.

It's really amusing. Every time there's trouble with the Badfort lot, he comes to help Uncle, and every time they try to stop him. But he works out a new route to puzzle them. There's no end to his resource.

Soon he arrived. He bumped a bit in his car, as he crossed the bridge.

Rudolph is short and laconic in his talk. He is thinner than Uncle, and quicker. He had brought with him in the car nothing but three large crossbows and a toothbrush.

"You'd better have the car looked at," he said to the Old Monkey. "Someone shot an arrow at the back wheel; it only grazed it, but I believe there's a slow puncture. The tyre seems to be going down a bit."

"Have something to eat," said Uncle, hospitably.

"Thanks, I'm not hungry. Shot down some breadfruit from a tall tree as I came along. I rushed the car along as it fell, and cooked it on the radiator. It was really excellent, like hot muffin."

The Old Monkey rubbed his hands. He is well used to Rudolph's promptness and resource, but this was something new, even to him.

"What's that on the table?" said Rudolph. "Oh, Sharpener Cordial. I'll have a glass, please. Wish I'd had some in the jungle."

"Did you have a good ride from Mother Jones's?"

"Oh, so so. I got on all right till I got near Badfort. Then I saw a chap watching me, big chap covered with jelly. He seems to live in the pay-box of a disused bathing pool near the marsh. I saw him reach for the telephone, but I put in a quick shot that knocked the instrument to bits."

Uncle looked at the Old Monkey. This was valuable information. They had often puzzled during the long winter evenings as to where Jellytussle lived.

"By the way," continued Rudolph, "they appeared to be holding military exercises in that field at the back of Badfort. They were throwing duck bombs at a big dummy elephant!"

Duck bombs burst when they hit you, and cover you from head to foot with a liquid which looks like lemonade but instantly turns into a tough jelly which is almost impossible to remove; in fact, you can't get it off for hours, and in the meantime you can only move very slowly, as if you were in a gigantic spider's web. You will not be surprised to hear that the Badfort people are always using them.

Uncle snorted, but just then the Old Monkey called out:

"Oh, I say, look here, sir! See what's happening at Badfort."

The windows were open, and a faint cheer was wafted across. They all got telescopes and field-glasses and looked out. A singular scene met their eyes.

An old man with a short grey beard was arriving at Badfort. He was mounted in a broken cart pulled by the Wooden-Legged Donkey. A piece of one of the wheels was right out, so that it jarred him painfully at each revolution; nevertheless he maintained an upright position, and an appearance of great dignity.

"That's old Nailrod Hateman, Nailrod's father," said Uncle. "This is a bigger thing than I thought."

Obviously the Badfort crowd were immensely cheered by the arrival of old Nailrod. Beaver Hateman seemed somewhat better, though he was still a good deal bent as he stepped forward. Filljug Hateman followed him with a small keg of hot Black Tom. The old man took very little notice of them. He accepted the keg of Black Tom, elevated it, and absently poured the lot down his throat. He was dressed in a sack suit of purple colour. Then he motioned to them to unload the cart. The luggage seemed to consist entirely of pumpkins, but the Old Monkey knew better. They were duck bombs.

Old Nailrod seemed to be addressing them. He kept pointing to Badfort, and frowning, as if remarking on the shabby appearance of the building. Then he contemptuously kicked on one side a little egg bomb, which a young captive badger was filling with glue, ink, and tin-tacks. He seemed to be preaching a sort of sermon to them, for they all looked very serious. Then he looked across at Uncle's.

All at once he saw Uncle and instantly took up a telescope to look at him. Uncle was just opening his mouth to laugh, when there was a hissing noise, and a steel dart struck deeply into his trunk.

He gave a loud trumpet of rage and despair, and then began to call in a soft voice for Magic Ointment and Doctor Bunker.

Meanwhile the Badfort crowd cheered loudly. Old Hateman calmly put his telescope away. It was a telescope combined with an air-gun, and you both sighted and fired at the same time. Quite a new weapon, and one that promised to be useful.

The Old Monkey reached for the telephone and called for

LEVENBURY 000000000

That's Dr Bunker's number.

They only get Dr Bunker when Uncle believes that he is seriously injured.

While he was coming, the Old Monkey was rubbing Uncle with Magic Ointment, which soon began to cure him; in fact, he was nearly all right when the loud braying of a horn was heard, and Dr Bunker drew up.

He was riding in a flag-decorated lorry with about

twenty of his students, and they all kept up a monotonous chorus as they pointed to him:

"He is great! He will cure you!"

Then they lifted from the floor of the lorry framed testimonials and letters of thanks, while one of them displayed a huge card on which was written:

> One hundred thousand people cured
> by Dr Bunker this month!

On the other side of the card was a picture of a hospital empty, and with all the nurses leaving.

The Doctor was a tall fat man with immense moustaches. As soon as he saw Uncle he said:

"This is a serious case!"

As he said this, his twenty assistants all bowed to the ground, and said in a low, monotonous chant:

"A serious case, but he can cure you!"

"Now," said Dr Bunker at last, 'just blow through your trunk to let me see if that's all right."

Uncle immediately did so, and blew so hard that the Doctor, who was standing right in front of him, got the full force of the blast and staggered.

He nearly fell over, and Rudolph laughed, but his laughter was drowned in a mighty chorus from the twenty:

"A cure! A perfect cure!"

When the Doctor had pulled himself together, he said in rather a surly voice:

"Not much wrong with the trunk, anyhow. How's your head?"

"Rather bad," said Uncle.

The Doctor pulled out from his pocket a small packet of tablets. "Headache Mixture!" he said. "Take three of these after we leave, and five minutes later your head will be as clear as a bell."

Uncle took the tablets and handed him two pound notes. Dr Bunker bowed his way to the lorry, and drove off to the accompaniment of some wind instruments which his students began to play.

Meanwhile Uncle swallowed the tablets, and finding, after about five minutes, that he had begun to feel worse, he beckoned to the Old Monkey.

"Just run up to the Old Man's and get a bottle of his Headache Producer (for enemies). Here's five shillings.'

The Old Monkey rushed off and soon returned with the bottle. Uncle took a dose, and began to feel more normal.

"That's done me good," he said, "and now, this evening, I think we might have a game of spigots. We can't always be watching against enemies, so I vote we have a little fun."

Uncle likes playing spigots because he always wins. You play it in this way: the Old Monkey puts some wooden boxes at the end of the hall, then you throw balls into them. It's quite an easy game, because the Old Monkey brings all the balls back. Uncle had a match with Rudolph and Cowgill and Butterskin Mute. They played twenty-six games and Uncle won them all. You can't beat Uncle as a thrower. He was quite willing to play even longer, but Rudolph was tired and wanted to turn in.

Cowgill and Mute went on for a bit longer and

Uncle rewarded them with good presents. He gave Mute a new lawn-mower, and he gave Cowgill sixty-five pounds of corned beef in five-pound tins.

So they all went cheerfully to bed, the Old Monkey too, for he always gets sevenpence halfpenny for fetching balls.

A QUIET MORNING

The next day, they all had a rest in the morning. There was almost complete silence at Badfort. The Badfort gang seemed to be having a late sleep.

"They were up late last night celebrating old Mr Hateman's arrival to help them with preparations," said the Old Monkey.

"Don't say 'old Mr Hateman' in that respectful way. I shall begin to think you are disloyal enough to admire him!"

"Sorry," replied the Old Monkey. "I didn't mean to say that!"

A sleepy feeling seemed to be over everyone that day. About eleven o'clock, the inhabitants of Badfort began to build a monster fire in front of the main gateway, tearing down window frames and doors from the upper storeys to do so.

"It's a marvel that there's any of that building left," said Rudolph. He had come down at last, and had breakfasted, and was now scouring the country with his powerful field-glasses.

"Oh, I expect they are welcoming a few people today," replied Uncle carelessly.

The fact is that these periodical campaigns against Uncle seem to be the occasion for a good deal of entertaining on both sides. Each party appears to be unable to move until a number of relatives and friends arrive to help.

Uncle had two powerful assistants arriving in the afternoon, and it was pretty evident that the Badfort lot were getting ready for someone to join them.

By common consent all parties seemed agreed on a peaceful morning, so they went out on the green outside Homeward and settled down by the side of the moat for a quiet rest. When they were all in deck chairs, with buckets of tea and coffee by their sides and crates of fruit and nuts at their elbows, Rudolph quietly produced a little well-worn volume from his pocket.

"I thought you might like to hear a few extracts from my diary," he said.

Whenever he comes he reads them some of his diary. He's a wonderful big-game hunter and traveller, but his diary is rather lengthy, and repeats itself a bit. Uncle can't bear it, and always goes to sleep when Rudolph reads it aloud, but the Old Monkey loves it, and so do Butterskin Mute and

Whitebeard. But Alonzo S. Whitebeard chiefly loves it because sometimes Rudolph will give a few pennies at the end of a reading; he is so greedy that he often begins to applaud in the wrong place in his eagerness to delight Rudolph.

So they sat there in a semi-circle, the water of the moat shining in the sun, and a beautiful feeling of quiet in the air.

Rudolph began to read.

"I'll start with yesterday's date, and then read backwards," he said.

"May 11th.   Arrived at Homeward. Had an excellent lunch en route of a breadfruit, which I cooked on the radiator of my car. Afterwards my brother was wounded in the trunk by a steel dart, fired with uncommon skill from Badfort . . .

"I say," grumbled Uncle, who wasn't asleep yet, "I don't like that phrase about 'uncommon skill'. It sounds as though you admired those hounds."

"It's all right," said Rudolph, hastily turning a few pages. "I'll just read a little further back:

"April 2nd. I am now in the celebrated Despair Valley. I have little hope of ever getting out. Over my head tower great cliffs of basalt. My last ration of dried musk-ox flesh is lying at my feet . . ."

Here Uncle began to snore gently.

"Not scores, but hundreds of wolves are moving stealthily up. I string my crossbow. I have just one bolt left—"

"Good!" said Alonzo S. Whitebeard, who felt that the time had come for him to say something.

Rudolph glanced at him severely.

The Old Monkey's eyes were alive with light, as he gazed in rapturous admiration at the great hunter.

"I find that I have one small duck bomb, preserved from a previous visit to Homeward. I hurl the bomb at the leader of the pack. It bursts and covers him with a yellow fluid which sends out a very curious smell. He grows suspicious, and raps with his foot on the ground.

"It is the signal of retreat.

"The other wolves slink away. The leader of the pack tries to do so, but the glue-like fluid makes him a prisoner.

"Moving away from me are no less than nine hundred wolves. Scanty would have been my chance, if they had come on."

The Old Monkey seemed delighted by this narrative. "Read us some more, sir!" he said eagerly.

"Let me see," said Rudolph, "the next few pages are rather ordinary.

"*April 19th.   Shot three grizzlies before breakfast.*
"*April 20th   Cross Never-Never Creek which the Indians say is unfordable at this time of the year.*

"Ah, here is something more interesting:

"*April 22nd.   An old chief came in tonight to say that the Volcano at Lester-Lester Range would shortly be in action. Said he knew this because a wizard, Snipehazer by name, had told him . . .*"

At this point they were interrupted by a sound of cheering over at Badfort, and, looking through field-glasses, they were able to see that someone important was arriving.

Uncle was awake by this time, and looking through a long telescope he exclaimed:

"I say, I really believe Hootman is coming out to join them."

There was no doubt about it, a shadowy figure dressed in a wisp-like sack suit was slowly emerging from a small door at the left-hand side of the fire. It was hard to make him out clearly – he was so vague and misty, but it was Hootman right enough – Hootman, the arch contriver of schemes against

Uncle. Hootman really is a sort of ghost, but a very inferior one. The other ghosts, of which there are many living at the Haunted Tower of Uncle's, will have nothing to do with him, and so he came to live at Badfort.

As soon as he appeared Beaver Hateman rushed forward, a plate of hot pork in his hand.

It looked strange to see the spectre holding the plate. Yet it appeared to be making preparations to eat the pork, for with its free arm it drew a sleeve across its shadowy mouth.

Just then Rudolph reached for his crossbow,

"Watch me," he said. "I don't think it will be possible to injure that phantom, but I think I can knock that plate out of its hand!"

There was a sharp twang, and a moment later the plate vanished.

Hootman threw up his arms, and gave a fine exhibition of rage. It looked very strange to see his ghostly indignation. Rudolph burst out laughing, and reached for his diary.

"I think," he said, "that today's entry will be unique in a small way!"

He began to write:

May 11th. Anger of a ghost: I have shot so many things that I began to think that there was nothing else for me to shoot, but today I think I even frightened a ghost . . ."

9

AT DEARMAN'S STORE

Two people were knocking at the moat gate. Uncle was glad to see them, for they were two specially useful fellows, Cloutman and Gubbins.

They often come over to stay for a time. Gubbins is a wonderfully strong man. He always arrives with a very heavy trunk and the first thing he does is to rush up the big staircase, carrying his trunk balanced on one hand. Everyone likes to see him do it.

Cloutman, on the other hand, cannot carry great weights, but he can strike terrible blows. One smack with his fist can make a lion stagger and fall. He has large bony hands. Uncle was very glad to see these two, as they are specially useful for subduing the Badfort crowd.

Just as he was welcoming them, a nasty laugh was heard in the distance, and Alonzo S. Whitebeard was observed to turn pale.

"I believe that's your stepfather, Whitebeard," said Uncle.

Whitebeard looked depressed, but reluctantly admitted that it was so.

He was coming along now, singing as he walked. His voice seems to have some kind of sickening effect, for the moment you hear it you feel rather ill, or at any rate seedy and depressed. He arrived at the gate, and then said with a ghastly smile:

"I've come to offer my services to you, sir, knowing that you may be attacked."

He made a silly preposterous bow as he said these words, and gave vent to a guffaw so abominable that a large glass jug on the table cracked from top to bottom.

Before Uncle could reply, Cloutman said:

"Excuse me, sir, but as we were coming along, I heard that old man offer his services to Beaver Hateman."

"Ha! Ha!" said old Whitebeard, with an atrocious chuckle that made everyone shudder. "That's a good joke, the best I've ever heard."

"Be silent," said Uncle, "and remove yourself or you will be kicked up!"

This threat had its effect, and the old man swaggered off with a scream of foul merriment that sickened all listeners.

The fact is that old Whitebeard is detested by everybody. The Badfort lot won't have him at any price; neither will Uncle.

After this unsavoury interlude, and as the Badfort people appeared to have settled down for an afternoon of planning, Uncle thought they might safely go out for a bit. A visit on the traction engine to a shop kept by Duncan Dearman in Badgertown would be a change.

Accordingly, they collected together a strong company on the engine and tender: Rudolph, the Old Monkey, Cloutman, Gubbins and Alonzo S. Whitebeard.

There was a certain amount of hissing and screaming from Badfort as they started, and a few arrows were shot, but there seemed to be a general agreement to leave each other alone for a while. The fact is that old Whitebeard has such a noxious influence that for some hours after he has been about, Uncle and the Badfort people feel fairly friendly towards each other.

So they went on merrily to Badgertown.

Duncan Dearman has a little shop in a side street just opposite Cheapman's huge store. All his goods are frightfully dear, so you can guess that he does very little business; in fact the only customer he has is Uncle, and if Uncle was not sometimes rather fond of showing off he would not go there either.

When they arrived at Dearman's, he was just changing a ticket on a thin, battered, tin milk jug. The ticket said:

YESTERDAY'S PRICE	£21
TODAY'S PRICE	£25

As he adjusted the ticket he wept loudly, and bemoaned his lack of customers.

Just then he caught sight of Uncle, and came running out with his face all smiles. He rushed up to him, and began to lead him into the shop.

"Come in, sir, come in at once!"

Uncle could hardly get into the shop, but there was a great armchair there into which he managed to wedge himself. When he was in it, the place was about full, and little Dearman had to climb about as best he could, crawling along the shelves, and standing on the counter. The others stayed outside and looked through the window, and they were joined by a lot of other folk from Badgertown, for a visit from Uncle was always a great event!

"Can I show you a nice clock, sir?" said Dearman, in an ingratiating manner, displaying as he spoke an alarm clock with one leg off, priced £30 7s. 4d.

Uncle didn't want the clock, so he showed him a shabby moth-eaten overcoat marked £21 10s. 0d. This was too small, so Uncle refused it.

There was little else in the shop, but after a long search he found an artificial pineapple, labelled "For the Fruit Stand" and priced £33 7s. 0d., and Uncle bought it at once.

Uncle is the last person in the world to put artificial fruit on his sideboard, but he can't resist anything that is capable of being thrown. He took out his money-bag, and paid at once in new pound notes and clean silver.

He wouldn't buy anything else, so he drank a mug of coffee that Dearman brought him, and then picked up the artificial pineapple, and heaved himself out of the armchair.

As he reached the door, he heard laughter. Then, looking down the street, he saw a sight that filled him with fury.

Beaver and old Nailrod Hateman had followed

him to the shop and they were actually giving a comic imitation in the street of the scene that had just taken place.

Old Nailrod Hateman had bought a halfpenny armchair from Cheapman's, and was sitting in it, while Beaver Hateman presented to him a number of articles: a broken spade handle marked £187 4s. 3d., a saucepan marked £88 5s. 7d. and an empty cocoa tin marked £25. As he offered these things, Nailrod Hateman kept saying in a loud imperious voice:

"No, that won't do; show me something else!"

They also had Filljug Hateman disguised as Whitebeard, pretending to weep and saying, "Oh, sir, you'll ruin yourself."

Large numbers of badgers were standing round, nearly splitting their little hides with laughter.

Even as Uncle looked, Nailrod Hateman extended his hand and took up a broken mousetrap with an enormous red ticket on which was written: "Only £500 4s. 21⁄2d. today, £21 9s. 0d. yesterday.

He said in a languid voice:

"I'll take that."

When Uncle saw this insulting mockery he turned scarlet, and, without waiting a moment, flung the pineapple right at Nailrod Hateman. It knocked him completely out of his chair. Beaver Hateman seemed to be too astonished to reply, so Uncle strolled haughtily by, and they all climbed into the traction engine and drove off.

Uncle got home in good spirits. He had lost his pineapple but he was very delighted to have had a return blow at Nailrod Hateman. The steel dart injury of the day before was now avenged.

When they got back to Homeward there was good news. The Marquis of Wolftown had heard that Uncle was likely to be besieged, and had sent him as a present two hundred cart-loads of honey and strawberry jam, and six thousand cases of condensed milk.

This was delightful, and Uncle's high spirits were further increased by an incident which occurred while they were having tea by the moat. Beaver Hateman appeared at the drawbridge carrying with him a white flour bag, which was supposed to be a white flag. "Flag of truce, young man," he said to the Old Monkey. "Tell Uncle that I want to go up to the Old Man's for medicine. Mr Nailrod Hateman's got a very bad headache."

Uncle said he could go, if Cloutman and Gubbins walked on each side of him.

All the way through the hall Beaver Hateman kept muttering, "Yes, this place is all right. Look at that golden jug, and those tapestries, and all that silver plate! We'll know what to do with it when this place belongs to us."

He was soon escorted out of the hall, but as he left

he turned to Uncle.

"Yes," he said, "it's all right knocking old men about with artificial fruit, and receiving cart-loads of honey and stuff the same afternoon; you've had a full day, I grant you. But there's tomorrow, and the day after, and the next day. Perhaps something's going to happen that will surprise you a little."

10

THEY VISIT WATERCRESS TOWER

It was a few days after, and Uncle was about to have
his music lesson. He has a great fondness for music,
but is rather a poor player. He is trying to learn the
bass viol, and there's a little man called Gordono who
comes to teach him. His real name is Thomaso
Elsicar Gordono. He's an Italian, and everyone calls
him the Maestro. The worst of it is he has such a
dreadful temper. He gets into a passion over his
music, and tries to throw himself out of the window
because he can't bear to hear things played badly. He
is always accompanied by a small lion, called the
Little Lion. No one knows his real name.

That afternoon, the Maestro came as usual, and
walking with him was his pet. Although he's grown-
up, the lion is hardly larger than an Airedale dog, but
he's fearfully tough and compact. He also has one
curious power. He can make himself heavy beyond
all reason. He does it in a moment. Try to get him out

of a room. You might think it would be easy enough, but the moment you try to move him you find your mistake. He doesn't resist you. He simply makes himself heavy, and though you'd hardly believe it, he must weigh about a ton! He seems to like music for he listens attentively to the Maestro.

That afternoon the Maestro played a brilliant waltz of his own composition on the piano, and then started to teach Uncle. Uncle is a bit heavy with the bow, and made one or two false notes. The moment he did so, the Maestro threw himself on the ground in a passion, grinding his teeth.

He got up and rushed to the window but realized then that he was on the ground floor. He looked rather sheepish, but contented himself with screaming a little. After a while he cooled down and the lesson proceeded.

When it was over, he said to Uncle:

"Have you ever been to Watercress Tower, where the Little Lion and I live?"

"No," replied Uncle.

"There you are! There you are!" said the Maestro. "Yet you can go over and over again to visit Butterskin Mute's wretched little farm! It's not fair!"

The Little Lion was squatting on a strong thick-legged stool. As the Maestro said these words, he made himself heavy, and the stool immediately collapsed.

"Now," said Uncle, "look what you've done! Spoilt a good stool!"

He knew the hopelessness of dragging or kicking the Little Lion out, so he said no more, but turned to the Maestro.

"It's true I've never been to Watercress Tower, but I'll come this afternoon, and — wait a bit — that's Butterskin Mute coming over the drawbridge. I'll bring Mute with me, and the Old Monkey."

"Righto!" said the Maestro with a smile. He was in high spirits all at once. One good thing about the Maestro is that his rages never last long, or else he would simply wear himself out. He was delighted at the thought of taking Uncle to see his dwelling place. The Little Lion stopped being heavy. He got on to his hind legs and briskly rubbed his eyes, as if preparing them for a good sight.

They set out almost at once. Mute was quite willing to go, for watercress is the one thing he cannot grow, and he had often wondered where Uncle obtained his splendid supplies. He emptied his sack of choice young cabbages on the table, and said that he would like to go immensely.

"You'll want bathing costumes," said the Maestro. "I always bring one in my bag and change on the way."

So they all took bathing costumes. The Maestro said that there was a good place at the foot of the tower where they could change.

"Shall we have to take any provisions?" said Uncle.

"Oh no," replied the Maestro carelessly, "there's always a bit going up there."

So they set out. They went to the end of the hall and took a tube labelled Biscuit Tower. When they got to the Biscuit Tower they found a junction, and another tube labelled Watercress Tower. They were glad to find that it was driven by Noddy Ninety. They went through a lot of tunnels.

At last they reached the base of Watercress Tower. It was a very wet place, and they could easily see the need for bathing suits. Right up the side of the tower was a gigantic salmon ladder. I don't know whether you have seen a salmon ladder in a stream, but they are like steps with water running over them. They all changed into their bathing costumes (except the Little Lion, who travels in his own coat all the time), and started up the ladder.

It was an exhausting business after the first two hundred feet, and Uncle stopped a minute and said to the Maestro:

"Do you come up and down this every time you want to go out?"

"Every time," replied the Maestro firmly. "There is an electric lift in the tower, but I can't stick the things. They make me feel wobbly inside and the Little Lion hates them so much that when he gets on, he makes himself heavy, and then the lift won't work."

"Well, I suppose there's nothing for it but to go on," said Uncle gloomily. "I suppose now you're going to tell me the usual tale about it being only twenty storeys higher up!"

The Maestro was so enraged at this speech that he threw himself right off the salmon ladder. However, he missed the rocks, and, after swimming about for a bit, grew cooler and began to climb after them.

"I vote we sit down," said Uncle, panting. "There's a pool here where we can sit down while the Maestro catches us up!"

It felt very nice there with the water rushing past. The walls of all the towers looked pretty too, for they had ferns growing on them.

They all felt rested when the Maestro arrived. He seemed to be in the best of tempers again, and had quite forgotten his annoyance. At last they reached the top. They arrived at a place where water came cascading out of a huge open door, and when they got inside they found themselves in a large room, with a stream running along the floor. They went through this and found themselves in another room about two feet deep in water, with stainless steel tables, chairs, bookcases, etc.

"I sometimes study here on a hot day," said the Maestro.

At the end of this room were two doors, with electric bells, and cards pinned beneath them.

One card said:

Mr T. E. Gordono

and the other:

Mr L. Lion

From underneath the doors came the stream of water.

The Maestro now drew out a latchkey and opened the door on the right. It opened on to a waterfall, or rather a flight of steps with water running down them. They waded up these steps, which looked very lovely with the foaming water pouring down them, and with lilies and ferns growing in the cracks of the stones. Then they found themselves on the shore of a gigantic lake on the top of a tower so huge that it seemed like a mountain. Most of the lake appeared to be overgrown with watercress.

On each side of the waterfall stood a little hut. On the door of one hut was

T. E. GORDONO

and on the other

L. LION

The lake looked fine, for there were cranes and herons flying around and enormous lemon-coloured fish swam lazily by.

The Maestro led them into his hut.

There was very little inside, except a grand piano, a violin and a camp bed. It was hard to see into the Little Lion's hut, for he dived in very quickly to have a rub down, and shut the door after him, but Uncle has very sharp eyes, and he noticed what looked very like a bottle of medicine on the table inside.

The Little Lion soon came out and joined them.

"Well," said Uncle, "you've got a snug place up here."

"Oh, it's all right," replied the Maestro. "But the rent's excessive!"

"The rent!" said Uncle severely. "I don't remember getting any rent from you."

"I don't pay you," said the Maestro.

"Indeed, and whom do you pay?"

"I always pay a man called Beaver Hateman. When I was looking for rooms in this neighbourhood, he met me, and said that he owned the tower, and that the lion and I could have rooms cheap."

When Uncle heard this, he trumpeted with rage. "Beaver Hateman!" he shouted. "Am I never to get out of sight and hearing of that chap? Here I am on the top of a lonely tower, preparing for a little intellectual conversation, and his hideous trail is here!

"Listen," he continued, "the man who charges you rent for these rooms is not only defrauding you, but his very presence is a menace. May I ask you what he charges?"

"He wanted fifty pounds, but I beat him down to twopence."

"Well, let me tell you that even at twopence per week you've been done. I only charge a halfpenny per week for large roomy flats, with electric light, and all conveniences."

When the Maestro heard this, he immediately rushed to the edge of the tower, but the Little Lion followed him, and, seeing that it would be a fatal drop, fixed his teeth in his trousers, made himself heavy and sat down,

The Maestro gave one pull, then, seeing the hopelessness of making a struggle, came quietly back to Uncle.

"I suppose you pay him regularly?" said Uncle.

"Yes, I pay him every quarter; that's two and twopence per quarter. I make him give me a receipt."

"I should like to see one of these receipts."

The Maestro reached up to a file, and took down a greasy piece of paper.

Uncle looked at it. It read:

```
to Bever hateman, Esq.,
rent of Rooms on watercress
Tower 13 weaks @ 2d.  5/6d
                        2/2
Recieved without thanks
                    B Hatman
```

"So he tried to make out that thirteen weeks at twopence came to five and sixpence. The scoundrel!"

"Yes, he said he wasn't any good at figures."

Uncle turned over the receipt. It was written on the back of an old bill which read:

To Thomas Minifer, Stationer.
 supplying 50 black books, with
 "hating book" inscribed on back
 50 @ 5/- . . . . £2 10s. 0d.

On the bottom was a note:

As this account has been presented in various ways during the past five years, we should like now to press for an immediate payment.

Uncle trumpeted again.

"This is vile!" he said. "He makes out his bill to you on the back of an unpaid bill of his own. I see he signed the receipt in red ink."

"No, he signed it in his own blood; he just stuck

the pen deep in his arm and wrote."

"His own blood! Is there any end to the man's detestable ways!" Uncle snorted, then went on:

"But wait a bit, you've been supplying me with cress week by week, for which I paid you the very substantial sum of twopence per week."

"Yes, I used that to pay the rent."

"So the money I paid for cress went into Hateman's pocket! It's a wonder I haven't been poisoned. Well, in future, you pay me. D'you understand?"

"Certainly. I shall be glad to do so."

Uncle sat down fuming, but the Maestro brought him some very good cress sandwiches, and, after devouring a few platefuls of these, he felt better. The sun was setting and the great lake was all golden, except for the patches of bright-green cress.

A gentle breeze blew, and the Maestro went to the piano and began to play. You'd be surprised to hear how well the music sounded up there. The Little Lion seemed to be carried away by it, for he sat perfectly still, except for a flickering half-smile, and the rhythmic wagging of his tail. The Old Monkey and Butterskin Mute were enraptured.

Uncle began to feel calm and happy.

"After all," he said to himself, "I have not come here in vain. I have exposed and removed a grievous wrong; the afternoon has been by no means wasted."

Before he left, he bestowed on the Maestro the sum of five shillings to repay him for some of the wrongly charged rent, and he gave the Little Lion a voucher for the same amount to spend at the Old Man's on medicine. That little creature is mad on physic and drugs (which he certainly does not need), for he snatched the voucher from Uncle as though he were gaining a fortune.

Uncle soon bade them farewell. They went down by the first lift they saw. It stopped for a moment at the bottom of the salmon ladder, where they collected their clothes, then took them most of the way back to Homeward.

Uncle was curious to see how the Little Lion spent his money, so, after tea, he slipped up the elevator to the tower where the Old Man has his medicine store.

He crept up and peeped through the window.

Yes, there was the Little Lion. He had already purchased a bottle of Headache Mixture, and one of Headache Producer (for enemies), besides two bottles of Rheumatism Mixture, and a flask of Stomach Joy.

Uncle smiled, and forbore to warn him, as he thought a sharp lesson might do the stubborn little creature good.

But the lion must have an inside of brass, for Uncle heard afterwards from the Maestro that he drank the whole flask of Stomach Joy and liked it, and seemed to be exceptionally bright and active next day.

11

A VISIT TO OWL SPRINGS

It was Uncle's birthday, and he had planned a celebration. He told the Old Monkey at breakfast that they were going to Owl Springs. The Old Monkey jumped for joy. If there is any treat that he likes, it is this visit. The springs are not up to much, and it's very hard to get a good look at the owl, but all the same there's something fascinating about the place.

People come from all round, especially when there is a rumour that the owl is about, but, as a matter of fact, the only person so far who had really seen the owl was the Old Monkey. One wet Friday night when everyone else had gone away he saw it quite clearly for about five minutes. Most people have not even had a glimpse of it, and those who have are notable characters for the rest of their lives.

They telephoned to Cowgill for the traction engine. Although it was Uncle's birthday, he had only received a few presents as yet, a packet of ginger-nuts from the Old Monkey, and some mangoes from Butterskin Mute, while Alonzo S. Whitebeard had simply given him a medal that he had picked up in the street. He gave it to Uncle because he thought it was no good, but he was surprised to discover later that it had a very useful quality that nobody had expected.

Uncle found this out by accident, while they were waiting for the traction engine. It suddenly turned blue when he stepped on to a little mound of earth, then became silver-coloured again when he stepped off it. He had the curiosity to dig the mound away a little, and found, just under the surface, nine half-crowns wrapped in grease-proof paper. It was evidently a buried-treasure detector. Uncle was delighted, for he had often wanted a thing of this kind, but Whitebeard was very depressed, and wished heartily that he had been generous enough to buy Uncle the halfpenny typewriter that he had been looking at for days in Cheapman's window.

At last they started, Uncle, the Old Monkey and Alonzo S. Whitebeard, with Cowgill as driver and engineer.

The road to Owl Springs goes through a deep valley. Lots of people were also travelling there that day, some on foot, some by car, but most by motor coach. A man called Onion Sam gets up these trips during the May to September season.

They chug-chugged along steadily. As they approached a place where the road was up, they heard the noise of hooves, and Beaver Hateman galloped up to them on his Wooden-Legged Donkey. He was followed by Nailrod Hateman on his lean goat, Toothie.

"Hallo, Uncle!" said Beaver Hateman. "Going to see the owl?"

"I hope to do so," replied Uncle calmly.

"Well, I don't think you will; I passed Wizard Blenkinsop on the road, and he assured me that the owl would not be seen after ten this morning. It's now half past nine and we shall be there in ten minutes, while you'll get there about eleven! So long, Uncle!"

He galloped off like the wind.

Uncle was rather irritated at this speech, but cheered himself up with a second breakfast of coconuts and chocolate ice-cream from an electro-plated bucket.

Beaver Hateman was right. It was nearly eleven when they reached the famous Owl Springs. The narrow valley was packed with people, who were walking round, dropping litter and looking at the springs. These springs are disappointing at the first glance, a mere muddy trickle of water coming down between bushes, but they are fascinating all the same, and it seems well worth while going there even if you don't see the owl.

Halfway up the valley is a large enclosure labelled
Trade Exhibition. Uncle was in no hurry, and seeing
that there was such a crowd, he thought he might as
well visit this first. They went in, paying a halfpenny
for the whole party at the turnstile. It was quite a
good exhibition with a large number of stalls.

One was kept by a dull, heavy ox. He appeared to
have only one thing on his stall, a box, pink in colour,
called BIRTHDAY BOX.

Uncle asked the price.

"A thousand pounds," replied the ox in a slow, dull
voice, "and I won't come down a farthing in my
price."

There was something about this box that took
Uncle's fancy, and though he thought the price high he
paid it in clean hundred-pound notes. The moment he
did so, the ox took from behind the counter a little
board marked stall closed and prepared to leave.

"Can you tell me the way to Cheapman's store?"
he asked the Old Monkey. "I've heard that you can
get lashings of hay there for a bob."

The Old Monkey directed him, and smiled as he
did so. A shilling spent at Cheapman's on hay would
provide any ox with a larger pile than he could
possibly devour during the rest of his life.

There were a lot of other stalls, but Uncle was
rather interested in a small quiet shop with a sign
which read:

> ### THE BOOKMAN
> Bookseller and Stationer

It seemed quite an ordinary sign, but The
Bookman was the actual name of the shopkeeper. He
was the son of a famous boxer called Wallaby
Bookman, who had married a young woman with
the curious name of Mable The. He had naturally
gone into the book trade on growing up.

The Bookman was sitting on a bench outside his
shop reading a small book, and every now and then
he marked some places in it with a carpenter's pencil.
When Uncle asked to see his shop he simply pointed
into the doorway with his thumb.

They went in. The shop consisted of a single room
built of thick square logs. On one side of it was a shelf
with about twenty books, They were all the same,
The History of Owl Springs.

"We've got this," said Uncle. "Let's get on to the
springs."

He walked out.

On their way Nailrod Hateman passed them.

"It's all over for the day," he said. "Oh, what a time
we've had! I saw the owl myself – looked straight at
it for more than an hour!"

This was most likely a lie, and they pretended not
to hear. A gleam of sun came out, and everything
looked rather pretty, in spite of the mass of litter left

by the excursionists. Just as they were looking at the thin trickle of muddy water, a wonderful thing happened.

From behind a low bush on the left, the *owl appeared*! He flew straight to a withered twig, and sat there looking at them.

Uncle reached for his cine-camera, and took some shots of the owl from different positions. He did not venture to speak for fear that the owl should go.

For twenty minutes the owl stayed, minutes filled with rapture. Then it gave a low hoot, preened its feathers, and slowly flew off.

They all kept silent for a time. Uncle's face was glowing, and as for the Old Monkey, he swung himself up to the branch of a near-by tree and hung there by his hands and feet.

At last they spoke:

"Congratulations, sir," said the Old Monkey. "I always wanted you to see it, and I was always sorry that you weren't there when I had that good look, three years ago."

Uncle said nothing for a long time. He was so full

of solemn joy. At last he drew a deep breath.

"Gratification," he said, "is a poor word to express my feelings at this moment. I am afloat on a sea of foaming joy and delight! For the time being, I will say little, but on many a long winter evening I shall expound to you with suitable words my feelings at this extraordinary event!"

"And I shall love to hear you," said the Old Monkey simply.

"In the meantime, leave me alone," said Uncle. "I want to travel back quietly, reflecting deeply on this glorious hour, and fixing its details in my memory.

12

THE BIRTHDAY EVENING

After a special birthday banquet that evening Uncle started to open his presents. It was impossible to examine them all at once, so, as it was chilly, Uncle directed his helpers to pile them up in a sort of semi-circular wall round the fireplace.

The fireplace is just like a little house; it has thick walls on three sides, and a little window at the back, looking out on to the moat. There was still room in this monster fireplace for a big table; Uncle's festival chair made of brass, with red velvet cushions; chairs for the rest of them; and also a great cauldron of hot ginger wine, which slowly warmed at the log fire.

"This is very pleasant," said Uncle. "And now I think we might have a look at the thousand-pound box I bought today."

They all gathered round the table, while Uncle examined the box. It was a queer box made of iron and wood with silver nails. It looked pinkish at first, then seemed to turn blue.

He tore off a piece of stiff parchment which was fastened over a hole in the lid, and found an end of touch paper. There was a note which read:

> Light this when the box is in the middle of the table, then look out for a big surprise.

He lit it.

At first it smouldered, then it began to burn with a small green flame, but very clear, and sharp as a sword. It trembled into purple, then pink, then started to fizz and to let out stars. You have seen those fireworks that come out like snakes – well, it was like that on a big scale. A great brown serpent came wobbling and gliding out of the box, and gradually spread its length over the table. It slowly turned a bright gold colour, gave one pop, and from its body came out hundreds of little balloons, blue, red, pink and green. These rapidly swelled out till they were about a foot broad, and floated about the room. It was pretty to see them.

There seemed to be nothing left of the snake, but instead a parcel lay on the table. Uncle began to open it.

It contained a pair of elephant's tusk-tips, cut out of diamonds big enough for a royal crown. Uncle stuck them on the ends of his tusks, and they shone in the firelight splendidly.

When Uncle had admired them for a time he said in an impressive voice:

"I might well have hesitated to spend a thousand pounds on this parcel. Instead of that, I said to myself: 'This is your birthday. Gratify that struggling ox!' What is the result? I have gratified myself and him, and we are both happy."

They were all impressed by this speech, especially Whitebeard, who seemed dazzled.

As the Old Monkey handed round glasses of the hot ginger wine, Uncle went on in a low, dreamy voice:

"That has always been my guiding principle. I was born in the jungle. My parents were poor. A young, tender elephant, I was thrust out into the world at an early age to make a living. My sole starting capital was a halfpenny, but I have built up my fortune on this principle – to do the other person and myself good at the same time."

Here Uncle drew out a handkerchief, and wiped away a little moisture from his eyes. He gets a lot of pleasure out of feeling sorry for himself when he recollects his early days.

"Nobody present," he said, "can remember the bitterness of my early struggles. Even the Old Monkey . . ."

There was a loud scuffling and shrieking in the

129

chimney. Then, with an appalling yell, a dwarfish little man was hurled right down the chimney into the cauldron of hot ginger wine. He made an awful splash, then floundered helplessly in the vat.

Uncle pulled him out, and set him by the fire to dry.

One look was enough to show them who it was. It was Hitmouse, and as Uncle looked up the chimney he saw glaring down on him the degraded face of Beaver Hateman.

"Ha, ha! Uncle," shouted Hateman. "I stuck it until you started talking about the Old Monkey, then I threw Hitmouse down to give you a fright; I also want to remind you that when you were talking about yourself you didn't mention the fact that you once STOLE A BIKE!"

When Uncle heard this he was so tremendously enraged that he filled his trunk full of the ginger wine, although it was so hot that it hurt him, and squirted it up the chimney at Hateman.

It struck him with such force that he toppled backwards and fell into the moat with a splash.

Feeling better, Uncle continued with his life story.

"When I had the Old Monkey, I prospered still more. It was then that I took over this castle from Wizard Blenkinsop. Everything would be perfect if it weren't for certain people who live in Badfort —"

As he said this, Beaver Hateman appeared at the

little window and began to shout in a loud voice at the window:

"Ha, ha! he STOLE A BIKE!!"

This was more than Uncle could bear. He rushed to the door. When he came back Hitmouse had disappeared. He had, so the Old Monkey said, slipped up the chimney again.

Uncle said sternly:

"Let us forget this disgraceful episode. And now, before we turn in, we will have a few games."

They had quite a number, including 'Whitebeard's Buff'. Uncle ties Whitebeard's whiskers round his head, and then Whitebeard has to find the rest of them. He looks funny – a tremendous mop of hair charging round the room. Uncle can play at it splendidly, because he puts out the tip of his trunk, and Whitebeard thinks that he has caught him while he's really quite a long way off.

After a lot of other games, they had light refreshments and then went to bed. In spite of the unpleasant incident at the fire, Uncle felt that he had had a really good birthday.

13

CHRISTMAS EVE AT UNCLE'S

It was now getting well into December, and the weather made it necessary for there to be a kind of truce between Uncle and the people at Badfort. The weather is always positively terrific in December, with deep snow, bitter frosts, and lots of blizzards. No one can equal Uncle at snowballing. He has always been the best thrower for miles around, and the way he can whizz a snowball through the air is really unique. Also, he draws fine snow up his trunk, and squirts it out with great force, pushing enemies over backwards into drifts.

There's a long-standing custom, too, that Hateman and his tribe should be invited to Homeward for the Christmas festivities, or at any rate for part of them. Uncle is always saying he is going to give this up, and the Badfort people are always saying they'll never come again, but somehow they turn up.

It was Christmas Eve, and one of the worst winter

nights ever known. Snow lay deep on the drawbridge and the frozen moat, but a cheerful company was assembled in Homeward.

Uncle had got off the last of his Christmas presents. For weeks motor lorries had been going out loaded to the roof with cakes, bread, hams, biscuits, chocolate and so on. During the few days before Christmas a gigantic presentation had been made to the dwarfs and other eager neighbours in the towers. At last they were all satisfied. The last Christmas card had been sent off, and all Uncle's guests had arrived except the Badfort crowd.

They were a gay party. Rudolph was there, the Old Monkey, of course, with his father and uncle, besides Mig, Cloutman, Gubbins, Whitebeard, Auntie and the Companion, Noddy Ninety and Don Guzman. Also the One-Armed Badger who had been really happy for the last few weeks, loading himself to the ground with bales of provisions.

Homeward was so resplendent with firelight that they hardly needed the electric lamps.

Then they saw dark figures approaching over the snow, singing as they came. It was the Badfort crowd, and the song they were singing was, as usual, something degraded, and like most of their songs, didn't quite rhyme, but, in compliment to the season, they were not singing anything insulting to Uncle.

"Hungry for sausage and MASH,
Or a newspaper full of fried SCOB,
I went to the Palais de FISH
And looked round for something to GRAB."

In front of the procession marched Beaver Hateman, carrying on the end of a pole a small tub filled with scob oil, which, I might explain, is made from the scob fish that they catch in the marsh. It burns a very dark red, and sparkles with a bright blue light.

When they got to the door, they piled up their bows and arrows on the threshold, besides some duck bombs they happened to have with them, and walked in unarmed.

They were wearing their usual sack suits, but they had tried their best to make them look festive, by tying on to them sprigs of holly.

They glanced hungrily at the table as they walked in.

Beaver Hateman was the first to approach Uncle.

"Good evening, Uncle," he said, extending a hand blue with cold, and with a spiky sprig of holly tucked away in the palm.

Uncle did not take his hand, but stood looking coldly at him.

"So you won't shake hands?" began Hateman. "I think we'd better go back for our duck bombs!"

"I do *not* refuse to shake hands," Uncle replied, "but standing at my side is my Aunt, Miss Maidy, and I want to remind you that it is always the custom to shake hands with a lady first."

"Oh, all right," said Hateman. Tucking the piece of holly up his sleeve, he shook hands with Auntie and afterwards with Uncle.

The rest were soon introduced. Even Hootman had come, for, being a ghost, he was quite at home on Christmas Eve; Jellytussle was also there, though he had to stand away from the fire, or his jelly would have melted.

It is not the slightest use getting the tribe to sit down at table. Uncle has tried it again and again, but they only smash everything. So they all sit on the hearth around the fire to eat, except Jellytussle, who slowly gnaws a joint of pork on the cool side of the room, and Hootman, who eats his provisions in a gloomy alcove.

They had a mighty feast. Uncle's table was so loaded with provisions that it had actually to be supported in places by casks of ham.

It seemed as though they would never finish, but at last the tables were cleared and they sat down for a time before having games.

There's one item that they always have at Christmas time, and that's an action song version of 'Good King Wenceslas'.

Uncle goes to the window and looks out, while everyone sings the carol, and then Whitebeard comes slowly up, gathering winter fuel, which he does to the manner born, for he has spent his whole life in gathering something or other.

Uncle went to the window. He had clothed himself in a red–and–gold dressing-gown, and looked every inch a king. He held a gilded marlinspike in his hand as a sceptre.

They all began to sing the carol.

Soon Whitebeard came into sight, bent nearly double as he searched for fuel. He was playing his part splendidly and everyone was pleased, when, all at once, a hideous laugh was heard, and Whitebeard's stepfather appeared on the drawbridge. The moment they saw him, all their spirits fell. He stepped right in front of his son, and looked at Uncle with an odious expression.

"Ha, ha, sir, you're doing 'Wenceslas', are you? Well, I'd better be the old man. My stepson won't do; he's too young. I can beat him at gathering fuel, and I can certainly beat him at the flesh-and-wine stunt!"

This was absolutely true.

As he said these words, Beaver Hateman stepped up to Uncle.

"If you admit Whitebeard's stepfather," he said, "we're all going home, and that's the truth!"

"Be silent!" said Uncle sternly. Turning to

Whitebeard Senior he said in a cold, terrible voice:

"Be gone!"

"Ha, ha! The great Uncle turns away a feeble old man on Christmas Eve!"

His laughter was so atrocious that even Beaver Hateman began to feel ill.

Uncle continued to address old Whitebeard in tones of ice.

"No man, whoever he is, shall be turned empty from my door on Christmas Eve. Take that bag!" He pointed to a large sack of cakes, sweets and nuts. "And now, remove yourself, or, even though it's Christmas Eve, I shall have to adopt an extreme course."

They opened the door wider, and Uncle went back for a run.

Old Whitebeard did not wait.

After this, they soon finished off the action song 'Wenceslas', though the interest in it was not as great as it had been.

When they had finished this, old Nailrod Hateman gave his conjuring display. It was very good, but a bit monotonous. It was called 'The disappearing pork pie'. Uncle put a pork pie on an empty table, and old Nailrod covered it with a handkerchief. When he took it off, the pie was gone. What he really did was to swallow the pie very quickly while he was flicking the cloth off. He did it with such immense speed that you couldn't see it go, only, if you looked very closely, you could see the bulge in his throat as he swallowed it. ·

He was quite ready to go on with this for a long time, but they soon got tired of his display, and played 'Whitebeard's Buff'.

After that Noddy Ninety gave his action song called 'At the Gates of Metz'. Ninety says that he was educated in Germany, at Metz. Nobody is old enough to contradict him.

He chanted the song in his piercing voice, emphasizing certain words:

"On a bitter winter's night
By the gates of METZ,
I waited in the fading light,
In my thin torn VEST.

"Only just across the way,
Was a sausage SHOP;
But it was no good to me,
Pfennigs I had NOT."

There were a lot of verses to this song and when he had finished, nothing would satisfy him but to start all over again, this time with the verse:

'On a bitter winter's night
By the gates of ULM,
I waited in the fading light
With my fingers NUMB.

Auntie and Rudolph cut in with an argument as to whether 'Metz' and 'vest' and 'Ulm' and 'numb' were rhymes. Noddy Ninety said, "We do modern poetry at Dr Lyre's School."

"Let's have supper," said Beaver Hateman. "We've had enough poetry for one evening.

After supper Uncle said:

"As a great treat tonight, I'm going to let you sleep in the Haunted Tower. I may tell you," he continued, "that everyone avoids that place; the last man who tried to sleep there came out in half an hour, unable to speak, and with his hair perfectly white."

Uncle couldn't have suggested anything better. It's a frightful business getting the Badfort crowd to go to bed, but the moment they heard of the Haunted Tower they were all eager to go.

"Good egg, Uncle!" said Nailrod Hateman. "I'm surprised at you thinking of anything so sensible: just the binge for Christmas Eve!"

Uncle was glad for them to go. He had stockings to fill, and other things to do, and so he was glad of this quiet hour.

So they all set out gaily to the Haunted Tower. You could hear their raucous voices echoing across the snow.

14

NIGHT IN THE HAUNTED TOWER

Beaver Hateman and his companions could soon see, looming up in the distance, the enormous black bulk of the Haunted Tower.

But before they reached it they heard singing in the distance.

"That'll be the Respectable Horses," said Hateman. "They always go round on Christmas Eve."

They soon came up with a group of three horses who were carol-singing outside the house of a man called Lilac Stamper.

He had a board fastened in front of his window on which were these words:

all singing prohibited.
Mr Stamper is writing a book.
He wishes for silence.
You sing at your own risk!

Stamper has publicly thrashed
three ballad singers, and has
caned four flute players.
HE will do it again!
THIS MEanS YOU!

In spite of this menacing notice they kept on singing, and they were singing very badly.

These horses are called the Respectable Horses as they always look so neat and tidy, and they are great friends of Uncle's. They would have been to see him that night, but they were too busy singing in aid of a Home for Retired Horses. It's wonderful to see how smooth and black their coats are. Near the throat they have a patch of white almost like a clergyman's collar, and they always have well-brushed hooves.

They do not like Hateman, but they always treat him respectfully, and, strange to say, he never attacks them. In fact, he sometimes takes their part.

That evening, for instance, although longing for a fight, Hateman went up to them and said:

"If Stamper attacks you, I'll thrash him!"

The Respectable Horses nodded, but did not interrupt their singing, which was really painful. Horses cannot be said to have good voices, and theirs were particularly dull and heavy. Still, they managed a few good notes now and then.

Beaver Hateman waited.

By and by Stamper's window opened, and his thin white face appeared. He handed out two pound notes which the leader of the Respectable Horses put into a tin which was tied round his neck. Then he closed the window.

Beaver Hateman was mystified.

"Why didn't he attack you?" he said.

"Oh, Mr Hateman," said the eldest of the horses, "I'm afraid you didn't read the little footnote appended to Mr Stamper's notice. It's in very small type. Let me lend you this quizzing-glass."

The eldest of the Respectable Horses carried an old-fashioned but powerful quizzing-glass suspended round his neck by a black ribbon.

Hateman took the glass.

"Where's the footnote?" he said.

The horse (whose name, by the way, was Mayhave Crunch) pointed to what looked like a greyish smudge on one corner of the notice. When Hateman looked at it through the quizzing-glass he found that it was in that very small type in which people sometimes print a whole page of writing in the space of a thumbnail. It read as follows:

Singers are however allowed to perform on the following dates: Jan 1 to Dec 31 inclusive and on all public holidays.

Hateman was indignant.

"The little skunk!" he said. "He's tricking us!" He tried to get Stamper to come out, but Stamper smiled and stayed by his cosy little fire eating roasted chestnuts, and as his window had been well rubbed with Babble Trout Oil it could not be broken, and the Hateman gang had to leave him alone.

Beaver Hateman was just going away when Mayhave Crunch jingled a money-box under his nose.

Hateman felt in his pocket, and drew out a handful of bad money, brass sovereigns, lead half-crowns, and very badly forged bank notes. At the bottom was a single good halfpenny, which he took out and gave to them.

They thanked him gravely, and passed on.

At last the Hateman gang arrived at the Haunted Tower.

As they opened the front door, a spectre leered at them, beckoned down a passage and then ran off. They went down the passage and arrived in a kind of hotel lounge. The walls were mildewed and hung with spiders' webs and the carpet was rat-eaten. There was a general air of decay and misery.

At a shabby reception desk stood a tall, cadaverous man.

He gave a loud shriek when he saw them, and pointed to two moth-eaten posters which hung side by side behind the desk.

One of them was headed:

BEFORE VISITING THE HAUNTED BEDROOMS

It showed a fat, prosperous-looking man walking along with a smile.

The other was headed:

AFTER VISITING THE BEDROOMS

It showed a lean miserable man with grey hair and his body bent almost double.

There was also a notice:

> When Visiting leave your valuables with the clerk. He will endeavour to return the same, but does not promise to do so every time.

"Hand over the keys," said Hateman.

"One key for the lot," said the clerk in a false, rattling voice.

He seemed to be fumbling about with the key. At last he handed it to Hateman on a small tray. The moment Hateman got hold of it he dropped it. It was red-hot.

It's a good thing that Beaver Hateman's hands are covered with thick horny skin. He burnt the outside

surface, but did not hurt himself at all. Hateman
didn't waste much time with the miserable clerk. A
bucket of coal happened to be standing near. He
picked it up and emptied it over him.

They went on to find the rooms. Beaver Hateman
fancied one that was labelled:

HAUNTED ROOM NUMBER 52314567 A15/J.A.I.
THE WHITE TERROR

Nailrod Hateman took

> NUMBER 52314568 A15/J.A.I.
> THE REMORSEFUL DUELLIST

Hitmouse said he would take

> NUMBER 52314569 A15/J.A.I.
> THE WAILING MURDERER AND CHAIN DRAGGER

Beaver and Nailrod went in, but Hitmouse, as you'll remember, is timid.

What he did was to wait till the others had gone in, and then lie down on the mat outside, where he thought he would be free from ghosts. He's never quite easy about ghosts, though they have all got used to them at Badfort, as Hootman every now and then has a ghostly friend over to see him.

But Hitmouse wanted to have the credit for being bold, and still to have a good night's rest. He wrapped himself up in the mat, and was just falling asleep when Beaver Hateman pushed open his door and came out to look for him.

"I say, Hitmouse," he said, "haven't you turned in yet? Well, you'd better come in here. The White Terror is an absolute wash-out, a very small ghost only about a foot high, and I'm not going to waste my time with it; I'm going into a room where there's something really terrific! Come on!"

Hitmouse didn't want to go, but Hateman took him by the collar and slung him in.

Once in the room, he could see nothing at first, and finding the bed comfortable he got into it, and was just falling asleep when he heard a low groan, and saw a very small ghost standing on a bedside table.

It stood there muttering:

"I did it! I took the strawberry jam!"

It began to scream in a small voice.

Hitmouse tried to stick a skewer into it, but as it was made of something like thick fog, this was no good. All at once he felt terrified of the little figure, and darted out of bed into the passage.

What he saw reassured him.

There was Uncle coming along the passage with the Old Monkey. Uncle couldn't sleep, and felt he would like to walk round and see what the Hateman tribe were doing.

Hitmouse ran blubbering up to him.

"Oh, sir," he said, "I'm glad to see you. It's awful in there. A little ghost, a rotten little ghost! ... Oh, I've fairly got the wind up!"

Uncle looked at him sternly.

"Cowardice, Hitmouse," he said in a firm voice, "is a detestable vice, and I grieve to see that you are its victim. However, since you are out, you might as well show us where Beaver Hateman is sleeping. I am rather anxious to see what effect the ghosts will have upon him."

"It's two rooms up, sir. I'll show you."

Uncle gravely walked up to the room indicated, and opened the door. He was followed into the room by the Old Monkey and Hitmouse.

He could not help smiling at the scene. The room

was lit by a very small lamp in the shape of a skull. There was an enormous bed hung with black velvet curtains, and right in the middle of it snored Beaver Hateman. He was asleep, and his great boots, studded with iron nails, projected over the bottom rail.

Standing at the foot of the bed was a tall thin ghost, with a puzzled expression on his face. His hand held a sword, and every now and then he groaned, took the sword by the middle, and tried to stab himself.

Beaver Hateman snored on,

After a while another ghost appeared, dragging a chain with iron weights attached. The noise made by this spectre was terrific, but it had hardly any effect on Beaver Hateman. He stirred in his sleep for a moment, and then shouted:

"Easy with the kegs. Don't rumble them over the floor like that, or you'll start the staves!"

By this time several more ghosts had arrived, and the room began to get crowded. They took not the slightest notice of Uncle and the Old Monkey, but directed their attention to Hateman, who was now gurgling in his sleep and grinding his teeth a little.

By and by another ghost arrived, carrying with him a pan of blue fire, which made things in the room a little lighter. They hadn't noticed him before. He was trying to wash his hands, and moaning. Nobody, not even the other ghosts, took much notice of him, so he went farther into the corner as if disappointed, and began to wring his hands quietly.

However, the most terrifying spectre of the lot was now appearing. A door opened in the wall, and out stepped a fierce-looking phantom, with skulls and crossbones round its neck and carrying a great axe in its bony hand. With this ghost were a couple of others, carrying a block, then two more, conveying a prisoner.

They made the ghostly prisoner kneel down. He gave a cry for mercy, but down came the great axe, and his head rolled into a basket. Hateman partly woke up at this, gave a yawn that rattled the windows, then muttered, as he dropped off to sleep again:

"That looks like old Uncle going his round!"

He then began to snore louder than ever. He had rolled round till his head was over the edge of the bed, and with his great teeth showing he presented a somewhat fearful spectacle himself. The ghosts appeared to think so too, for they wavered and grew more and more insubstantial. At last one of them stepped forward and began to wail. His voice was piercing, and so strident that they all had to stop their ears. But it had little effect on Beaver Hateman. He is thoroughly used to screaming, for Hitmouse often sleeps in his room at Badfort, and, having a really bad conscience, regularly screams in his sleep.

So, when the spectre began to wail, Hateman took no notice at first. At last, when it yelled till the whole place shook, he stopped snoring for a moment, half lifted his head, and said in his sleep:

"Hitmouse, if you don't stop yelling, I'll . . ." Then his sleep became even more heavy, and his snoring settled down to a deep steady drone. His head, which was hanging out of bed, sank till it rested on a small stool at the bedside. This compressed his throat, and the noise he began to make then was simply unbearable.

The ghosts faded away till they were all gone.

Uncle and his companions stepped out of the room too. Uncle was secretly laughing.

They went down the corridor, and entered Nailrod Hateman's room. He wasn't asleep, but was watching an old ghost, who was trying vainly to pick up a phantom sovereign from a crack in the floor.

"That's your two hundred and seventeenth attempt, old lad!" Nailrod said cheerfully. "And remember, when you've got it, it's no good. You can't spend it! Ha! Ha! Ha!"

The old ghost, however, took no notice of him, and began to grope again in the crack.

"Well, I must say, you're very persevering!" said Nailrod Hateman.

Just then he looked up and saw Uncle standing in the doorway.

"Hallo!" he said. "Come and watch. It's a case of 'If at first you don't succeed, try, try, try again!' It reminds me of those yarns you used to tell us about how you succeeded in business."

Uncle was in no mood for controversy, or even reproof. He simply gave Nailrod Hateman a searching, severe glance and moved on.

They found Hootman in the passage in a very bad temper. He had gone to a room farther down with the title:

> BATTLE OF ALL THE SPECTRES
> AND
> THE STRANGLING WIZARD

He had been most disappointed, for no ghost had appeared at all. The fact is, ghosts look on Hootman as partly one of themselves and they detest him so much that not one of them will go near him, except the one or two who visit him at Badfort, and these are ghosts who have been driven out of the tower.

The consequence was that he had been awake for the best part of the night in a damp room with nobody to talk to.

By now, it was time for Uncle to go home, so they set out. They arrived safely, and had a late sleep on Christmas morning. So did the Badfort crowd. It was nearly twelve o'clock when they turned up for lunch.

"How did you sleep?" said Uncle to Beaver Hateman.

"Oh, very well indeed, undisturbed by ghosts or anything else!"

The Hateman tribe always go away soon after dinner, because their comparatively good manners are by that time getting near breaking-point.

So when Beaver Hateman said he must be off, Uncle did not try to delay him.

"Well, goodbye, Uncle. Are the sledges of provisions ready?"

The sledges were ready, but Uncle did not like the tone of this remark. It took his valuable presents too much for granted, so he said gravely:

"The sledges *are* ready, but I wish you would have the common civility to say 'Thank you'!"

"Oh, stow it, Uncle. You owe us something. You know jolly well that you'd be bored stiff if we didn't have a dust-up occasionally! Well, goodbye, and remember this: that the next time we meet you'll get something to make you look less pleased with yourself!"

15

THE SWEET TOWER

Christmas had not been over very long before much hammering and knocking was heard to come from Badfort. In spite of this Uncle decided to take a little time off to go exploring.

"I'm running short of sweets," he said, "and I'd like to know what is in that big green tower at the back. I've looked at my plan, and it said: 'Tower Number 279A; Sweet Store and Chocolate Warehouse. Servitor in charge: Samuel Hardbake.' I've never seen Hardbake yet, and I thought we might have a good look round and bring back a supply of eatables."

They all approved of this and Uncle said they needn't carry much stuff, only a few baskets. They had very hard work to get the One-Armed Badger to travel light, but they got off at last, Uncle, the Old Monkey, Gubbins, the One-Armed Badger and Whitebeard. They didn't want to take Whitebeard much, but he begged hard to come, so at last they let him.

So far as they could make out from the plan, the way to get to Sweet Tower was to take the circular railway to Lion Tower, then change on to a sliding chute to Swan Tower, walk across the top, where there's a spring machine that shoots you up to a little brown tower only thirty storeys high, then from the top of that tower there's an escalator to Merry-Go-Round Flat, a place where there's a free fun fair always going. Then you get to the Black Stag tunnel and ride on trolleys for about a mile, go up the elevator, turn to the right, then on to the big swing boats which swing you on to Buzzard Tower. After that it's easy.

In one corner of Buzzard Tower there was a little rusty switchback railway labelled 'To Sweet Tower'. It hardly looked as though it would work at all, but it started right off with a scream, tearing down culverts and jumping great chasms at such a speed that you could hardly see anything. The journey only lasted about half a minute. Then it ran suddenly into a wall of what looked like soap, and stopped. When they looked back, and saw right in the distance the dim outline of Buzzard Tower, they began to realize how far they had come.

It was Sweet Tower all right.

There in his office at the entrance was Samuel Hardbake, busily entering up some items in his ledger.

He looked up as they came.

"What's this!" he said. "Visitors ain't allowed except on the third Friday of every second month. That's today, and the boys from Dr Lyre's school are here already. My hands will be full up with them, so you can take yourselves off."

"Wait a bit," said Uncle. "I am Uncle, the owner of this place."

"Oh, are you? I have my doubts. Let's have a look at you."

He put on another pair of spectacles and looked at Uncle for a long time, comparing his figure with a framed portrait that was hanging in the office.

"Well, you look a bit like him," he said reluctantly; "but what about these fellows?" He glanced at Whitebeard. "I don't like the look of your companions. Mind, if you take any sweets away you must sign for them, whoever you are."

"By the way," said Uncle, "you referred just now to a visit from Dr Lyre's boys. I never gave them permission to come."

"Oh, didn't you? Then what's the meaning of this?"

He reached from his desk a paper with Uncle's crest on the top. It stated that Dr Lyre's boys were to be allowed to view the Sweet Tower and that each boy was to be permitted to take away as many sweets as he could carry. It was signed in Uncle's flourishing hand.

"This is a forgery," said Uncle sternly. "Well, I think we'd better go into the tower, and when the Doctor comes I'll have a word with him."

The tower was a wonderful place, with hundreds of rooms all filled with coconut ice, toffee, mint rock and every kind of chocolate.

They paused in a great hall which was walled with toffee and floored with slab chocolate. While they were looking round they heard a sound of cheering, and Dr Lyre appeared at the head of his boys.

Uncle asked him the meaning of the permit.

"Why, it was this way," said the Doctor; "an inspector called in at the school the other day and said that he had been sent by you to inspect the boys. He heard the top form read, and then he took the chalk and wrote a sentence on the blackboard for them to read. A strange sentence it seemed to me. It was this:

UNCLE IS A BOASTER!

"I expostulated of course, but —"

"Stop!" shouted Uncle. "The abominable sentence you have quoted gives me the key to the identity of this so-called inspector. What did he look like?"

"Oh, he was rather roughly dressed. He wore a sack suit, I think. All the same, I rather liked him: I'm just a shade deaf, but I think he said his name was Hateman. I know he told me you had appointed him to be an inspector."

"All right!" said Uncle, with a hissing intake of breath. "I begin to see how things stand, but go on, I might as well hear the whole disgraceful story. What did he do then?"

"I asked him to lunch, and for an inspector he had an abnormally large appetite, but he liked my book about Lion Tower, and took a couple of copies."

"Did he pay you for them?"

"Why no, not at the time. He said he would send me a cheque for five pounds the next day, but it hasn't come yet. I expect he's a bit absent-minded like myself."

Uncle smiled bitterly.

"Then," continued the Doctor, "he was so pleased with the boys' reading that he gave the school a month's holiday there and then. He also said that he would get you to send a letter giving the boys permission to visit the Sweet Tower, and take away a sackful each. The letter arrived next day. It was brought by a curious little chap about the size of Noddy Ninety. His name, he said, was Mr Isidore Hitmouse."

"Very good," said Uncle sternly. "Call the boys together; I will have a word with the whole school before they inspect the tower."

They were soon drawn up, and awaited Uncle's speech with eager faces.

Uncle was very grave. For some time he looked

over the ranks of boys with a far-away but sombre expression. At last he spoke.

"Boys," he said, "I am sorry to inform you that you are here today under a forged permit, a permit deliberately made out by a man so grey in sin, that it seems barely possible that such a person should exist at all. He has now added forgery to his other misdeeds, and above all he is trying to be generous at another person's expense. However, I will settle with him later, and now, so that you may see that my liberality exceeds even that of a forger, who does not own what he gives away, I will arrange for you to receive not one but two sacks of sweets today, and I will also write out a permit whereby the whole school shall visit Merry-Go-Round Flats free of charge."

There was terrific cheering as Uncle announced this, and afterwards they all went right through the Sweet Tower. It's full of surprises.

"Not a bad place," said Uncle, as he sat down for a moment on a divan made of mint rock, and looked through a barley-sugar window into an interior courtyard paved with glacier mints.

"I think it's lovely," said the Old Monkey in a rapturous voice. "Oh, look at that man. He's bringing chocolates in a wheelbarrow to mend that hole in the pavement!"

They were rather amused, when they arrived at a big hall at the very top, to find Noddy Ninety was playing cricket. He had brought his bat and set up three big sticks of mint rock as wickets. Some of the boys were bowling at him with aniseed drops the size of cricket balls. He hit them every time into the same place, a huge sack which hung from the hand of a chocolate man. When the sack was full, the man, who was on a pedestal, overbalanced and fell with a resounding smash.

Old Whitebeard had been quietly eyeing a

presentation box of chocolates with the intention of sticking it away under his beard, but, just as he was lifting his arm, Noddy Ninety sent down a very fast aniseed ball, and caught him on the elbow. It jarred his funnybone, and he thought it best to retire quietly to the background.

After that they went up to the boiled-sweet room. This is a perfectly enormous place right at the top of the tower. A cascade of hard sweets of all colours, red, green and blue, came pouring out of a spout, and made a beautiful rainbow-coloured pool on the floor. They all gathered sackfuls from time to time.

After that they went to the Fun Fair, and then returned home, everybody in a very satisfied state of mind, especially Doctor Lyre, for Uncle ordered five copies of his book about Lion Tower, and paid for them on the spot.

But their satisfaction was short-lived.

As they neared Homeward they heard a low clanking hum, and an aeroplane appeared from behind Badfort and flew towards them. Rudolph, who was out near the moat, was already running for his crossbow.

It was a miserable and rusty plane, and seemed to cough and hesitate in the air. A number of tins of petrol were loosely tied on with rope. Beaver Hateman seemed to be flying it. Rudolph tried to shoot it down, but though he peppered the figure in the front seat with many bolts from his crossbow, the plane still came on, dripping oil and making a creaking noise.

They found out afterwards that the figure of Beaver Hateman was a dummy, and that Hitmouse was really flying it, crouched in the rear seat and using a dual control.

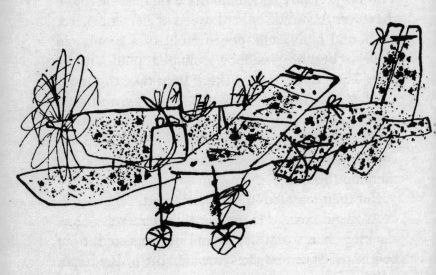

The dummy fell out just as the plane was flying off, and they found that it had been hit in nineteen places. Not one of Rudolph's shots had missed. When the plane arrived overhead, a shower of leaflets fell out, also a large bomb, filled with glue, ink, and tin-tacks, but luckily it fell in the moat.

They picked up one of the leaflets which read as follows:

TO ALL FREE CITIZENS:

This is to announce that we have at last completed our plans against Uncle, the arch-bully, tyrant and boaster. WATCH HIM! His grandeur will fade,

WATCH HIM!

Uncle made the Old Monkey gather up all these pamphlets and burn them.

He was uneasy, however, and after a time he said:

"Cowgill tells me the helicopter he's been working on is so improved that he can take me up now. Some of us will go over to Badfort, hover a little and see what they're up to."

In fact only one person could go with Uncle, for he is rather heavy, and Cowgill, who had made the helicopter and understood it, was the best one to go.

They took off from the top of the tower in which Uncle lives, and soon they were almost stationary, and, thanks to Cowgill's ENGINE NOISE MODIFIER,

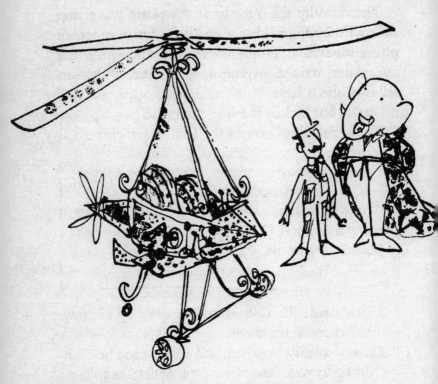

almost silent in the air above Badfort.

Uncle forgot the danger of an occasional arrow and took no notice of the one or two duck bombs which were catapulted up at them from a wooden erection which looked like a see-saw. This was a unique experience, this view of the enemy fortress from the air.

"Badfort is hollow!" he said in surprise to Cowgill. "Those towers in front are entirely deceptive. Why, what an untidy-looking place it is with that shabby field in the middle and the rickety galleries running all the way round. Can you go a little lower, Cowgill, I want to see what those offices are at the side."

"It's not safe to lose much more height, sir," said Cowgill.

"Oh, rubbish!" said Uncle, who was too interested to feel danger. "Why, I do believe they are moneylenders' offices! So that is where they get their cash!"

"There's Flabskin coming out with a bag of money!" said Cowgill.

"You're right! And as for pawnshops, Cowgill, there must be at least a hundred of them. Look at the degraded wretches streaming in with sack suits and hating-books!"

"And there's a place where you can pawn yourself, sir," said Cowgill.

"What do you mean, pawn yourself, Cowgill?"

"Oh, I've heard a lot about that," said Cowgill. "It's an old Badfort custom. A man can go in and get ten shillings on himself, and then go and sit on a shelf as a pledge."

"But what does he do with the money?"

"The usual thing, I believe, is to send out for a keg of Black Tom, sir, and sit on the shelf drinking it."

"Disgraceful," said Uncle, adding hastily, "but what then?"

"I believe he throws the keg at the proprietor, and escapes!"

"Atrocious behaviour," said Uncle. "Pass me the glass, Cowgill, and go a little lower if possible; I want to read the menu outside that café."

"No lower, sir, I dare not risk it!" said Cowgill.

"I can just read it!" cried Uncle, leaning perilously out in his excitement: 'Gossip Muffin, 1/2d., Envy Jelly, 1d., Cruelty Sausage, 1/2d., and Muddle Jelly, 1/2d.! What an atrocious list of comestibles!"

"Shall I gain height now, sir?" said Cowgill, looking anxious.

"One moment!" said Uncle, sharply. "What is that long wooden building on wheels behind Badfort? It looks like a Noah's Ark! That's what they've been hammering at."

"Look out, sir," shouted Cowgill.

A yell of derision came up from one of the dusty galleries below and a dart whistled close past Uncle's trunk. The shock made Uncle tip perilously forward. For one frightful second it looked as if nothing could save him from pitching right into the crowd which had collected below. The lurching of the helicopter was sickening, but Cowgill was able to control the machine with an effort and Uncle righted himself, breathing heavily. He and Cowgill looked at each other, acknowledging the full horror of what they had just escaped.

"Let us return to Homeward," said Uncle with as much dignity as he could command; "I have seen enough. Those are the people who wish to depose me! I need say no more!"

16

THE DANGER

"Well," said Uncle the next day, yawning, "no hammering from Badfort today! It's pleasant to be quiet for a bit, but I almost miss the miserable oafs. If some of them would turn up I'd be able to sift this matter of the school inspector and the Sweet Tower."

He picked up a duck bomb, which somebody had left behind on Christmas Eve, and skimmed it over to Badfort. There was no reply. Nobody seemed to be there.

"Where are they?" he said pettishly to the Old Monkey.

It was a dull morning. Not a single letter came and there were no callers except a thin man who was trying to sell a skeleton key guaranteed to open any door in Homeward. Uncle sent him off with a big bag of bananas. Rudolph was wolf-hunting at the back of Homeward; it's very nice out there, and has never been really explored. There are some mysterious green lights at night that have often puzzled Uncle, but he is still too busy trying to get the hang of his own house to spend time on them.

Cloutman was writing an interminable letter, holding the pen in his great fist as if it were a pistol. Alonzo S. Whitebeard was dozing on the sofa, secretly counting over the coins in his pocket.

Everything felt flat.

"What are those rascals doing?" asked Uncle again. "That big portable building intrigues me, I must say."

Just then Captain Walrus came in.

"Good morning, sir," he said. "I want to tell you that our neighbours are up to no good. I passed Joe's on the way to Cheapman's this morning, and they were all laughing about something. He's got some new stuff called 'Scream Fizz', which is very popular. But they can't even sit down and drink their vile brew decently. They all stand round and scream in chorus:

> 'He stole my glass of scream fizz
> Once but never again.
> He came with laughter on his lips
> And went away with pain.'

"Oh, they're a set of scoundrels! But some of them can sing properly if they want to. They've got a chap there called Sigismund Hateman, who is a really splendid singer. He's going to sing this afternoon in the field in front of Badfort, and they tell me that people are coming from all parts to hear him."

Uncle was deeply interested in this account. He also felt very much puzzled. What could they be up to? Instead of attacking Homeward they were singing. It seemed very strange. Uncle scratched his head as he tried to understand it.

At last he spoke to Captain Walrus.

"Where did you say this singer was going to perform?"

"In the big field over there, and he's going to start just after lunch. You can see the people rolling up already."

It was true. Thousands of badgers were streaming over the plain, and a great company of idlers from Wolftown were already there.

Uncle ordered dinner, and afterwards said:

"Well, you can all go and hear the star Sigismund if you like. I'll stay here."

The Old Monkey's eyes shone. He loves singing, and he loves being in a tightly packed crowd, because he runs over the heads of the people to the front row. They try to catch him, but are all too tightly wedged, and he enjoys the sensation.

"It's very good of you to let us go, sir," he said gratefully.

"No, it isn't," replied Uncle. "I don't want you here while you are longing to go and hear that traitor sing, and I don't want to hear his wretched singing myself. You can all clear out."

There's a kind of mud pond at the edge of the moat and when there's nobody about Uncle loves to wallow in it. He doesn't do it when anyone is there, because he thinks he would he made fun of.

They all set off and left him, and as soon as they were well over the drawbridge Uncle took off his purple dressing-gown, and walked down to the mud pond. Nobody was about, so he plunged in, and wallowed blissfully in the warm mud. He spent about an hour in this way, and was just having a pleasant doze on the bank, when he heard tremendous cheering in the distance.

In spite of himself, he got up and climbed to the moat bank. Right in front of him was a meadow shaded by trees. In it were gathered an enormous crowd of people. Standing in the midst of them, on a large barrel, was Sigismund Hateman.

Sigismund began to sing. From where he was standing, Uncle found to his annoyance that he could not hear a word, only just the faintest whisper of a tune.

The song ended. Then came the mightiest outburst of cheering that Uncle had heard for a long time. Everybody listened eagerly and all appeared to have forgotten their quarrel. Then there was a dead silence, and Uncle could see the Old Monkey running to and fro over the people's heads.

The next song was a quiet one. Uncle could hardly hear it at all. He began to feel much annoyed. He looked round. There was still nobody about, so he felt he could safely leave the castle. He strolled quietly over the drawbridge, and began to walk towards the crowd, keeping in the shadow of the bushes and trees. At last he came near enough to hear.

Sigismund Hateman was just finishing a Spanish song about a sick goat tormented by wasps. He sang it very sadly. His subject was not promising, yet Uncle found himself sniffing, and two large tears fell down on each side of his trunk. Everyone seemed to be touched; even Beaver Hateman pulled out an old dishcloth which served him as a handkerchief, and gave a loud sneeze.

There seemed to be no end to Sigismund's repertoire of songs; he sang tragic, narrative, and comic songs, one after the other; and it was a tribute to him that so mixed a crowd kept dead still in order to hear him.

He announced his subjects before he sang them.
All at once, he gave out in his high speaking voice:
"My next song is a comic parody of 'The Village
Blacksmith'." Then he began to sing:

> *"Under a spreading chestnut tree,*
> *The village tyrant stands;*
> *Uncle, a mighty man is he,*
> *With large and sinewy hands,*
> *And the muscles of his waving trunk,*
> *Are strong as iron bands.*

> *"Week in, week out, from morn till night,*
> *You can hear his boastings blow,*
> *You can see him swing his loaded trunk*
> *With measured beat and slow,*
> *And he often kicks his neighbours up*
> *When the evening sun is low.*

> *"Lying, swindling and boasting,*
> *Onward through life he goes;*
> *Each morning sees some crime begun,*
> *Each evening sees its close;*
> *Somebody bullied, somebody done,*
> *Has earned a night's repose."*

When Uncle heard this song he was full of
indignation, but he thought it best to go away

quietly, so he stole back to the house. About ten minutes later, the concert broke up, and his followers hurried away, and managed to get back before they were attacked. The moment they arrived, Uncle asked:

"How did you enjoy the concert?"

"Oh, it was grand," they all said.

"I happened to be walking near, during the last item," said Uncle gravely, "and I want to say this once and for all, I'm profoundly disappointed in the lot of you. You listened to that abominable song and liked it! Now it's no use your saying you didn't, and it's most disloyal of you! Whitebeard, I was going to give you threepence this afternoon, but you can go without it! As for you, sir –" he turned to the Old Monkey – "you actually ran over people's heads to hear an insulting song about your master!"

"I didn't know it was about you, sir. He announced it as 'The Village Tyrant'."

"Then you ought to have come right away, the moment you heard the first lines, but there, I've given up all hope of finding decency or loyalty anywhere!"

Just then the Young Monkey came up, stuttering. He pointed to the window.

They looked out and Uncle saw the large portable building which had reminded him of a Noah's Ark being brought out from behind Badfort. It was about a hundred feet long, and fifty broad, and was being

pulled along by as motley a crew as ever tugged a
weight. More than a hundred persons were drawing
on the ropes. Beaver Hateman, mounted on the
Wooden-Legged Donkey, was the leader, and behind
him were all the principal inhabitants of Badfort,
assisted by a mixed crowd of captive badgers and
others.

When they had dragged the building out into the
meadow where Sigismund had been singing, they
nailed to the front of it a huge sign:

> PLEASURELAND CINEMA
> Continuous Performance. Come in thousands!

The booking office was opened, and at once a crowd of badgers filled the place. From Homeward they could hear shrieks and squeaks of mirth from the building. At the end of every half-hour small doors were opened at the side of the building, and the spectators were driven out, for they were reluctant to leave so soon.

Most of them paid another halfpenny to see the next part of the film. It was only a halfpenny to go in, but it really cost much more, for everyone was driven out every half-hour. The film was called "The Unicorn's Dream" and it must have been really splendid. People who had been driven out could be seen borrowing money or even selling themselves into slavery to see another instalment; for you really paid quite a lot to see the whole thing.

The Old Monkey and the others were dying to go, but they dared not ask permission, so they spent the evening quietly in the large dining-room.

Uncle amused himself by showing one or two of his treasures to Alonzo S. Whitebeard, who loves to see things that are costly.

He opened a silver cupboard to show him a strange device. There was a golden spout, and from it there continually dropped shillings. They fell with a jingling sound into a little wooden keg mounted on rails. When the keg was full, automatic machinery took it away, and another one came up in its place, while the old one moved away to the treasury. These shillings represented the annual rents continually coming in from a gigantic tower away at the far end of Uncle's castle. They were collected by a trusty agent called Oliver Hoot, and just to show you how vast are Uncle's holdings I may mention that he has never yet seen Hoot, nor inspected the tower, which is called Goldfish Lodge. He means to go some day soon, but the way there is hard and puzzling, so he's waiting till Oliver Hoot comes to show him over.

Meanwhile the rents keep coming in through a tube. He actually gave Whitebeard a peep at his treasury through a twelve-inch-thick glass window protected by a flamethrower. They looked into an enormous room built of solid steel six feet thick. He only gave him one peep, but Whitebeard saw the flash and dazzle of diamonds, and the milky radiance of pearls set off by the red fire of rubies. He felt a bit dazzled, and couldn't see clearly.

Uncle, growing tired, said:

"I think I'll go out for a short walk. You can all amuse yourselves around the fire. I don't want anyone to come with me, not even the Old Monkey."

Before he left, he gave the Old Monkey a two-

UNCLE

shilling piece, for he seemed surprised at Uncle going out without him, and was downhearted.

Uncle set out. It was getting late, and all the people had gone. It seemed a very good time to have a look at the Pleasureland Cinema,

181

17

THE DISASTER

When Uncle came to the door of the cinema, everything was perfectly quiet. He waited a bit, but there seemed to be nobody about, so he decided to go in. There were some little windows high up which gave a dim light, but he drew out an electric torch from his pocket and snapped it on.

It looked very much like any other cinema, only smaller. There were some rather expensive seats labelled twopence and right in the middle of them there was a monster armchair marked threepence. Uncle went and sat down in it, and looked at the screen. It had a curtain over it, on which were some strange pictures, but he couldn't make out what they were in that dim light. One seemed to be of a wharf with boats. As he leaned forward for a closer look, he heard a sudden snap behind him, and a harsh voice shouted:

"Got him at last!"

Uncle jumped up, and rushed to the door of the cinema. It was closed and locked, but he thought little of that. He knew well that with his trunk and tusks he could soon demolish a flimsy door like this one. He threw his weight on the door, and it began to give. Another good push, and it yielded altogether.

Then came the sinister surprise.

Outside the door there was a great network of solid steel bars, and beyond these he saw the leering, hideous face of Beaver Hateman.

"Ha! Ha! Uncle," said the latter. "We've got you at last. You can try as hard as you like, but you won't get out of this!"

Uncle snorted with fury, and made a mad-bull rush at the flimsy side of the cinema. To his surprise, the wooden walls were backed by solid steel.

Again and again he rushed, but in vain. Then he rushed at the screen. To his surprise and horror, this covered a solid iron wall.

At last, with jarred tusks and bruised limbs, he came furiously back, and sat down in the threepenny armchair.

Meanwhile, Beaver Hateman was busy taking down the wooden doors, and opening others at the sides. Then he gave a bubbling howl, which was his rallying cry, and all at once his followers appeared.

Nailrod and his father, Hitmouse, Mud-Dog, Mallet Crackbone, Sigismund Hateman, Flabskin and all the others were there. Hootman hovered at one of the side doors.

They carried with them crossbows, duck bombs, skewers, and bladders of vinegar.

When they saw Uncle, they all began to howl and shout with delight.

Uncle was reassured, for he knew that the noise would soon bring his own followers up, and in this he was right. There was a loud whistle from Homeward, and Rudolph, the Old Monkey, Cloutman, Gubbins, and the rest poured over the drawbridge. They left Cowgill and the Old Monkey's father, however, to defend the house. Captain Walrus also came, trailing behind, laden almost to the ground with marlinspikes and belaying-pins.

"Let's knock the swine out," shouted Cloutman as he ran.

"Ay, that we will!" replied the Captain. "I shan't be happy till I use every one of these belaying-pins on those pirates!"

"Let me get hold of Beaver Hateman," said Gubbins, extending his mighty arms, "and I'll hug him till he squeaks for mercy!"

They were quite near the cinema, when Beaver Hateman shouted out to them:

"We've got old Uncle, and there is a stone weighing ten tons over his head. If one of you throws a spike or a belaying-pin, down comes that stone and

Uncle is flattened!"

"Is that true, sir?" shouted Gubbins, who was the nearest to the cinema.

Uncle looked up.

To his horror he saw that the whole roof of the cinema was composed of a great stone suspended by a single chain, and this chain, in turn, was fastened to an immensely strong rope. By the side of the rope, with a sharp sword in his flabby paw, stood Jellytussle.

It's seldom that Jellytussle speaks, but just then he looked down and said in an oily but cruel voice:

"It's true, Uncle! One slash and you're flattened out!"

Uncle is cool in emergencies, though inclined to be irritable over ordinary annoyances. He called out to his followers:

"Do nothing for the present! I fear these miscreants are speaking the truth for once.

"That's a nasty remark!" said Beaver Hateman savagely. "But wait a bit, and you'll know what revenge means. However, I'm going to keep cool too for the present. No, friends, don't throw your duck bombs yet! Now, it's no good getting excited, Uncle. These are my terms.

"A MILLION POUNDS! No less. I've gone into debt over this binge. I've raised all the money I could to buy this cage and the biggest dump of Black Tom and food ever known to celebrate. I've sold myself as a slave to nine different people to raise the cash. If Uncle produces a million pounds, and also signs a statement to the effect that he stole a bicycle as the start of his fortunes, I'm inclined to say, 'Treat him a bit rough and then let him go!' But, mind you, it must be a million pounds."

He turned to his henchmen, who were gibbering with excitement. "In the meantime, you can all have one shot each as a treat, just to show him what we're made of. Now all together!"

There was a hiss, and dozens of darts buried themselves in Uncle's hide, and at the same time he was deluged in poisoned vinegar. Meanwhile a deafening shriek arose from his tormentors.

"I can't stand this!" cried Cloutman. "We must attack!"

"If you do," said Beaver Hateman, "down comes the stone!"

It was no good, they had to wait.

Meanwhile, Uncle drew out as many of the darts as he could. Pierced, insulted, and streaming with vinegar, he was yet an imposing sight.

At last he stood up and waved his hand for silence. As he stared haughtily round the circle of bandits, they all felt small for the moment.

Then he spoke.

"I must say," he said, "I thought you had reached the bottom of human iniquity. Now I see that I am mistaken. It is like looking into a loathsome tank. You see one form of horror and think, 'That's the worst!' and then there's a slight stirring of the turbid fluid, and another form, more monstrous, more —"

"Shut up!" shouted Beaver Hateman. "We don't want a speech! Will you pay the million pounds or not? Now, out with it, or down comes the stone!"

Uncle paused. He was in a difficult predicament. The question was, would they liberate him if they got the money? He waited gloomily, lashing himself with his trunk in painful thought.

Just then there came a loud report, and a crimson flare lit up the sky behind them. There was a dismal screaming, and Flabskin rushed up shouting:

"The Black Tom dump's afire. Someone must have lit it!"

Meanwhile, huge flames were rising into the sky. It was true. The vast pile of kegs and baskets had been fired by someone, and now the whole place was radiant with the red glare. Beaver Hateman wavered. His desire to save the dump was so great that he was almost prepared to leave the cinema.

At last he shouted: "Down with the stone, Jellytussle! Let's try to save the dump."

But just as Jellytussle raised his sword to cut the rope, there was a twanging sound, and a well-aimed crossbow bolt knocked the weapon out of his hand. Rudolph had crept round to the back, and had been waiting for his opportunity.

Meanwhile the Old Monkey and Mig had managed to get an oxygen blowpipe at work on the bars behind the screen.

The tide had turned!

"Make a rush, sir!" shouted the Old Monkey. "Just near the screen."

Uncle did so, and in a moment found himself in the cool night air, free, and ready to deal out a terrible punishment. Trumpeting with fury, he turned on his tormentors.

They had all run away to the dump and were watching the burning kegs with cries of lamentation on their lips. It was impossible for them to get very near the dump because of the heat, and everything was as bright as day in the terrific glare.

Then, like a mighty avalanche, Uncle was upon them, and he was followed by Cloutman, Gubbins, Captain Walrus, Rudolph and the rest, while Alonzo S. Whitebeard followed close behind.

The Badfort crowd put up a most determined
resistance, but nobody could stand before Uncle that
night. Trampling with his feet, piercing with his
tusks, lassoing with his trunk, he was a veritable
tornado. Meanwhile Cloutman was singling out
individuals and stunning them with one blow of his

fist, while Old Walrus laid about him with belaying-pins and marlinspikes in true sea-dog fashion. The twang of Rudolph's crossbow seemed to be everywhere at once.

They got some very hard knocks themselves. Old Nailrod Hateman threw a keg of blazing Black Tom right over Gubbins and he had to rush into the water of the marsh to put the fire out. Uncle himself was half-blinded with vinegar and pierced with dozens of darts, but he seemed hardly to feel them.

At last he came face to face with Beaver Hateman. Uncle tried to kick him up, but his kick came at the wrong angle.

It merely sent him along the ground. He turned nineteen somersaults before he found his feet. He looked like a human wheel spinning along the ground. Just as he at last ceased his whirling, and stood for a moment to take a breath, Uncle saw his opportunity. There was a quick rush, and a sharp thud, a loud cry, and then the body of Beaver Hateman soared majestically into the crimson sky over the burning dump.

That was the end of the resistance. All the Badfort people faded away, and Uncle and his followers were left on the field triumphant.

They marched home, merely pausing to set the cinema on fire, and they soon crossed the draw-bridge.

As they entered, Cowgill, who is a good trumpeter, blew a joyous blast.

They hurried into the hall. Hot baths were prepared, Magic Ointment was provided, medicine and bandages were made ready, and, only an hour after the great fight, Uncle was well-nigh himself again.

As he sat down, he said:

"Well, I think that's the best night's work I've ever done! Tomorrow shall be a day of public rejoicing!"

18

THE DAY OF PUBLIC REJOICING

The next day dawned cloudless. It seemed as if all nature were prepared to revel with Uncle. The air was like crystal, except that in front of Badfort the dump was still burning and throwing up a great column of black smoke, which fortunately blew away from Uncle's and right over the top of the house of Hateman.

Uncle got up in high spirits. His wounds were nearly healed, and he spent the morning in receiving deputations, and also congratulatory telegrams from all parts of the country.

Many presents also arrived. The Marquis of Wolftown outdid himself, sending no less than a hundred trains filled with hams, lard, dried goats' flesh, etc. Cheapman sent an army of a thousand badgers, who marched in single file, each carrying on his head a box of provisions.

The King of the Badgers, poor as he was, had still

managed to send six stalwart policemen carrying boxes of choice dates and fruits, as well as a little case containing some of his family jewellery. I may say that Uncle returned this, and with it such a handsome gift in cash that the King was quite well off for about a year after.

An unknown magnate called Rosco, who lives beyond the green lights in the marshes, sent a hundred wagon-loads of butter, and twenty kegs of first-grade water-melon pickle.

There was also an illuminated address, hastily prepared by the badgers, with a photo of Uncle, and three hundred and fourteen lines of praise.

They were going to finish up that night with a great festival banquet and a display of fireworks, but, in the meantime, Cowgill, that most ingenious man, had managed to make a vast supply of daylight fireworks. I don't know whether you have seen these, but they go up like rockets, then explode, making many very curious shapes in the sky.

Some of them made clouds like lions, some like unicorns, but the best of all were some huge rockets, which when they exploded made a great pink cloud in the sky on which was the gigantic figure of an elephant, with uplifted trunk. These were loudly cheered.

During the day Uncle made preparations for a feast on the green in front of Homeward.

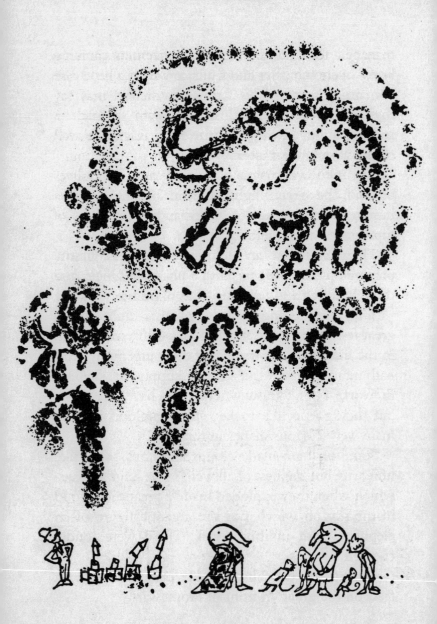

Decorations began to appear. The most remote towers were hung with silk curtains and flags.

Cowgill was in his element, for his staff of engineers were preparing an elaborate scheme of flood-lighting and illuminations. Right above Homeward, they were rushing up a monster sign: 'Uncle the Victor'. Bells rang, songs were shouted. The Old Monkey was particularly happy, because Uncle had told him that he never intended to go exploring without him again.

Butterskin Mute arrived about noon, driving a wagon loaded with ferns and beautiful flowers, and he was followed by about twenty farm carts loaded with his finest vegetables.

It took them nearly all day to make the preparations. Invitations were out early, and the

railways and elevators were black with passengers coming to the feast.

Uncle had arranged for many jugglers and singers to be at hand to entertain the waiting crowds. Meanwhile the banqueting tables were being set out, and a huge festival chair of solid gold studded with turquoises had arrived from Cowgill's works.

They had very little to eat during the day: there was not much time. As soon as one deputation had gone, another appeared on the drawbridge. All the presents were piled up in one place. There was no attempt at order, they came so fast. You saw casks of lard, hams, Turkish delight, chests of tea, side by side with ornamental chairs, cups and goblets.

At last all was ready. Dr Lyre and his boys had come, and also Auntie and Miss Wace, the Maestro and the Little Lion. So had Don Guzman and the two leopards, the Respectable Horses, and the Old Man and Eva. Everybody was there.

At six o'clock in the evening the banquet began, and it continued till nine, when, at a signal from Uncle, the whole castle was illuminated by millions of electric lights while the great sign flashed above their heads in red, purple and yellow.

"This does me good," said Uncle to the Old Monkey as he leaned back in his chair. He was wearing his diamond trunk-tips, and gold-studded boots, and a special purple dressing-gown embroidered with gold and rubies.

"I was never so happy in my life, sir," said the Old Monkey, with glistening eyes. "The main thing is that you're safe and sound!"

Uncle made no reply, but put his hand into his pocket and pressed a five-pound note into the Old Monkey's paw.

Then the fireworks began, and continued for more than an hour. They were stupendous. Some rockets were so huge that they seemed like barrels on the end of scaffolding poles. Then they burst in the air, turning the sky into a lake of dazzling light.

At last the fireworks were over, and Uncle began to distribute his gifts. He had decided that the whole pile should be given to the assembled multitudes, and, besides that, he had added a pound note for everyone, and an enormous sack of mixed foods and goods. So big were these sacks, that the dwarfs in particular found it impossible to move them, and had to hire transport.

At last the multitudes began to fade away, but before they went Uncle made a speech:

"Friends and followers," he said, "we are all assembled today to rejoice over the defeat of a set of human skunks. (Loud cheers!) I am very proud today, and yet, I am in a somewhat humble mood – so much happiness makes me feel almost solemn. I wish to say this, that I have today sent a cheque for £2,000 to the owner of the bicycle, which I once, in my callow youth, er — appropriated for my own temporary use. I have also sent him six hundred casks of herrings (cheers), a thousand kegs of Turkish delight (loud cheers), and fifty thousand first-grade cheeses! (Terrific cheers!) I think, after this," said Uncle, mildly but firmly, "that I shall hear no more of a certain song. Now disperse, and I hope to meet you all again on many occasions. Be upright, pay your rent, avoid brawling and disorder, and you will find Uncle a friend and protector at all times."

As he ended, the cheering was deafening, but at last they began to go away, and Uncle sat down for a quiet chat with the Old Monkey.

Meanwhile at Badfort also a celebration was going on. Beaver Hateman had persuaded his followers that, in spite of being kicked up, he had scored a great victory over Uncle. Their stocks were low, but a Syrian, called Abdullah the Clothes-Peg Merchant, who lived in the marsh, had sent them presents. He sent them seven wagons loaded with dates and dried goats' flesh of an inferior quality and also he paid Beaver Hateman's ransom to the nine people to whom he had sold himself as a slave, though he needn't have troubled to do this, because, as Beaver Hateman said: "If they want me they have got to fetch me!" He also gave them £9 7s. 6½d. in money. Also they had managed to save some of the Black Tom which had run down from the dump without taking fire.

They had all gathered in a circle, and were having a festival evening.

The dump was still slowly burning, and at about eleven o'clock one or two more kegs caught fire and burned up with a very strong purplish blaze. In the light of it Sigismund Hateman got up to sing. Beaver Hateman appeared to be quite well again, and he was accompanying him on a small guitar.

This is what they were singing. I don't think Uncle heard it, for he had just turned aside to receive one last deputation, but the Old Monkey, listening carefully, heard every word.

"I went into the cinema
On a cool and frosty night;
I sat down in the threepenny chair,
And then I got a fright . . ."

He didn't hear any more, for there were cheers and laughter at this point.

Before Uncle went to bed, he said to the Old Monkey: "I really think we've finished with Badfort this time."

The Old Monkey shook his head doubtfully as he went up the stairs.

UNCLE
CLEANS UP

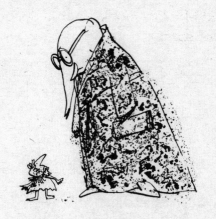

To
Stella, Grace, John and Hal

1

TEA ON THE LAWN

After Uncle's victory over the Badfort crowd he felt he could look forward to a peaceful summer.

"I really think we've dealt with them this time," he said, but the Old Monkey, his faithful friend and helper, was not so sure.

It had been a great victory. Uncle and his supporters had driven off Beaver Hateman and his gang after a fierce fight.

Now it was a time of celebration – of fireworks and banquets and messages of congratulation. Letters, telephone calls and greetings telegrams poured in. And so many visitors came to see Uncle that for a time he behaved with extra politeness and did a good deal of entertaining.

One fine afternoon he asked several important neighbours to tea on the lawn outside his immense castle of Homeward.

"Let's do the thing properly," Uncle said to the

Old Monkey. "What about some of those big striped umbrellas? They'd look very festive set up along the edge of the moat."

"Oh yes, sir," agreed the Old Monkey, "and Cheapman has a good stock at a halfpenny each."

Cheapman's Store is in Badgertown. It is a delightful shop where you can get all sorts of splendid things for a halfpenny.

So the tables were set out under the gay umbrellas. The many-coloured towers of Homeward, with switchback railways and chutes strung almost like glittering necklaces between them, looked magnificent in the sunshine. A little distance across the moat lay Badfort, the home of Beaver Hateman, Uncle's enemy. The sight of this huge dingy fortress, always in need of new glass for broken windows, was a constant annoyance to the inhabitants of Homeward. However, the Old Monkey and Cowgill, Uncle's engineer, had placed the umbrellas so that the party would face the massive drawbridge that spanned the blue waters of the moat – a much more pleasant view.

"Pity the King of the Badgers can't come," said Uncle.

The King of the Badgers is one of Uncle's best friends and neighbours, but he was away arranging a loan from a foreign banker.

Unfortunately, Uncle's brother, Rudulf, the

big-game hunter and traveller, could not be at the party either. After giving valuable help to Uncle in his great fight with Beaver Hateman and the Bads, he had gone back to his exploration of the Lester-Lester Mountains.

"We'll ask Ivan Koff and Len Footganger," said Uncle.

Ivan Koff comes of a noble Polish family. He has splendid manners, and looks well when he is dressed up, but he is rather touchy. For instance, if he sees someone with a slightly larger egg than he has, he thinks nothing of throwing a teapot at that person's head.

Len Footganger appears to know all sorts of important people. He dresses well, but a funny thing about him is that though he wears a well-cut morning coat he wears no shirt with it. Still, this doesn't matter as he spreads his tie over his chest and wears a lot of medals. They are made of rather thin tin, but he explains that he has left his real ones at home. He always carries a great book, *The House of Zillagicci*, which he says is a history of some near relatives.

Uncle also asked a very respectable person, Thomas Glot, who lives in a little hut that juts out over a waterfall.

Several of Uncle's supporters were asked to meet these notabilities.

Don Guzman, who looks after Uncle's oil lake at the base of a distant tower in Homeward, was asked. He says he has a huge estate in Andalusia.

Alonzo S. Whitebeard, who is a friend of Uncle's in spite of being rather miserly, was allowed to come on condition that he combed his beard and put on a clean shirt; he agreed, because there is nothing he likes so much as a free tea.

And, of course, Butterskin Mute, Uncle's gardener, who grows such large cabbages and lettuces, came as well. Uncle had asked him to leave his rake behind and not to wear his smock. Without these things he looked rather uncomfortable as he wears nothing underneath except a pair of maroon-coloured trousers and a frightful singlet with brown marks on it. The fact is that Mute is not much of a person for dress, but the moment he smiles you forget this! In any case the Old Monkey lent him a frogged coat with brass buttons on it, so he looked fairly well.

Altogether they made a very smart group. Uncle's purple dressing-gown, and, of course, an elephant's dressing-gown is very big, added a splendid touch of colour. The Old Monkey makes a good waiter and the tea-party looked like being a great success.

They had thin bread and butter with eggs and jam, and some very small cress sandwiches. Some of the guests found Uncle's egg-shell china difficult to manage, but Uncle had no trouble as he was able to lift cups with a little tip at the end of his trunk. Still, he found the cress sandwiches rather a trial. There seemed to be nothing in them, and an egg was not much use to him either. He doesn't like teaspoons, which is understandable, and in fact he was secretly wishing for one of his solid meals of ham, buckets of cocoa and nets full of cabbages.

Thomas Glot ate cress sandwiches in a dignified way, taking very small bites, and between each bite uttering well-balanced remarks about the weather and the state of the crops.

Footganger also ate very elegantly, but I must say he ate a great deal. An egg was soon gone, and, as for cress sandwiches, his fingers hovered over them like butterflies, and in no time, it seemed, the plate of sandwiches was empty. The Old Monkey kept bringing him more, but he had hardly put down a fresh plateful when there was Footganger languidly looking at the empty plate and lifting to his lips another cup of tea.

Don Guzman did not worry over the unsubstantial provisions because he was narrating a terrific story about his estate in Andalusia, to which he hoped to retire very soon and where, it appeared, he kept no less than ninety boarhounds.

Uncle can't bear long stories of any kind, and he was beginning to feel bored by Don Guzman when the Old Monkey, hurrying up with a fresh plate of sandwiches, whispered in his ear:

"Oh, sir, look across the moat! See who's coming!"

Uncle turned to look towards the dusty unmade road which led to Badfort. The Old Monkey was right. Two shabby carts were making their way towards the moat.

The first cart, pulled by the Wooden-Legged Donkey, held Beaver Hateman, who was wearing a particularly ragged sack suit and a battered silk hat with a flag sticking out of the top. This cart also carried a rickety old table and chairs with some legs missing, and a collection of torn black umbrellas. Hitmouse, a wretched little person who is the chief reporter on the *Badfort News* and who lives in a Nissen hut outside Badfort, was sitting by Hateman. He was bristling, as usual, with skewers, and writing in a hating book. The back of the cart seemed filled with a large jelly of a bluish colour, and this, of course, was Jellytussle, a most spiteful character.

The second cart was driven by Nailrod Hateman, while Sigismund and Filljug Hateman crouched among a number of rusty tea-urns and cardboard boxes of food.

Hootman, a kind of ghost, who spends his time plotting against Uncle, was wafting himself along somewhere between the two carts.

"Take no notice of them," said Uncle. "Don't flatter the miscreants by giving them your attention."

But as the Badfort party set up their tables just across the moat it was impossible to ignore them altogether, especially as Uncle was getting tired of the smallness of his repast, and the Badfort crowd had got together from some source or other quite a solid feast. They had large hams, loaves of bread and buckets of tea, and soon began to eat these things in hideous imitation of the polite party so near to them.

Beaver Hateman took a well-cooked ham between his fingers and thumb, and said in a high-pitched voice as he passed it to Nailrod:

"Have another sandwich, Count!"

"No, thank you, but won't you take one of these

little cakes?" replied Nailrod, balancing a whole loaf on a very small egg-cup. "They're so light!"

Hitmouse brought Filljug a plum-cake on an imitation lace mat torn out of newspaper.

"I'm such a small eater," said Filljug in a high squeaky voice. "It always takes about twenty bites for me to eat a macaroon."

Uncle was getting very hot. There was no doubt that the Hateman gang were deliberately insulting him.

Then Beaver Hateman took a whole bucket of tea, and in some mysterious way held it in the crook of his little finger.

"I'm so glad I've got this little attachment on the end of my trunk. It's so handy for holding egg-shell china!" he said in a loud offensive voice.

Still Uncle controlled himself, and went on eating, though with a faint heart, the cress sandwiches that were set before him.

All at once Thomas Glot threw down his cup of egg-shell china, and shouted:

"This is a rotten show! Those chaps over there know how to do a tea much better than you!"

Uncle was surprised and hurt, but he was still more upset when Footganger suddenly yelled:

"I've been here two hours, and hardly had a bite!"

This was most unfair, for they had devoured twenty eggs and nineteen platefuls of sandwiches, besides emptying six three-tiered cakestands of their contents.

"Besides," Footganger went on, "it's so jolly slow! Look, I'll show you a bit of life and action!"

Footganger rose, and balanced a silver teapot on the end of his toe. Then, with a skilful movement, he jerked it on to his forehead, and dipped his head so that tea began to pour out of the spout into his mouth. It was frightfully hot, but he didn't appear to mind that. Then he began to spin the sugar basin on the heel of his boot.

Thomas Glot could juggle too, for he took a plate of sandwiches and threw them into the air, in such an artful way that they came down in a stream, and he stood underneath and snapped them up as they fell.

Meanwhile Beaver Hateman, made bold by the remarks of the visitors, snatched a large fish that was swimming by in the moat, and threw it at Uncle. It hit him on the side of his head with a slack wet noise.

Uncle flushed, and lashed himself thoughtfully with his trunk. He hesitated to begin again the old wary battle with the Badfort crowd. Yet action seemed almost thrust upon him.

"I am a person of peace and order," he began.

"Shut up!" shouted Beaver Hateman. "We don't want to hear the old bike-thief!"

That decided the matter.

Uncle had been extremely patient, but this allusion to an incident of his University days was too much. Once, in his hurry to get to an examination, he had borrowed a bicycle without permission and, being very heavy, broken it. The Badfort crowd never forget this and never let Uncle forget it either. It irritates Uncle more than anything else.

Uncle noticed that the Old Monkey had propped up one of the table legs with a large stone club. It is not usual to take weapons to a tea-party in your own garden, and Uncle had come quite unprepared. Now, ready to his hand, lay the means of delivering a swift answer to these continued insults.

Uncle stooped, picked up the stone club, and hurled it at Beaver Hateman.

It took him by surprise. The first sign the miscreant had that Uncle was in action again was something like an earthquake in the region of his right ear.

This prompt and vigorous action revived Uncle. He was at once his old autocratic self, and turned his back on the Badfort crowd. He even smiled graciously as he watched Footganger balancing chairs on his nose. Then Thomas Glot carried along a table on his back without spilling a drop of tea or milk. As Glot was on his hands and knees under it, the table seemed to run along the ground and up the steps into the hall of Homeward. It was an amusing sight.

Soon Beaver Hateman pulled himself together again.

"You big bully!" he shouted. "I've done nothing to you, and you've injured me badly – maybe *mortally*!"

This did not seem to be true, for he paused and drank off the contents of a jug of iced soup while he was getting his breath.

"I suppose you don't call throwing a flat-fish at your neighbour during a party an injury?" inquired Uncle in masterful tones.

"No, I don't," said Beaver Hateman. "And let me tell you, that I'm going to attack you soon in a very unusual manner. I've been doing a little quiet inspection while you've been giving parties and I've 'acquired' – note that word – a copy of your book on the secret passages of Homeward. My friend Hootman has done a bit of nosing around, and we've found passages leading into your old castle that you've never dreamed of! Ha, ha, you'll soon find out what we're up to!"

Uncle ducked, but not quickly enough to avoid a teapot that Beaver Hateman flung at him with a lightning movement. By the time that he had got the fluid out of his eyes, the scoundrels were well on their way to Badfort.

Uncle went into Homeward in a thoroughly bad temper. However, he found in the hall a letter that cheered him up.

It read as follows:

FLINT, FLINT, FLINT, BURROUGHS, FLINT,
MACKINTOSH, COATES & STAINER, GOBBLE COURT

Dear Sir,

We beg to inform you that our esteemed client Mr Laurence Goatsby was so impressed by your conduct in dealing with certain bandits that he has decided to make over to you the sum of £1,000,000 (One Million Pounds) to be used for any good purpose you may have in mind.

He wishes, however, to make two small conditions:

(1) The name of the foundation to be The Laurence Goatsby Benefit.

(2) A small statue of Mr Goatsby, which our client
      will dispatch in advance, to be placed in the hall
      of your residence Homeward.

If you agree to these terms Mr Goatsby will himself in
due course bring you the cash in gold ingots.

Yours faithfully,

FLINT, FLINT, FLINT etc.

Uncle read this letter to the Old Monkey.

"We'll have to think this over," he said. Then he
added, "This has not been a bad day after all, but I'm
getting a bit tired of these polite tea-parties, so we'll
have meals as usual in future.

2

A VISIT TO WHITEBEARD'S

Uncle was not long in sending a reply to the lawyers, and a few days later he had a telephone message from them. The Old Monkey took the message.

"Mr Goatsby is coming at eleven this morning," he reported to Uncle, "and bringing the statue with him."

Mr Goatsby drove up in a gigantic motor. The statue was wrapped in packing cloth, and firmly fixed on a roof luggage carrier.

Goatsby was a singular-looking man. He had great projecting ears, and such small eyes, hidden behind such thick glasses, that you could hardly see them. After a little refreshment, he began to argue with Uncle as to the place where the statue was to be put.

"It would be best in front of the fireplace," Goatsby said, snappishly.

"I'm not so sure," objected Uncle. "It would be

awkward to sit round the fire with a statue in our midst.

"I don't see why!"

But Uncle refused to budge.

Goatsby sulked for a minute or two, then had a fresh idea. He walked over to the main picture in the hall at Homeward, the magnificent oil painting of Uncle opening the dwarfs' drinking fountains.

"That's the place," he said, "right under that old picture."

Uncle very rightly objected to this.

"It would destroy the effect of the picture," he said firmly.

At last they placed it in an alcove, where it was fairly noticeable, though Goatsby was not too pleased. Uncle had to tell him that his million-pound gift, though useful, was by no means indispensable. So in the end Goatsby gave in and drove off saying he would return in a few days with the money in the shape of gold ingots.

It was funny that the moment he was left alone with it Uncle felt that the statue of Goatsby began to get on his nerves. It was so very plain-looking. Even the Old Monkey confessed that he wanted to knock off the hateful projecting marble ears.

Uncle was even beginning to consider sending the statue back and doing without the million pounds, but Whitebeard begged him not to.

"Well," said Uncle, "I'd like to get away from it for a bit, anyhow. I think I'll come and stay with you for a day or so, Whitebeard."

Whitebeard turned very pale.

It is true that he had often invited Uncle to come and stay with him, but he had never dreamed that he might actually come. Whitebeard is such a miser that the very thought of providing a meal for himself makes him shudder, and the thought of providing for Uncle put him into a high fever.

Still he could hardly get out of it. He had been staying with Uncle, off and on, for nearly a year. So he gave a ghastly smile, and said it would be a pleasure, but that, being a poor man, he was afraid that his house would be badly stocked.

"That's a pity," replied Uncle, "for I was thinking of bringing Cloutman, Gubbins, Cowgill and the Old Monkey. Still, I dare say we shall manage, for I remember some months ago giving you three barrels of tinned food. You thanked me warmly, and sent them to your house to be used in case of siege, or if visitors came. Those were your very words. These will be ample for the first day, and by that time you will have had time to look round and order in further supplies."

Every word he spoke was like a poisoned dagger turning in Whitebeard's heart.

"We'll go immediately after breakfast," said Uncle.

"Wouldn't it be better to wait till after lunch – or even till after dinner?" begged Whitebeard.

"No," said Uncle, "we'll start in good time, and then you'll have all the morning to prepare a substantial lunch."

Next morning Whitebeard swallowed twice his usual breakfast as a tonic, and also so as to need less of his own food at lunch-time.

Uncle had, however, got among his morning mail a pamphlet on 'The No-Breakfast Slimming Theory', and decided to try it at once.

"I'll go without breakfast this morning," he said to the Old Monkey, "except for a bucket of cocoa. If I feel a bit faint, I'll make up for it at lunch."

Whitebeard looked up with a sickly smile.

"Old Gleamhound says that going without breakfast is very good for most people, but very bad for elephants," he said.

"Don't worry, I'm only going to try it for one day," said Uncle, reassuringly. "Tomorrow when I'm staying with you I'll have breakfast as usual."

At last they started. Several of them were going on the traction engine which was pulling a tender as well. All the people that Uncle had mentioned went, as well as the Old Monkey's father and the Muncle, though the Muncle didn't travel on the traction engine. He had put on a pair of special electric boots; he switched on the motor and they carried him along. The Muncle is always thinking about boots and shoes, and he has lots of pairs, big travelling ones that run on wheels, some smart lemon-coloured ones, and some that are so highly polished that they look like steel.

Cloutman and Gubbins were rather late and had to start without any breakfast. However, as they told Whitebeard, it would be easy to make up at lunch.

They had quite a safe journey. Badfort was quiet, except that a great fat cat, almost the size of a tiger, was hurled violently out of a window into the moat as the traction engine chugged past.

At last they reached Whitebeard's farm. It's hard to see it at first, for it is surrounded by a very high hedge of sharp thorns. Whitebeard dismounted, and unlocked the gate. The moment they were inside and the gate was shut again, he had to climb speedily back on to the engine, for down the drive came a small herd of lean muscular pigs with sharp tusks, and they made straight for him. The fact is that Whitebeard doesn't feed his pigs, and the result is that they have grown lean and wild and are very fast runners. Also they have developed the habit of fighting in packs like peccaries, and are very dangerous.

"It's asking for trouble keeping them so short," said Uncle. "One day they're going to hurt you, Whitebeard."

"Well," replied Whitebeard, "if there's anything left

over from lunch, I may give it them!"

This was not likely to happen, for Whitebeard gathers up fragments of meals in a bag which he hides under his beard and saves them for himself. He eats them in the middle of the night with tremendous relish.

When they got in, they all sat down in a perfectly neat room with a door at the end of it labelled 'Larder'.

Whitebeard told them to be seated. They looked a massive and hungry company sitting there, as Whitebeard went with trembling hands to the larder, unlocked the door, and then gave a shout of surprise.

"Oh, I say," he said, "there's hardly a thing in the cupboard! Someone must have been stealing my supplies!"

Uncle knew perfectly well that this was a lie. It might be all that Whitebeard had in that cupboard, but it was not all his store.

"Scatter, boys," said Uncle, "and search the house for hidden supplies!"

All Uncle's followers are good at finding secret passages and hiding-places, and it was not long before Cloutman gave a joyous cry: "Come here, sir. Just look at that!" A whole wall of the room had moved on rollers, and inside was a really well-fitted grocer's shop, with a counter, scales, a till, shopping baskets and string. On the shelves was one of the best displays of provisions that Uncle had ever seen.

As a matter of fact Whitebeard is so miserly that he can't even bring in food from his own store without pretending to strike a bargain with himself. He pretends there is a shopman there, and offers eightpence for a ninepenny tin of salmon. He then pays the money into the till and feels he has struck a good bargain.

Uncle looked grave. "Whitebeard, you have lied to me. I'm sorry to say it of a personal friend, and I would take a stronger action, if I did not remember how well you served me in a supreme hour of peril by wheeling up that truck-load of stone clubs. You will now serve us with your costliest and choicest provisions, and those in unlimited quantities!"

Whitebeard was horror-struck.

"Oh no, sir!" he gasped. "Not *choicest*! Not most *costly*!" Then, in a kind of shriek: "Not UNLIMITED QUANTITIES!!"

However, Uncle thought Whitebeard needed a lesson, so they all sat down to a mighty feast.

"That's my ninth tin of preserved ginger," said Cloutman to Gubbins, "and really, I think it tastes better than the first!"

The room they were sitting in looked out on the garden where there was a statue of Whitebeard.

"Strange," said Uncle, "I don't remember seeing that statue before, Whitebeard."

"I've never seen it myself," said Whitebeard. At that moment the pack of lean angry pigs came round the corner and made a rush at the statue which they thought was Whitebeard himself. As the pigs rushed up, the figure was quickly drawn back on a plank into a recess in the wall. Two of the pigs rushed after it, and the flap was then quickly closed.

"I come here," said Uncle, rather crossly, "to get away from one statue, and here is another. I seem haunted by statues!"

The Old Monkey ran upstairs to look out of a window, and came back with the explanation of the mystery.

"Beaver Hateman and a sort of shadowy chap are loading those two pigs into a cart pulled by the Wooden-Legged Donkey," he said.

"Well," said Uncle, striking his trunk on the table with a resounding blow, "that's clever! I can see that the ghost Hoootman is behind this. It's far too smart for Beaver Hateman. There'll be roast pork in Badfort tonight!"

As he spoke, they heard a loud shriek, and an old man came sprinting round the house pursued by the rest of the wild pigs.

"That's your father, Whitebeard," said Uncle.

"Oh dear," said Whitebeard, "I didn't know he was coming."

Whitebeard's father is a detestable man. His son

appears almost lovable by his side. He dresses in would-be fashionable clothes, and has a laugh which makes every living creature shrink away. But at the moment he was not laughing at all; he was screaming, and I may say that his scream is far better than his laugh.

As he came round for the second time, he saw Whitebeard in the window. "Alonzo!" he called in a piercing voice. "My son! My son!"

But a great black boar was snapping at his heels, so he tore off again.

As he came round for the fourth time, he was slowing down. "This can only end one way," said Uncle, gravely.

But he was wrong, for Whitebeard's father suddenly stopped, drew himself to his full height, and gave vent to a laugh so sickening that every pig paused. Then he laughed again. So abominable was his merriment that the swine seemed to lose strength.

With an odious chuckle he stooped forward and said:

"The pigs, the dear little pigs, how I love the DEAR LITTLE PIGS!!"

And he tried to put his hand on the head of a pink sow that had been foremost in the chase, but he laughed again so foully that the pigs began to shrink away into the bushes. Also a number of plants and

shrubs near by began to droop and wilt.

Laughing hideously, Whitebeard's father then walked towards the house.

Whitebeard turned to Uncle, looking worried.

"This has been a day of great strain to me, sir," he said, "and if my father is allowed to come in I feel that I shall be seriously ill!"

Others felt the same, and Uncle took up a seven-pound tin of corned beef and threw it haughtily at the detestable man's feet.

"Now, be off!" he said.

And to everybody's surprise and relief Whitebeard's father went.

3

UNCLE'S TREASURY

When Uncle came back from Whitebeard's, he settled down to his usual breakfast routine.

The Old Monkey came cheerfully in with two buckets of cocoa and a great basket of breadfruit and bananas. But Uncle, instead of reading the paper, was looking gloomily at the statue of Goatsby.

"I don't like the way its ears stick out," he said.

"No, sir, nor do I," agreed the Old Monkey. "And it's got such a sneering expression. I don't feel at home with it in the room."

"I suppose I'll have to get used to it," said Uncle, turning his back on the statue. "The gold ingots will be coming this afternoon."

"Where will you be putting them, sir?"

"In my treasury. We'll all go together to deposit it."

"Oh good, I've never been to the treasury," said the Old Monkey, in high spirits once again.

Uncle collected a strong company together to

move the gold ingots. He sent for Cloutman and Gubbins and Captain Walrus, while Noddy Ninety was also told to come, for he's a shrewd old chap, and good at watching against treachery. Ninety, although very old, likes to dress up as a schoolboy and go to Dr Lyre's school in Lion Tower. He knows the work so well by now that he starts in the bottom form on Monday and is in the top form by Friday afternoon. He is also very good at cricket. He works on the trains of Homeward during the holidays.

The gold ingots arrived in ten large wagons. The gold was in the form of polished bricks and bars, and looked very handsome shining in the sun.

Uncle had told Cowgill to be prepared for the transport of heavy materials, and he was ready with a number of motor-lorries.

Uncle's henchmen made an imposing sight drawn up in the hall, and Goatsby seemed very much impressed by the massive figures of Cloutman and Gubbins and the venerable, but tough form of Noddy Ninety.

"Didn't know you had all these chaps working for you!" he said. "Well, it will take the whole lot of them to shift this stuff. Do you know that it takes two strong men all their time to lift one of the smallest of these ingots?"

Uncle motioned to Gubbins, and Gubbins, without the slightest effort, picked up two of the largest ingots and flung them into a truck.

Goatsby was amazed. "This is a valuable helper of yours!" he said, in rather a jealous voice.

"Oh, the others are just as good in their way," replied Uncle. "Cloutman, for instance, can strike down a lion with one blow!"

"Let's get the stuff in," said Goatsby, irritably. "I suppose you have a suitable place to put it?"

"Yes," replied Uncle, in a grave, dignified voice, "my treasury."

He took from his pocket a small key, and went into a room adjoining the hall. Then everybody heard a loud, piercing noise rather like a buzz-saw and Uncle motioned them to approach. What they saw surprised them.

The whole floor of the room had risen up to the ceiling. Where the floor had been, a long smooth passage of brilliantly lighted steel sloped gently downwards.

"Drive the lorries in carefully," said Uncle, "and then everybody can sit on them and we'll start. Are you all here?"

They were all there except Alonzo S. Whitebeard, who was discovered in a fainting condition. The sight of so much gold had made him positively ill. However, Uncle happened to have in his pocket a packet of Gleamhound's Faintness Producer for Burglars. On it were the words: 'Guaranteed to protect the timid housewife. Simply place a couple on your adversary's tongue, and he falls into a deep coma.' As Gleamhound's remedies work backwards he slipped two into Whitebeard's mouth and he revived, and stretched himself admiringly by the side of a large ingot.

The lorries glided down the sloping passage and after a long journey drew up at a huge barrier of massive steel.

Uncle's treasury is guarded by a very good sentry called Oldeboy. As the lorries stopped they saw him looking out from his sentry-box which had a flame-thrower fixed on the top of it. Oldeboy is only about sixteen, but he is always pretending to be old. He admires Noddy Ninety so much that he copies him in every way possible, even wearing an artificial beard and large spectacles. He is very sharp-witted and makes a first-rate sentry.

"Stand, every one of you, and then come up to the light!" he said and switched on a powerful electric lamp.

"Have I got to do this?" asked Goatsby crossly.

"Let's have a look at you, one by one, or I'll turn the flame-thrower on you!" was Oldeboy's answer to that.

When he had examined them he turned to Uncle.

"Right, you can unlock the gate, sir. I have to be careful, you know. Only last week a fellow arrived disguised as Whitebeard. He was all beard and whiskers. I wasn't satisfied so gave him a taste of the flame-thrower. That scorched his whiskers off, and who do you think it was?"

"I know – Beaver Hateman," said Uncle. "That man's foul trail is everywhere!"

"He went off down the passage like a firework, sir."

"You've done finely, Oldeboy, finely!" said Uncle.

"Need I go to Dr Lyre's school any more sir?" asked Oldeboy. "It makes me feel too young."

"You stay while you can! It's a fine school!" shouted Ninety.

"You can guard my treasury for the time being, but your studies must continue," said Uncle. "In the meantime here is a little present I have been keeping for you."

He handed Oldeboy a bottle labelled 'Gleamhound's Youth and Beauty Foam. Turns a withered, wrinkled hag into a peach-complexioned sylph in a few minutes. Simply rub in.'

"Oh, sir," said Oldeboy, "I want to look very old!"

"Listen to him," said Ninety in disgust. "What I'd give to look as well as he does in a school cap!"

"Don't you know that Gleamhound's medicines work backwards? You'll find this effective. Try it."

Oldeboy rubbed in the lotion and in a moment had the wrinkled face of an old man; his very eyes looked dim and his face seemed to fall in.

"And," said Uncle, "in case your mother doesn't like your looks, here is a little tin of Gleamhound's Old Man Ointment."

"I thought we were coming to a treasury, not a beauty parlour," said Goatsby.

Uncle felt annoyed at this, but he said nothing, only giving the signal for the lorries to move on. At last they reached the treasury, passing through nine steel doors – each of which had to be unlocked – to get there.

Uncle's treasury resembles a vast cave lined with steel. Valuables are piled everywhere in majestic confusion. The vast room is about half full, but Uncle directed the lorries to be pushed into an open space in front of a mighty pile of gold. Then he directed Cloutman to unload the gold bars.

As a matter of fact Goatsby's million pounds worth of gold didn't seem to make much difference. "You have to look twice to see if it's there, don't you?" said Uncle.

This seemed to be too much for Goatsby, who turned away from the pile of gold and said:

"Well, let's get back."

As a matter of fact Uncle wanted to get home by six o'clock as he was expecting a very special parcel by the second post, so he gave the signal to return.

The journey to the treasury had made Uncle

forget Goatsby's statue, but as soon as he got back to the hall of Homeward its ugliness made him shudder. The marble ears seemed to stick out even further, and it was depressing to think that having accepted the gold ingots he now had this hateful object in his living-room for ever.

"Oh, look at my statue!" cried Goatsby. "It's not very well dusted, is it?"

"You had better remove it if you don't like the way it is kept," said Uncle, breathing heavily.

"Oh no, your room would look so empty and drab without it! I'm sure you won't mind me coming every week and bringing a feather duster!"

This insult to the Old Monkey's housekeeping was too much for Uncle. "Look," he said, "to tell you the truth I'm tired of your statue, Goatsby. You can take it away."

The Old Monkey jumped for joy.

"What about the gold ingots?" said Goatsby, with an odious smile. "No statue, no ingots."

Uncle went to his desk and took out his cheque-book.

"I will pay you for the ingots and that will finish the matter! That is unless you would like me to take the gold out of the treasury again."

"Oh, we can't go through all that again!" said Goatsby. "I'll take the cheque."

"You'll have to cash it here," said Uncle. "There's

no bank in the country that could meet such a sum. And I reserve the right to pay in cash or goods. I'll think the matter over. You can present the cheque tomorrow. But you can remove your statue now. It may be a good likeness, but it takes away my appetite and spoils my breakfast."

Goatsby said nothing, but took the cheque. Then he did a very strange thing. He began to dance in front of his statue. They all watched him while he bowed and scraped and whirled for a long time.

After he had gone with the statue Uncle sighed:

"Well, that's a relief. I must say. I'm much puzzled though by Goatsby's conduct. That dance, what did you make of it?"

"I don't know I'm sure, sir," said the Old Monkey. "It was as though he had won a victory, but how could he have done?"

"Very mysterious," said Uncle.

A few minutes later a telegram arrived from Badfort.

DEAR OLD CLEVER-BOOTS, GOATSBY JUST ARRIVED. THE GOLD HE BROUGHT YOU IS GILT LEAD. TOMORROW WE CASH CHEQUE AND HOLD FESTIVAL BANQUET.

BEAVER HATEMAN

Uncle turned pale as he read this. He felt very depressed and so did the Old Monkey.

As for Whitebeard, despite the medicine he had recently taken, he was lying on the floor in a state of collapse.

"A cheque for a million!" he kept muttering.

"I'll tell you what, sir," said the Old Monkey. "I'll give you all my savings to help you out."

This was very generous of the Old Monkey, for he had got together, in one way or another, a hundred pounds. He does Uncle's accounts, but even so he doesn't really understand the meaning of a million pounds.

"No," said Uncle. "Thank you all the same. I shan't need that, but I shan't forget the offer."

Incredible as it may seem, there did come a time when Uncle actually needed the Old Monkey's money, and very badly, in a terrible emergency.

"I must honour my own cheque," said Uncle, "but I've got to save my face somehow; the question is how!"

"We must think of something!" said the Old Monkey. "We can't let Goatsby win over this."

"I've got it," said Uncle suddenly slapping down his trunk, "I'll ring up Wizard Blenkinsop and see if he can show me a way out."

"Oh, splendid, sir," said the Old Monkey.

Uncle went to the telephone and asked for Wizard Glen 88.

Blenkinsop replied at once, and Uncle explained the matter. The Wizard said that the best way was for them to come and see him and meanwhile he would think out a plan.

They decided to set out that very night, for Uncle felt he couldn't sleep till something was settled.

They left Whitebeard weeping and swallowing pie and sandwiches in order to recover his strength.

4

THEY VISIT WIZARD BLENKINSOP

It is not very far to the Glen. They did not take the traction engine as the road there is very rough. It was coming on wet, so they wore mackintoshes. Uncle's mackintosh is just a big tarpaulin that fits him like a haystack, but the Old Monkey has rather a smart, bright yellow one with a belt. It doesn't suit him very well. It has such a huge collar that it makes his face look too small, and, as he was wearing an enormous yellow sou'wester as well, he seemed all mackintosh.

But they shuffled along. Uncle had some clips inside his mackintosh to hold one or two stone clubs; otherwise they didn't take much.

It seems easy enough to get to the Glen, yet when you try it's hard. You go by railway right through the castle, and get out at a little station called Cake Loop. Right in front of you is a signpost: to wizard glen.

The road is good for the first few yards. Then it becomes very muddy, then very slippery, then full of

round pebbles that turn under your feet. Then like jelly. They could see the Glen right in front, yet it took more than an hour to get there, and all the time it kept getting wetter and wetter. The rain was coming down like a river as they reached the entrance.

A downcast-looking man was sitting by a brazier. He was wearing three mackintoshes and an overcoat. He had a great drum of carbide by him. He kept casting lumps into the brazier, and they burnt in the rain. The more the rain came down, the bigger the flame, but it gave out a most atrocious smell.

"Who's that?" he shouted in a dismal voice as Uncle came up. "I can't see you."

With these words he emptied half a drum of carbide into a puddle and lit it with a match. A great sickly-yellow flame sprang up and the smell became, if possible, worse.

"Oh, it's Uncle," he said at last. "I hardly knew you in that tarpaulin. And is that the Old Monkey? He looks just like a walking mackintosh. Well, push on, Blenkinsop's expecting you, but you must be careful. It's very wet further on!"

They passed him. It grew darker, and much wetter, and soon they reached a bend in the Glen where the thunder roared and the lightning flashed all the time. The ground was a foot deep in water and blue with electric flashes.

But all at once this changed, and they found themselves out of the storm. They looked back and saw behind them what looked like a wall of water, blue with flares and roaring with explosions.

Right in front of them was a black, square house with i. blenkinsop on the roof in letters of flame. By the side of the door was a brass plate which read:

I. BLENKINSOP — WIZARD
Branch Office at Sable Gulf

They rang the bell, and a sandy-haired boy came to the door.

"You want to see Mr Blenkinsop? Well, he's just having his supper, but come into the office and I'll ask him."

The office was a very ordinary place, except that some of the chairs kept getting bigger and then smaller, and a great white cat was weighing parcels in a corner.

The cat seemed to take a fancy to the Old Monkey, and, seeing one of the parcels had come undone, took a piece of dried fish out of it and pushed it along the desk to him with a ruler.

"Put that fish back!" said a piercing voice.

The cat hastily began to wrap up the parcel again, but he soon stopped to write a hasty note to the Old Monkey: 'He can see through walls!'

The Old Monkey shuddered.

Just then the young man came back and said:

"He says you can come in now."

When they entered Blenkinsop's office they found him sitting at a roll-top desk. He was a little man with cloudy eyes and wore old-fashioned breeches and stockings. He also took snuff, but he was quite up-to-date in his brand; for a tin of Gleamhound's Paralysing Snuff (Anti-Burglar) stood on the table, and the Old Monkey could read on the label:

> *'Simply throw one pinch into a burglar's face. He immediately becomes helpless for hours.'*

Blenkinsop took a refreshing pinch as they came in, and tossed his supper dishes into the mouth of a four-foot-high rubber frog that stood by his desk. The mouth immediately closed, and a swishing, washing-up sound followed.

"Now I am ready," said Blenkinsop, "and as this is a regular consultation my charge is two guineas."

Uncle took out the money and laid it on the table.

"Thank you," said Blenkinsop. "Now I will give you my opinion. This is a serious matter, and I have thought it out myself. The smaller difficulties I usually refer to my oracle machine!"

He pointed to a machine in the form of an iron statue.

"I use this a good deal," said Blenkinsop. "It's only five shillings for an opinion. You write the question on a card, put it into the statue's hand, turn a handle at the back, and a typed answer comes out of the little door in front. Here are some ready for the post.

Uncle took one of the cards, and read:

> *Question:* I cannot keep my eggs from going bad. Have tried water-glass, but at the end of ten years they are slightly musty. What shall I do?
>
> *Answer:* Place them in a wooden box smeared with lime juice. They will be fresh at the end of fifty years, but do not open them before that time or they may be stale suddenly.

Then another:

> *Question:* How can I be cured of baldness?
>
> *Answer:* Smear the head with water-resisting glue; and then sprinkle with chopped badger hair.

"Now I think," said Blenkinsop, "That each of those answers is a good five shillings' worth! By the way, they should be posted. Where's Goodman the cat? And my little instrument for seeing through walls? Oh, I say, the idle rotter! He's watching a rat-hole!"

He gave a loud shout:

"Goodman!"

Goodman at once left the rat-hole and came into the office.

"How often have I told you: no mouse- or rat-catching during office hours!" said Blenkinsop.

"It was a huge rat," said Goodman sulkily. "He was after the office paste!"

"That's no excuse. You know you only do it for pleasure. Here, take these cards and post them, and be quick about it!"

The cat seemed unwilling to go.

"The post is right down the Glen," he said, "and I shall get wet! And, besides, I'm working overtime for nothing! I reckon to stop at six. And I haven't had that rise in wages. Three saucers a day is rotten pay. Rotten!"

"You shut up," replied Blenkinsop, "or I'll put a spell on you. Now be off to the post!"

"Can I lend him my mackintosh, Mr Blenkinsop?" asked the Old Monkey.

"If you want to," said Blenkinsop, rather crossly.

They had great trouble in getting the mackintosh on to Goodman. It was far too big, and kept slipping. At last they bundled it on, and the cat, looking like a great waterproof parcel, started slowly down the Glen.

"Idle, slovenly, sleepy rascal!" said Blenkinsop.

Uncle said nothing, but he thought that the wizard was rather too hard on his employee, and this view was confirmed now that the cat had gone, because there was a joyful squeak, and the office became filled with great rats.

"Drive them out!" shouted Blenkinsop, furiously.

He ran in himself, striking right and left, but was not in time to prevent a grey-whiskered fellow from dragging a small parcel down his hole. Meanwhile the young man in the office, whose name was Walter Meal, was not lifting a finger to help. He was pretending to add up a column of figures, and had got them all wrong, as Uncle saw. He took no notice of the rat hunt.

They settled down after a while, and then Blenkinsop gave Uncle his opinion about Goatsby and the million pounds. It was this:

"Pay Goatsby, but pay him in pig iron and have it melted into a solid immovable mass in front of Badfort!"

Uncle was much struck by this idea. He would save his face by honouring his cheque, and Beaver Hateman and his gang would be scarcely any better off. A solid mass of iron could cost nearly as much to cut up as it was worth.

"What a brilliant idea!" he said. He was so pleased with it that he gave the wizard a big five-pound piece as well as the regular fee.

They were now ready to return home, but the Old Monkey had no mackintosh, so they had to wait.

At last they saw Goodman, the cat, coming slowly up the path. He looked a miserable object. His front paws were in mackintosh sleeves that dragged on the ground, but he hobbled on steadily.

"Did you post them?" said Blenkinsop.

"Well, sir, the pillar-box was under water, but there was an otter there who seemed a decent chap. He dived down to put them in."

"You unspeakable ass!" shouted Blenkinsop. "They'll all be spoiled! Look here, Goodman, you can clear out, and I'll get another cat."

The Old Monkey whispered to Uncle. He had often wished they had a cat, and he had taken a real liking to Goodman.

Uncle nodded. They were getting over-run with mice at Homeward, and Goodman would make a nice companion for the Old Monkey. Besides, he himself had taken rather a fancy to the strange creature.

So it was settled. Goodman had no mackintosh, but Uncle said that he could walk along inside his tarpaulin.

The wizard was not altogether pleased, but he was always changing his cats and a miserable little tabby had been round asking for work at low wages – two saucers a day. So perhaps he could try it for a time.

As for the cat Goodman, he
was absolutely delighted, for
the Old Monkey whispered
to him that he'd get
unlimited milk and fish, and
that his boss was very kind
to animals.

I must say that Goodman
is a very interesting creature.
He's much larger than most cats, and very playful,
though he looks grave and thoughtful. He told the
Old Monkey that he thought he could help Uncle a
lot because he could walk very quietly and find out
things.

They got back rather late, and Uncle gave
Goodman a can of milk that fairly took his breath
away – about a gallon – and then told him that he
could sleep by the hall fire, but he was to sleep very
lightly, and keep listening. He would be allowed to
doze a good deal during the day because Uncle
wouldn't have so much for him to do except
wrapping up parcels and stamping letters. Goodman
loves stamping letters. He licks the stamps as if he
enjoyed the taste of the gum, and puts them all on
straight.

"Right you are, sir!" replied the cat. "And I'll tell
you this. If a mouse or a rat so much as shows his nose
in this hall, I pity him. He won't do it twice. The

whole bally crew will get the wind up. Let them show their noses, only their *noses,* at the hole, and they'll think it's the end of the world! There were a hundred great rats that banded themselves together once to try to do me in. They came in platoons down a place called Cheesy Hole. Do you think I cared? I did 'em in, I tell you, I did 'em in!"

"Don't talk so much," said Uncle, but he was secretly smiling a little.

"Right you are, sir," said Goodman cheerfully. "I'll have another saucer of milk. Three saucers a day, the wizard gave me, and nothing extra for overtime – carrying letters and parcels, and in my spare time – and I was also supposed to catch fish for Mr Blenkinsop!"

At last they turned in. Uncle slept well, for he thought he could see a way through the mesh of difficulties that surrounded him.

5

THE BIG CASTING

When Uncle came down the next morning the first thing he saw was the cat Goodman chasing a piece of brown paper round the room. The moment he saw Uncle, he straightened up and began to sort the letters. When Uncle sat down to breakfast, he found on his plate two fresh trout. Goodman had been out exploring and had caught them for him.

Goodman behaved very well at breakfast. He had a seat next to the Old Monkey, and he drank his milk like a gentleman. His only lapse from good manners was when Uncle gave him one of the fish. Then he rushed from his chair spinning the trout along the ground and pouncing on it. But Uncle excused that because Goodman was not used to sitting at the table, but usually drank from a saucer on the floor and looked for rats at the same time.

He only had one really bad habit. He loved to read the morning paper, and on this first morning he jumped on Uncle's chair and tried to look over his shoulder. Uncle couldn't stick that. He decided to order Goodman a paper of his own.

In any case, Uncle had little time to look at any paper. He had to push on with preparations for getting the million pounds' worth of iron melted down in front of Badfort. He rang up Cowgill, and Cowgill thought it would be a big job, but said he believed he could manage it.

The difficulty was getting the iron there.

At last Uncle thought of a plan. There are a million dwarfs who are his tenants, and he decided to employ the lot for one day as carriers, and to let them off a week's rent besides giving them a free feed of fish and rice.

That left Cowgill free to manage his hundreds of portable furnaces for the smelting. These arrangements took some time, but at about ten o'clock they were ready, and Uncle put on a specially rich gown of purple, and waited contentedly in the warm sunshine.

Soon there was a great rattling and changing at Badfort. They had erected Goatsby's statue just outside the front door, and crowds of Beaver Hateman's friends were filing past it, singing and laughing.

Then they formed a procession and set out gaily to cash Uncle's cheque for one million pounds.

In front was a cart drawn by the Wooden-Legged

Donkey and the lean goat, Toothie, and sitting in the cart were Beaver Hateman in a new red sack suit, Nailrod, Sigismund Hateman, old Nailrod, Flabskin, and Oily Joe. They filled the cart to over-flowing; in fact, Oily Joe and Flabskin sat on the ledge at the back and were always falling off.

Beaver Hateman was blowing a trumpet and rattling a great money-box.

By the side of the procession walked that odious man, Alonzo S. Whitebeard's father. He was playing very badly on an accordion, 'See The Conquering Hero Comes'.

At last they reached the moat bridge, and Beaver Hateman got down. He pulled the cheque out of his pocket and said in a menacing voice:

"Well, Uncle, we've come for the million pounds. This is your cheque, isn't it?"

Uncle smiled.

"It is," he said.

"I suppose you're going to try to get off paying?"

"You'll be paid all right, but remember that you can be paid in either goods or money, as I wish," Uncle replied.

"Stop talking. Cash it and be quick about it!" said Beaver Hateman.

Uncle answered this rudeness with one calm and impressive sentence:

"I've decided to pay you the whole sum in the

form of pig iron which will be melted down in a great mass in front of your house this afternoon."

Beaver Hateman was furious.

"I don't want iron, you oily old shark!" he shouted.

"Well, that's all you'll get," said Uncle with a smile of quiet triumph.

Beaver Hateman now tried to put the cheque back in his pocket, but he had forgotten the length of Uncle's trunk. In a moment Uncle had seized it and torn it up.

"Now," he said, "push off! . . . Oldeboy, have you got that flame-thrower ready?"

"Yes, sir," exclaimed that ready youth, emerging from a clump of bushes with what looked like the nozzle from a fire engine in his hand.

"Well, turn it on when I've counted ten!"

But before he had, the Hateman crowd were walking sulkily back to Badfort. They have a wholesome dread of Oldeboy's flame-thrower.

Whitebeard's father, however, did not go with them. With a ghastly smile he came up and offered his services to Uncle.

"Can I do anything for you, sir?" he asked. "You heard me playing 'The Conquering Hero' for you."

"You were playing it for Beaver Hateman," shouted Uncle.

The sight of Whitebeard's father is nearly enough

to make Uncle lose his temper. Now this flattery sickened him. Turning on the lying, shifty old scoundrel in righteous indignation, he took a quick run and fairly kicked him up!

It was a magnificent kick. The body of the old hypocrite went up, up, up, in the sunlight, looking far more attractive than it had even done before, and then came down, down, down, on the hideous statue of Goatsby that disfigured the front of Badfort. That monstrosity with its hateful projecting ears was knocked to bits.

"Well," said Uncle, "perhaps that was a shade violent, but I just had to do it, and I will say this – a better kick I never made."

 After a light lunch, the great removal began. Uncle's plan was to make several journeys, and from the distance the dwarfs looked just like a swarm of ants carrying sticks and leaves. By six o'clock the whole million pounds' worth had been taken across, and then the little men sat down to devour their meal of fish and rice. You could hear their jaws making

a faint rustling sound like leaves stirring in the wind.

The Cowgill's work began. He had gathered together, during the day, a hundred portable blast furnaces. They were wheeled into a semi-circle in front of Badfort. As night came on, the sight was magnificent. From the hundred flaming furnaces, melted iron was pouring in streams. They cast the great mass of iron in a hollow place, and it took two or three days to melt it all. At last it was done, the furnaces were wheeled off, and in front of Badfort was a low dull-red mound of solid iron. It cooled down into an almost unbreakable mass.

Beaver did his best to sell it, but it took too much carting, and very few people wanted it.

The Wooden-Legged Donkey pulled over a few loads to Cheapman's, but he soon rebelled at the hard work. Even Beaver Hateman's great offer: 'A ton of iron for a single ham – fetch it yourself' met with no response. Finally he had to admit that the stuff was no good to him.

But he sent a threatening letter to Uncle:

To Uncle, the old crab of Humbug Lodge.
    Hootman is making a catapult and the whole of your iron will be returned to you in ton pieces. I hope they hit you and crush you flat!

Uncle took no notice of this except to laugh, but he felt more serious when he saw the machine they set up to throw over the pieces of iron. That doubtful character, Abdullah the Clothes-Peg Merchant, was helping Hootman to construct it. There was an immense spring in it which was coiled down by the aid of hundreds of captive badgers.

Uncle could only hope that, like so many of the Badfort schemes, it would not work.

Unfortunately it did work, at least once, for Uncle had gone to the front door of Homeward to welcome the King of the Badgers when a great lump of iron came zooming through the air and hit the outside dining-table, burying it deep in the ground.

"Oh, sir," cried the Old Monkey, "what an escape!"

"Don't worry," said Uncle, "the labour of breaking off a piece that size must be almost unbearable. They won't do it often."

On the whole, in spite of the catapult, Uncle was very pleased with the iron scheme, and the King of the Badgers was so full of admiration for the way Cowgill had managed the big casting that he came on a special visit to see Cowgill's works.

The King of the Badgers often comes to see Uncle and is very friendly, but it's a pity that he often seems to be hard up. He never buys at Cheapman's for some reason, and such a lot of his subjects are taken into captivity by Hateman that he is always having to ransom them, and this keeps his kingdom rather poor.

Uncle took him with great pleasure to see Cowgill's works, which are part of Homeward. It is a very interesting place as there are all sorts of workers there including a lot of birds. Crows, especially, are very good at screwing on nuts in awkward places. They fly up with the nut, and then, grasping it with their beaks, they fly round and round in circles, and they get it on splendidly.

Cowgill had got all his portable furnaces stowed away, and everything in such good order, that the King bestowed on him one of highest honours, the Order of the Golden Goat.

With this on his coat, Cowgill felt six inches taller. Uncle also gave him seventy cases of mixed fruit and twelve hundredweight of choice lard, besides a silver tripe bowl, so he felt very happy indeed.

UNCLE CLEANS UP

257

6

THEY VISIT THE FISH-FRYING ACADEMY

For a long time Uncle had intended to visit the Fish–
Frying Academy. You may remember that on the roof
of a great lonely tower he had noticed a big square
door battened down, with the words 'Fish-Frying
Academy – Goods Entrance' on it. He was a little
doubtful about going so far from Homeward as he
was pretty certain that Beaver Hateman was planning
a tremendous return blow, but they all felt that they
wanted a change so he decided to go. He got Captain
Walrus to come down and watch the door of
Homeward, with the help of Cloutman, Gubbins and
Alonzo S. Whitebeard. Captain Walrus was quite
pleased. He brought down a great box of
marlinespikes and belaying-pins.

"Now," he said, "let the swabs come, and they'll
regret it for the rest of their days!"

Uncle decided to take Cowgill this time, as
another little reward for his splendid engineering.

Also Uncle had heard that it was very hard to get into the Fish-Frying Academy, so they might need to break open that great door, and then Cowgill and his tools would be invaluable.

Also, of course, they took the cat Goodman, and I really believe that he would have done something desperate if he had been left behind. Goodman has a strong turn for adventure and reads a lot of detective stories. Sometimes he lies on the floor in the library gently turning the leaves with his paws and purring loudly at exciting  places. When he gets to a very thrilling part, he mews, and sometimes he leaves the book and rushes round the room.

Of course, the One-Armed Badger went. There is nothing he likes better than going on an expedition with Uncle and loading himself to the ground with things that might be wanted. Today he had outdone himself by devising a great pack that so covered him that you could scarcely see him at all. He looked like a great bale of goods shuffling along. Meat-juice, lint, bandages, cocoa, hams, mince-pies, bottles of milk, preserved fruits, clean socks, telescopes, compasses, axes – there was nothing that he had forgotten.

Cowgill brandished a great four-foot spanner.

"If we do meet any doubtful customers, sir, this will be as good as a stone club any day."

Uncle rather doubted this. He has such a liking for stone clubs that he feels uncomfortable without one when he is going on a journey. All the same, the spanner would be a good stand-by.

He had found out, after some trouble, the best way to the Fish-Frying Academy. You walk along the outside of Homeward until you come to a little room called 'waiting-room'. Then you go in, and simply wait. There's no way out of this room, except through the door by which you came in, but if you wait for a time the whole room begins to move and takes you with it.

On the wall is a card with this message:

Passengers to the Fish-Frying Academy must be content to wait their turn.

✦

There are always more visitors than we can accommodate.

✦

Keep quiet, do not cough or sneeze, or sing.

✦

Passengers requiring lunch can telephone Hungry 87659.

✦

Passengers can play games if quiet, but Tiddlywinks, Noughts-and-Crosses, and Halma are strictly forbidden.

✦

——————— SLOGAN FOR TODAY ———————

'Patience in the waiting-room means joy in the Fish-Frying Academy.'

Uncle read this notice through, yawned, and sat down on the one decent chair in the place.

"We might as well have a spot of lunch," he said.

They were all agreeable to this, and the One-Armed Badger soon had a splendid repast ready. When it was finished, Uncle said:

"Well, I vote we have a game. If I had Tiddlywinks with me I should play. I'm the master of this castle!" He turned to the One-Armed Badger. "Next time you come this way, bring a set of Tiddlywinks with you."

They felt a bit sorry for the One-Armed Badger; he thought he had brought everything. He offered to go and fetch a set.

"No!" said Uncle. "You'll get left. It doesn't really matter." And he gave the One-Armed Badger a threepenny piece as consolation.

"But I'll tell you what," said Uncle, as another hour dragged by, "I think we might manage a game of spigots. The room is rather small, but I fancy we could do it. There are half a dozen of those round Dutch cheeses and six cake boxes."

Just as he said this someone shouted: "Hold tight!" And they felt the room move.

The next instant they felt a jar, and the same voice shouted:

"This way out!"

To their surprise one of the sides of the room had

vanished and they were looking down a long tunnel like those in the Underground. They walked along till they came to two branching passages, one labelled 'To The Academy' and the other 'To The Sinking Parade'.

"I wonder what the Sinking Parade is," said Uncle, as they took the other passage.

After a few steps they found themselves at the foot of an immense escalator. It went up very slowly, and more and more people kept getting on to it.

At last they found themselves outside an enormous door of brown wood with the words 'Fish-Frying Academy' on it in brass letters.

Inside they had to pass through a turnstile where a little sharp-featured woman told them to turn out their pockets.

"We've had some bad thefts of fish lately," she said, "so we look as you go in and we look as you go out."

Uncle was a bit uncomfortable about the cat, for Goodman has an idea that it's all right to steal postage stamps and fish. He never takes anything else, but it seems impossible to cure him of these two faults.

However, there was no time to worry about this now, for a menacing roar came from the people behind who were having to wait while the One-Armed Badger's huge bale of goods was being examined.

"Seems to me this place is more bother than it's worth," said Uncle.

At last they reached the first department of the Fish-Frying Academy. A lot of boys were sitting at desks earnestly reading books and repeating sentences.

The teacher, a lean, anxious-looking man called Will Shudder, greeted Uncle.

"They're not allowed to touch a fish till they've been two years in this department," he said, "but now and then they get through in a year and a half. Here's one of our scholars who is getting moved up in seventeen months. Come here, Figby."

A pale boy, wearing an eyeshade and two pairs of spectacles, came up.

"Now Figby has got a good hold of the *theory* of fish frying. He can repeat by memory nine hundred and eighty-one ways of cooking hake. Would you like to hear him?"

"No, thank you," said Uncle hastily, and they passed on.

Just as they were moving, Uncle heard a woman say:

"Look, there's Edgar in the crab-and-whelk class! Doesn't he look nice?"

She pointed to a small obstinate-looking boy who was busy writing in an exercise book.

"How's he getting on?" she asked the teacher.

"Well, ma'am," replied Will Shudder, "I'm sorry to say he's not doing too well. He actually brought a real crab to the class the other day, and offered to prepare it for the table. He said it only wanted turning out of its shell. Of course, we couldn't allow that, and now he's engaged in writing out a thousand times: 'Crab cooking is difficult, and takes months of careful study before one can even begin to understand it.'"

Just as he said this, the small boy took the exercise book and threw it on the floor.

"This fish-frying stunt is *soft*!!" he cried.

The teacher held up his hand in horror.

"Oh, I'm afraid that means expulsion!" he said. "You'd better come over to Professor Gandleweaver. He *may* give you another chance, but I'm very doubtful!"

"Oh, Edgar!" wailed his mother. "After all the trouble we took to get you into the Academy!"

But Uncle stepped in.

"I think, madam," he said, "that I can give your son a part-time job in my kitchen, say for two hours a day."

"Oh, sir!" said the woman. "This is good of you. Come out of the class at once, Edgar."

She was all smiles because it's a grand thing to work for Uncle.

They went on to a huge hall. In the middle of it, before a range, stood Professor Gandleweaver. He was a short stout man with shifty eyes, and he did not look very learned. Yet he must have been, for he had all sorts of diplomas pinned up on the wall behind the range.

In front of him, on a small table, was a single hake.

"Now, good friends," he exclaimed, in a pompous voice, "you're going to have a treat. I'm glad to see a bigger crowd than ever today, including the celebrated owner of the castle. I hope you didn't mind having your pockets turned out at the gate, but the fact is we've had some pretty bad cases of fish-stealing lately. A haddock vanished a few days ago, and yesterday a couple of herrings, though dead, managed to swim off!"

This was a joke, and was greeted with roars of laughter.

"But," continued Gandleweaver, "it's no laughing matter. Fish is dear. The expense of carrying on the Academy is heavy, and the cost of frying is always rising. However, you have come to see a bit of first-class frying, and I promise you you shall not be disappointed!"

He was just flouring his pan before greasing it, when the cat Goodman darted upon the hake, and dashed out of the room with it.

Gandleweaver turned to Uncle with a furious look.

"You are a scoundrel, sir," he said. "You brought

your cat here purposely to steal fish!"

Uncle waved his trunk in silence.

"I regret this incident, as much as anyone here," he said. "The cat who accompanied me has the unfortunate impression that fish and postage stamps are common property—"

There was a howl of rage from the crowd. They clearly didn't believe him. But Uncle waved for silence once again and continued:

"However, in order that you may suffer no loss, I will send you—" he shouted the next words:

> "10 stone best hake,
> 7 stone plaice,
> 100 first-grade crabs
> and 20 cod-fish.

"I think, after this," added Uncle, mildly but impressively, "that everyone will be satisfied."

Gandleweaver came forward all smiles, but Uncle turned haughtily away.

"I may say," he said, in tones of ice, "I shall take my own measures with my cat, but I am not altogether satisfied with conditions here!"

The crowd began to hiss, and, as Uncle didn't want a row, he decided to withdraw and take action later.

The moment he and his party got out of the crowd, they were forgotten. The Professor had started

frying a conger eel in an enormous pan, and this is one of his star turns; and nobody thinks about anything else when he does it.

Goodman was waiting outside the door of the Academy. As soon as he saw Uncle, he brought the hake and laid it at his feet in spite of screams of rage from the woman at the entrance.

"Be silent, madam," said Uncle. "I must remind you that this is my castle."

"Excuse my taking this fish, sir," said Goodman, "but that old Gandleweaver is a liar. Did you notice the pan of stale batter he was using? And his pockets were bulging with money. I never like a chap whose eyes are like a rat's. Now I've had a lot to do with rats—"

"Shut up," said Uncle. "You let me down by your conduct, and I've half a mind to punish you severely."

"Oh, you wouldn't do that, sir. I thought I was doing you a good turn, getting you out early. You'd never have stuck his lecture on frying. Why, it takes him half an hour to get the fat hot, and he talks and laughs the whole time. You'd never have the patience, sir!"

Uncle knew this was true, so he said no more. They took the hake back for supper, but it tasted horrible, so they gave it to Alonzo S. Whitebeard, who doesn't mind how things taste so long as they are free.

7

IN THE LIBRARY

The next day Uncle decided to go with the Old
Monkey to have a cup of coffee at Gasparado's
Restaurant.

Gasparado's is situated in the market-place of
Badgertown. It's rather a doubtful restaurant. Uncle
doesn't know that customers are sometimes hit on
the head, robbed and left to cool off in the little
Italian garden at the side of the shop. He goes there
occasionally simply because the top window
overlooks the market-square, and is so well hidden
that he can't be seen. That's an attraction to Uncle.

He ordered a bucket of special coffee with a cup
for the Old Monkey. Gasparado brought it himself,
and greeted them with an oily smile. "It's very good
of you, sir, to patronize our quiet little house," he
said.

Uncle only grunted. He doesn't like Gasparado
much. Gasparado went away, and Uncle, after

drinking his coffee, picked up a paper called the Badfort News. He does not take this paper regularly, but when he comes across a copy in a café he eagerly reads it. This was what met his eyes:

ANOTHER OUTRAGE

We are horrified to find that the Tyrant of Homeward has added yet another to his long list of crimes. He went yesterday to the excellent Fish-Frying Academy of Professor Gandleweaver, and there carried out a contemptible theft. He took with him a degraded cat that he had specially trained to steal fish. This feline burglar seized a valuable hake from the Professor's table.

Uncle looked up from the paper with a frowning face that disturbed the Old Monkey. Just then they heard shouting and laughter in the square, and, throwing down his paper in disgust, Uncle looked out of the window. The Old Monkey ran to stand beside him.

What they saw surprised them.

There in the square were Beaver Hateman, Nailrod Hateman, and Sigismund

Hateman. Beaver Hateman was playing a guitar, and Sigismund and Nailrod were singing a duet. They had a great portrait of Uncle on a board, with the newspaper cutting pinned on to it, and above it in red letters were the words:

THE WORLD'S TRICKIEST FISH-SNEAK

Crowds of people surrounded the singers. Flabskin and Jellytussle and many others of the gang were there to lead the responses. They called their song 'Question and Answer' and this is how it went:

Nailrod and Sigismund sang the first line, and the

rest of the gang replied, while Beaver strummed his guitar and old Nailrod kept time on a drum.

"Would you like to know just how to steal a fish?"
"Yes, sir! Yes, sir! That is my wish."
"Would you like to hear the trickiest way?"
"Yes, sir! Yes, sir! Tell me today!"
"How would it be to get a trained cat?"
"Go on, sir! Go on, sir! There's something in that!"

They sang these verses and several more to a rather lilting tune, and then Beaver Hateman went round with a collecting box. People were laughing at his song, and humming it, and he seemed to be collecting a fair amount of money.

Uncle ground his teeth.

"If only I had a stone club!" he said.

Gasparado had been listening behind the door. Now he came in with a treacherous smile, and said:

"I have a ver goot stone club hanging up in de hall. It is curio that my broder brought me from Borneo. I hire him to you for thirty shillin'. It is dear because of de sentimental value!"

Uncle was desperate for vengeance, so he paid the thirty shillings and crept softly down the stairs.

All would have gone well, if that little wretch Hitmouse hadn't been on the look-out.

The moment Uncle and the Old Monkey

emerged he shouted:

"Look out, here comes old Snorty!"

Before Uncle could swing his club the singers had vanished down a narrow entry, while Hitmouse dived down a drain.

Uncle looked round, and then tossed the club back into the restaurant with a haughty gesture.

"Pah!" he said to the Old Monkey. "Let's get away. The atmosphere is absolutely polluted."

They went back to Homeward, and there in the hall was the teacher from the Fish-Frying Academy, Will Shudder.

"I came to tell you, sir, that I've lost my job. The Academy has been closed down. All the boys rebelled after your last visit. They all want to work for you and think the fish-frying business is a wash-out."

Uncle rubbed his hands. All his annoyance was forgotten. He had been uneasy in his mind about the boys undergoing Professor Gandleweaver's fish-frying course.

"Well," he said, "I am glad to hear it. I may be able to find posts for some of the boys, and the younger ones can go to Dr Lyre's school. At any rate, they will be better there than at Gandleweaver's!" He paused, and then added: "I suppose Gandleweaver is still keeping up his fish-frying displays?"

"Oh, yes, he'll keep them up so long as he can get mugs to come and watch him. Between you and me, sir, he *can't fry*! He almost always burns the fish, and he uses abominably stale batter!"

"I can believe it," said Uncle. "Well, I think I can find you some useful work. How would you like to be a librarian? I've got a big library that wants classifying. A penny a week, free rooms and board!"

Shudder's weary eyes gleamed. He had long hoped for such a post.

"Oh, sir," he said, "what a wonderful chance! I promise I shall be systematic and work hard."

"The post's yours then," said Uncle, "and we might as well go and have a look at the library!"

They went there at once. The library is a most interesting place. It's quite near the dining-room, but hardly anyone goes there except Goodman the cat. Uncle himself used to be a great reader but since taking his degree he has read very little. However, he still orders books, and for some years these have piled up in the library. He orders at least a thousand books every year, and there is a vast pile there waiting to be put on shelves.

The building consists of a stupendous hall which goes all round the bases of four big square towers that are set about a lake. It's really four rooms in one, and the rooms are so big that if you want to go from one of them to the one opposite it's easier to row across than to walk round. A good boat has been provided for this. Although this lake comes right up to just below the windows, the hall is perfectly dry. It has books going up so high that you can't possibly see where the top rows are, but luckily there's a patent step-ladder with a chair at the back. Simply press a button and the chair soars right up to the ceiling, so that you can easily reach the topmost books.

The library walls are of a brown colour with rich red silk curtains. It looks very grand, but at the time when they saw it it was rather blocked up with great cases of books.

In it there are nine immense gas fires in fireplaces shaped like dragons. You light the gas, and the dragons become red-hot. It looks fine on a winter evening. It's evident that the place is honeycombed with secret passages, for there are all sorts of peculiar knobs and handles in places where there are no books.

In the middle of each of the four parts of the room is an ink fountain. A jet of ink shoots into the air from a black bowl, and falls softly back. It's a handy place for filling fountain pens and ink-pots. Also on a counter near the door there's a very convenient little stationery machine. This is shaped like a bear. Hit him in the right eye, and he shoots out a postcard from his mouth. Hit him in the left, and he shoots out a sheet of paper and an envelope. Hit him on the nose, and he shoots out a small flat box with ten sheets of paper and ten envelopes. And the funny thing is he never seems to run short.

Will Shudder had one look at the place and then began to cry.

"What's up?" said Uncle.

"Excuse me, sir," said Shudder, pulling himself together, "but I feel a bit upset with pleasure. I shall be perfectly happy here. I shan't need any wages — just a little of the plainest food, and I'll sleep among the books!"

"No you won't," said Uncle. "The Old Monkey will find you a room, and you shall have the wages I promised you, and eat at our table!"

"Oh, thank you, sir," said Will Shudder. "At that wretched academy I got no wages at all, and I had to live on stale fish and batter, and it was so frightfully dull!"

"Why did you stay then?"

"Gandleweaver promised me a partnership."

"It's high time you got out of all that. But, Shudder, there's one thing you might do for me here. I'm expecting a big attack from Badfort any day now. Just keep an eye open for anything unusual!"

They all went to have lunch after this. Shudder sat next to the cat. He tried to stroke him, but the cat is a very outspoken creature, and told him not to.

"Paws off!" he said. "You and I are going to be pals all right, but I can't bear being stroked. It makes me feel silly. I don't mind having my tail pulled. In fact, I rather like it. If you get hold of my tail and pull me along a smooth board, it's a real treat. Still, you and I will get on all right because we both like books. When I was working for the wizard it got very tiring watching a rat-hole for hours, so I used to have a book by me and read by the side of the hole. It didn't prevent me catching 'em. Not a bit. I've even stunned 'em with a book before today!"

Soon after this, Shudder and the cat went into the library for the afternoon. Shudder lit up the stoves and the place looked fine. He saw at once that it would take years to get the books thoroughly straight.

The cat took down a very interesting book and there was no sound except the faint turning of leaves, occasional slight mews, and the scratching of Shudder's pen.

There was a quiet almost sleepy atmosphere, but Goodman was wide awake. When an enormous rat peeped round the corner and began to nibble at the cover of a big book bound in leather, he got the surprise of his life. Goodman made one bound and was on him like a streak of lightning. He only just escaped and was ill for a long time afterwards.

8

THEY CALL AT CADCOON'S STORE

There was a little shop at the top of a hill near Uncle's that was called Cadcoon's Store, and Uncle had often thought of going there. The difficulty was to get away. There was so much to do at Homeward, and Uncle was practically sure that the Badfort crowd were about. Shudder told him that he was certain that he had heard someone swimming in the lake last thing at night when he went to shut up the library.

The cat Goodman had also found an empty Black Tom bottle on one of the sills.

All this made Uncle somewhat reluctant to leave his house, but one morning he received a letter.

It was from Cadcoon:

Honoured Sir,
I have long wished you to visit my store and
sample my goods, but I know that your time is

much taken up. However, I have received a
threatening letter from Beaver Hateman, in
which he says that he is coming today to obtain
provisions from me free of cost.
As he will be safely away from your district, I
suggest that you pay me a visit with some of your
friends. I should like you to see me deal with that
bandit.

Yours respectfully,
JOSEPH CADCOON

P.S. Try our Jumping Bean Rusks. Something new
as a breakfast food.

"Good," said Uncle to the Old Monkey. "The way
seems clear. I will take you and Gubbins. That will be
enough, I think."

"What about me?" said the cat Goodman, who
had been listening very eagerly.

"I think we had better leave you at home, my
young friend, you might be stealing fish again!"

"Let him come, sir," said the Old Monkey. "He
worked very hard yesterday with letters and parcels,
and I haven't seen a single rat since he came."

In the end Uncle allowed him to go on condition
that he behaved gravely and decently. They also took
the One-Armed Badger. This time he was only
allowed to carry empty cases and boxes, so that he
could fill them at the store.

Cadcoon's Store was situated at the top of an extremely steep hill. It was really a wonder he got any customers, because it was very difficult indeed to climb up to the store. People often slipped in the winter and rolled down from the top to the bottom. Still he had a fair number of customers. His stuff was not very cheap, but it always had a peculiar rich flavour that made you want to taste it again.

They found it very hard work to get up the hill, but at last they reached the top, and paused for a moment to get their breath. Just ahead of them, on a sort of platform, stood Cadcoon's Store. It didn't look like a shop, but more like a house. It was very neat and had pretty curtains at the windows. These were made of panther-skin, and Cadcoon was very proud of them. From these bow windows you could look right on to the porch.

"If he's expecting Beaver Hateman I hope he's rubbed those windows with Babble-Trout Oil," said Uncle. "They just ask to be broken, sticking out like that."

"What's Babble-Trout Oil?" asked Goodman.

"Any glass rubbed with it is unbreakable," said Uncle. "Useful stuff."

"I'm sure Mr Cadcoon will have a good supply," said the Old Monkey, "to protect his curtains."

The funny thing was that though Cadcoon's Store was noted for good provisions, the only food they

could see as they stood in the porch was one loaf of white bread on a shelf behind the front door. Cadcoon soon came to the door. He was a neat, gentlemanly man, and he welcomed them in and took them upstairs, where there was a large room covering the whole top of the house and with views to every side.

"I've been thinking out a nice meal for you," he said. "What do you say to bread and butter?"

"Thank you," said Uncle, though he thought it sounded a little on the plain side for visitors. He changed his mind though, when he tasted it. This was real Cadcoon bread and butter. You took a bite. It tasted like bread and butter, and yet there was something special about it. You took another bite and your pleasure increased. The cat Goodman was provided with a large brown pan of milk; it looked ordinary enough, but he drank it with the liveliest satisfaction, purring loudly, and every now and then shouting: "Splendid!"

While they were enjoying the unexpected flavour of these delicacies, Cadcoon said:

"I expect Beaver Hateman any time now, and I'm going to deal with him. I know, sir, that you are the best subduer of this bandit, but I would like you to have a little rest today. Settle down and enjoy yourselves. Here's another plate of bread and butter. I will be downstairs washing the works of my clock with very thin gruel while I'm waiting. The thing goes slow, and I have the idea that thin gruel squirted into the works may do some good."

He went downstairs, and for a few minutes all was quiet.

Then in the distance they heard heavy snorting.

Someone was coming up the slope.

They all moved to the windows, and very soon a hot red face appeared over the edge of the platform.

Beaver Hateman had come by himself for once. As you know, he usually brings many supporters. He soon reached the front door and banged the knocker down so hard that it seemed as if the wood must split.

Then he gave a mighty shout:

"Bring out food, the best you've got, and hurry up!"

Cadcoon pulled aside the panther-skin curtains and put his head out of a little side window.

"Where's your money?" he asked sharply.

"Money? Me? Don't be a fool!" Beaver Hateman leapt forward and seized hold of Cadcoon's nose.

"Now, you rascal," he yelled, "bring out those provisions or I'll twist your nose off!"

Cadcoon could hardly speak, but he managed to mutter in a stifled voice: "Release me a little, I can't speak!"

Hateman loosened his grip, and told him to say what he had to say quickly.

"I'll come to the door and hand you out a loaf of my special bread, Mr Hateman," said Cadcoon humbly.

Hateman was reluctant to let him go, but did so at last.

"I want more than a loaf," he said, "a lot more, and hurry up, you slimy viper!"

Uncle, the Old Monkey and Goodman saw Hateman bang his fists on the bow windows, but the glass was too well rubbed with Babble-Trout Oil to break.

Then they all hurried out on to the landing so that they could look down into the hall and see what happened when Hateman and Cadcoon met at the front door.

The first thing they saw was Cadcoon reaching for the large white loaf that stood on the shelf by the door.

With a lightning movement Cadcoon opened the door and flung the loaf at Beaver Hateman. It hit him with great force on the head and sent him spinning along the platform. As they watched he disappeared over the edge, and they could hear him bellowing and roaring as he rolled down the slope.

"Oh, sir," gasped the Old Monkey, "that's no ordinary loaf!"

He was right. As they found out later the loaf was made of wood skilfully painted to look like a crusty loaf.

Goodman was down the stairs and outside in a flash. He came scampering back from the edge of the platform to report.

"Beaver Hateman's picked himself up. He was rubbing his head and saying horrible things. Shouting them too. I've never heard such things. Do you know what he said about—?"

"That's enough, Goodman," said Uncle. "I don't want to hear his vile remarks! I only hope he has learned a lesson."

Then Uncle turned to Cadcoon.

"I am much impressed by your quiet efficiency," he said, "and now let us have a look at your store."

Cadcoon led the way. He keeps his food in iron safes to protect it from flies and bandits.

Uncle bought a lot of things including a number of boxes of Jumping Bean Rusks. The One-Armed Badger was soon so laden that Uncle did not think it safe for him to carry the provisions down the slope, so Cadcoon lowered them to him by ropes. They saw no further signs of Beaver Hateman and it was not long before they were home.

Late that evening Cadcoon sent them a little poem describing the day's adventures. It was beautifully written on violet parchment in yellowish ink, and was very long – at least twenty verses.

The Old Monkey began to read it aloud to the others.

"I was washing in gruel the works of my clock
For the thing was inclined to go slow,

When I heard at the door a thunderous knock
And a voice bellowed loud: 'Bring out dough!'

"I went to my little side window and pulled
My panther-skin curtains aside.
A thumb and four fingers closed tight on my nose.
'Bring me money – or grub,' the voice cried.

"'Bring me sausage and cakes,' repeated that voice,
'Bring me buns, or your nose I shall nip—'"

At this point Uncle began to snore. He does not
like poetry, and he had had a very heavy day.

9

CADCOON'S SALE

In the early hours of next morning, Uncle was awakened from a refreshing sleep by the Old Monkey.

"There's a big blaze, sir! I'm afraid that Cadcoon's Store is on fire."

Uncle bundled himself into a dressing-gown and looked out of the window. On the top of Cadcoon's hill there was a blaze that looked like an erupting volcano.

"That must be Cadcoon's Store," said Uncle. "It's doomed, that is quite clear. There is hardly any water on that hill."

As they watched, the flames grew higher and higher till they lit the whole countryside. Then there was a tremendous outburst of flames and sparks, and gradually the fire began to die down.

"Oh, sir, what can we do?" asked the Old Monkey, anxiously.

"We'll go and see if there is anything to be done for Cadcoon himself," said Uncle, "but the store has gone, I'm afraid."

While they were dressing, Cadcoon crept over the drawbridge. His neat suit was blackened, and his face woebegone and grimy.

"Oh, sir," he cried, as soon as he saw Uncle, "this is a sad night's work! Everything's gone up in flames. My panther-skin curtains gone! Not a rag left!"

It was too much for the little man, and he laid his head on the table and sobbed.

Uncle, however, was able to cheer him.

"We've got some panther-skin curtains in our furniture department and you can have them," he said.

Cadcoon was overjoyed. "Oh, sir, this is too good of you. Are you sure you can spare them?"

"Panther-skin curtains are rare," said Uncle, "but I can fix you up all right."

Thus encouraged, Cadcoon took an early breakfast, and Uncle gave him a glass of Sharpener Cordial. Then he began to look better.

"Somebody set it on fire," he said, "and I know who that somebody was. It was Beaver Hateman. But the difficulty is to prove it."

The cat Goodman, who had been rubbing himself against Cadcoon's legs and trying to comfort him, said quickly:

"It was Beaver Hateman, right enough. There's an old rat that brings his friends in from the country, and I thought I'd trace him home last night. D'you know where he lives? I will say he's got a first-class hole up there on a sunny hillside with a good view—"

"Go on," said Uncle.

"This hole is not far from your shop, Mr Cadcoon. I didn't want to climb that hill twice in one day, but I had to trace that wily old rat and stop him bringing his relations down to Homeward. In front of me, in the dark, I could hear heavy breathing, and soon I caught up with Beaver Hateman riding the Wooden-Legged Donkey and carrying a tin of petrol!"

"Ah, a tin of petrol!" said Uncle. "Useful evidence, Goodman!"

"But it doesn't prove anything and my house has gone!" sighed Cadcoon. "Still," he said, cheering up a little, "the safes are still there and some of the food in them may be eatable, in fact freshly roasted. I think I'll have a sale, and with the money I get, and my savings, I'll start building again. I've got the panther-skin curtains, anyway, thanks to you. That's a good start."

Then he became downcast again.

"But how can we let people know in time?" he wailed.

"Leave it to me," said Uncle.

He turned to the Old Monkey.

"Ring up for the traction engine," he told him.

"But, sir, it'll never get up Cadcoon's hill."

"We'll take it through Badgertown to the foot of the hill – and keep sounding the hooter; and I will tell the crowd through a megaphone where we are going. I object to advertising," he added, "but this is a good cause."

They set off almost at once. The sight of Cadcoon, grimy and singed, on the traction engine beside Uncle filled the badgers with sympathy, and soon they were flocking up the hill to the smouldering ruins.

When Cadcoon unlocked his safes he found, as he had thought, that some of his food was splendidly roasted. The butter, of course, had melted and run about, but Cadcoon scooped up several buckets of it. It would be splendid for cooking.

Just as the crowd was eagerly bidding for the goods, Uncle heard the Old Monkey gasp:

"For shame!"

Uncle looked round and saw Beaver Hateman, Flabskin, and old Nailrod Hateman stroll coolly up.

"You take my breath away!" said Uncle. "Setting Mr Cadcoon's shop on fire and then daring to come and bid at his sale!"

"Who says I set the place on fire?"

"My cat Goodman saw you going up the slope

towards the shop with a can of petrol last night!"

"Your cat!" hissed Beaver Hateman, "A nice witness! He's a common thief, a contemptible fish-sneak! All you've got is one thief as a witness. But I can bring scores, hundreds, to say I was nowhere near Cadcoon's last night! Come on, Flabskin, where was I?"

Flabskin scratched his head in a horrible sort of way and said:

"You were down at Oily Joe's clearing out the till!"

"That's no good," said Beaver Hateman. "Let's

291

have another witness. Here's my father, dear old Nailrod Senior. Now you can believe a father when he speaks about his son, can't you?"

"I can believe some fathers," said Uncle.

"Come on, Dad," said Beaver Hateman. "What was I doing last night?"

Old Nailrod thought for a while.

"My son Beaver spent the whole of last night reading a good book," he said at last. "He only left his chair once, to get a lemon biscuit from the sideboard."

"You're lying," said Uncle indignantly.

"I can bring lots of witnesses!" said Beaver Hateman.

"I don't want to hear them," said Uncle.

All the same he wished he had one more witness to confirm Goodman's story. Just then the Respectable Horses appeared. There are four of them, three sisters and a brother, and they are always neat and polite. Their black coats looked very shiny against the ash and muddle of the burnt-out store.

"Ha, ha," said Hateman, smiling falsely at them, "here are my friends, the Respectable Horses. They won't believe the lies you've been telling about me."

"I'm sorry to say, Mr Hateman," said Mayhave Crunch, the eldest of the horses, "that what we have to say may be displeasing to you, but we must tell the truth."

"Why?" asked Flabskin.

"Shut up!" said Beaver Hateman, hastily.

"Continue, Mr Crunch," said Uncle.

"Last evening we were taking a pan of warm boiled oats to an elderly mule who is ill with influenza. He lives just below here. We found him shivering violently and with very little hay to warm him. He said that just before we arrived Mr Hateman had ridden up to his stable door and demanded dry hay. In spite of our friend's protests, Mr Hateman piled the hay on the back of the Wooden-Legged Donkey and led the way to the store carrying a can of petrol."

"There's gratitude for you!" said Beaver Hateman. "I've never been against you horses, never hit you or thrown anything at you, and this is your return. All right! I've done with mercy after this. I'm going to fight with the gloves off!"

"Have you ever had them on?" asked Uncle.

"Yes, I have," said Hateman. "I've never done half the bad things I wanted to, but I'm going to start, and quickly too!"

Before Uncle could guard himself, the ruffian had picked up a bucket of warm melted butter and thrown it in his face.

Unfortunately Cadcoon happened at this moment to be in his largest safe getting out some goods for the sale. Like lightning, Beaver Hateman slammed the door, shutting Cadcoon in. As he made a rush for the path he also pushed Goodman into a vat of warm vinegar, tripped up Gubbins, and threw a jar of salad-dressing over Mayhave Crunch.

Then he was off, leaving confusion behind him.

Uncle was shouting and spluttering. Gubbins was staggering about, half stunned. Poor Goodman struggled out of the vinegar vat, his fur clinging to him. But the worst off was Cadcoon, shut in the safe. He was pounding on the door and shouting.

"Attend to Cadcoon first," said Uncle. "The smell of all those roasted provisions must be stifling. Unless we release him he will be suffocated. Goodman, go as fast as you can to Cowgill's works for the oxy-acetylene blowpipe!"

"Yes, sir," said Goodman, smartly, and was off down the path.

"The way he runs!" said the Old Monkey admiringly. "His fur will be dry before he gets there!"

Uncle, regardless of his own discomfort, went to the safe and tried to encourage Cadcoon. It's very hard to speak to anyone in a safe, the door fits so closely.

"How are you, my friend?" roared Uncle.

"I can hardly breathe!" came the faint reply.

"We've sent for Cowgill!" Uncle told him. "Have courage and eat a little of the provisions to keep up your strength!"

But Cadcoon did not answer. They thought they

heard a thump inside the safe as if somebody had fallen over; then there was silence.

"This is very worrying," said Uncle, and added to the Old Monkey: "Is Cowgill in sight yet?"

The Old Monkey went to look over the edge of the platform and reported that Cowgill and his men were on the steep hill path already.

"But they're having an awful struggle with the equipment, sir," he said.

"Go and help, then," said Uncle, "and take Gubbins."

As soon as the blowpipe was hoisted on to the platform they set to work and the lock was soon cut out and little Cadcoon, very white and in a dead faint, was lifted into the fresh air.

There was no water so they had to fan him with their hats.

Luckily Uncle found he had a box of Faintness Producer for Burglars in his pocket. He put two tablets in Cadcoon's mouth and the little man opened his eyes almost immediately.

"Where am I?" he asked.

"You're all right," said Uncle, "and in your own home. Your own ruin, I should say."

"How did I get locked in the safe?"

"Need I say?" said Uncle. "It was Beaver Hateman."

When Cadcoon heard this, in spite of his weakness, he seemed to expand to twice his size, his hair bristled, and he dashed to the ground two great jars of pickled cabbage that were standing by. This seemed to relieve his feelings for he grew calmer and turned to Uncle.

"Sir," he said, "I owe you an apology. Once, I must own, when you kicked that man up I thought, privately, that you were a little hard on him, but now I see my mistake. You were too lenient, far too merciful."

Words failed Cadcoon. In spite of the medicine he was still weak.

"He will pay for his atrocious action," said Uncle; "and now let us all sit down and revive ourselves with a meal. Cadcoon, lie on that rug and have a drink of Sharpener Cordial."

In spite of everything, they had quite a jolly meal. The air on the top of Cadcoon's hill was fresh and gave them a good appetite, and the food Uncle had bought at the sale tasted really splendid.

Next day they went on with the sale and it was quite a success. Cadcoon got enough money to start rebuilding, and he went to stay with Uncle till he felt really better.

10

THEY GO TO LOST CLINKERS

When Uncle came downstairs a day or so later he found Goodman reading the paper, and also eagerly eyeing a wasp that was flying round the big treacle tub that stands in the middle of the table.

As soon as Uncle appeared he took a flying leap and jumped on to his shoulders, purring loudly.

"Good sport at Badfort this morning, sir," he said. "The police are there!"

"Not before time," said Uncle.

"Beaver Hateman's been having meals on credit at a little restaurant run by a chap called Winkworth. When at last Winkworth asked for his money, Beaver Hateman and Flabskin dashed out, so he sent the police from Badgertown to arrest them. And there they are, twenty of them, great big chaps they are—"

"Don't talk so fast," said Uncle. "Calm down a little."

"Well, there they are waiting for him to come out.

That's all, sir."

"They'll wait a long time," said Uncle. "But I tell you what, we'll have a day off to go exploring. It's pretty evident Beaver Hateman won't leave Badfort for a while, so we'll just have a trip I've long wanted to make, to Lost Clinkers."

The Old Monkey clapped his paws. He loves going to new places.

Will Shudder was glad to go because he wasn't feeling very well. One of the stoves in the library had started leaking and a day in the country was just what he needed.

There are cheap trips to Lost Clinkers on the Badgertown Railway, so Uncle sent Goodman to get the tickets and to inquire the time of starting. The tickets were only a penny each and this included lunch on the train. Not much of one – only watercress, melons and a few biscuits – but the badgers love these things.

"The stationmaster has put on a special trip for you, sir," said Goodman when he came back. "Seven hundred badgers are going on the afternoon trip, and he thought you might like a quiet look round before they arrived."

"Very obliging of him," said Uncle. "I shall not forget his thoughtful kindness. We'll start at once."

They didn't have to go to the Badgertown Station, for the stationmaster had the train run right up into the siding outside Uncle's lard department. So they all climbed in and glided off. When the ticket collector came round Uncle gave him three pounds to pay for the special train and also a threepenny bit for himself.

The scenery was very pretty at first. There were lots of woods, with great purple flowers as big as shields, and some ponds full of yellow fishes, but the nearer they got to Lost Clinkers the uglier it became.

Lost Clinkers is really an old deserted gasworks; it's not much to look at but the air there is very good. There were great piles of cinders and rubble and everything was black with soot. At last the train began to run beneath blackened arches and between bluish pools that looked as though they contained chemicals, and finally drew up in the very yard of the gasworks.

"I'm specially glad to come today, sir," said Will Shudder to Uncle, "because I have a friend living at Lost Clinkers – a writing master called Benskin. He gets a free room in the gasworks, you see."

"Rather an awkward place to get pupils, isn't it?" said Uncle.

"Yes, he has to travel round to other places giving lessons."

At first when they got out of the train they couldn't see anybody, but soon they found the writing master frying some small fish over a cinder fire.

Shudder introduced him to Uncle.

"I'm very glad to meet you, sir," said Benskin. "I've been intending to come to Homeward just in case there was someone who would like to take lessons in fancy and copperplate writing."

"Come by all means," said Uncle. "I shan't require you myself. My signature is well known and I don't intend to alter it. Most of my business letters and accounts are done by the Old Monkey and this cat."

The writing master looked deeply interested.

"That's the first cat I've ever seen that can write," he said.

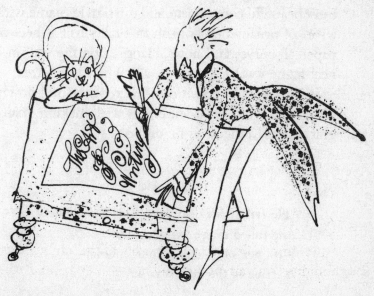

"Then there's Cloutman here, a fair writer, but he holds his pen like a pistol. Gubbins is very slow. They could both do with a polish up."

"Oh, I'll come, sir," said Benskin eagerly. "I have to seize every opportunity. I earn my living through my writing desk. That reminds me, Shudder wrote a little poem about my work. I liked it very much and had it hung up in my office. Just have a look in. I should like you to see my specimens of fancy writing too."

Uncle went with him to the Gasworks Office. Benskin had his writing desk in the window, which was a large one. There were some splendid specimens of his work. He can draw swans, deer and geese without taking his pen from the paper. He writes the most beautiful copperplate, and can sign his name with a sort of ornamental flourish that takes half a sheet of paper, all curves and bows. Hanging on the wall in a neat frame was the poem to which he had referred.

It was called 'Prepositions'. He read it aloud slowly to Uncle with great emphasis and making many graceful movements as he did so.

PREPOSITIONS

"He earned his beef *through* his writing desk,
And toiled in the twilight dank,
With pen of gold and flourish bold,
A scribe of the loftiest rank.

"He kept his beef *in* his writing desk,
And fastened it with a lock —
A solid hunk of the savoury junk,
With suet firm as a rock.

"He took his beef *from* his writing desk
And laid on the lid his prize,
While a haggard man to his window ran
And looked in with envious eyes.

"He carved his beef *by* his writing desk,
On the oaken window board,
And with glittering steel, and fork like an eel,
He served forth his flavourous hoard.

"He ate his beef *on* his writing desk—"

"What do you mean — 'fork like an eel'?" interrupted Uncle.

"He whirls it round and then wriggles it in, like this," said Benskin, demonstrating with his pen, "but you must admit, sir, that it's a good poem. Lots of people don't know what a preposition is. So, when I give writing lessons, I often give this poem as a copy, and so I teach writing and grammar at the same time."

The cat Goodman had been eagerly listening to

this, and all at once he burst out:

"Oh, I think that's splendid, Mr Benskin. I've often wanted to learn grammar. I can read all right, taught myself at the wizard's. He got lots of letters from people, and, having rather bad sight, he used to call me in. 'Now, Goodman,' he would say, 'look at that letter. Tell me what that word is. Write it out, you fool, if you can't read it! Make a copy of the words!' So I found myself writing out words which I didn't know. It was more like drawing than writing at first. Then I learned to read a few of them. At last I learned to read jolly well, and Blenkinsop often got me to read him spells from his wizard's book, but grammar I never learned. It must be splendid!"

"Not half so good as writing," said Benskin. "Here, just let me see you sign your name."

The cat took the pen and signed his name in bold but rather spluttering letters, CANUTE GOODMAN.

"So that's your name, CANUTE?" said Benskin curiously. "I must say you write extraordinarily well for a cat, but not like me."

He took a fresh sheet of paper and a gold pen, and first wrote 'Canute Goodman' in exquisite copperplate. Then he surrounded the whole name with graceful flourishes, birds, flowers and scrolls. The cat watched him with its eyes nearly bursting out of its head.

"Oh, I should love to do it like that!" he said.

"You can learn," said Benskin, "if you try!"

"Oh, I'll try. You'll find me at it all the time."

Uncle was getting tired of this conversation, and here he interrupted.

"I have no objection," he said, "to my cat having a *reasonable* amount of education, but I don't want it to become a craze. He has heavy and responsible duties day by day, and I say to you, Goodman, don't overdo things. Don't get mad about things. Steady must be your motto."

Goodman seemed a bit over-awed, but this didn't last long, for he caught sight of a rat running along a beam in the gasworks, and rushed after it so fast that they could just see a white streak in the air.

Uncle smiled. "And now," he said, "we are here not on business but on pleasure. I propose first of all that we have lunch in the retort house."

It was nice and cool in the retort house, and the One-Armed Badger soon had ready a splendid lunch, including more than twenty bottles of ginger ale and raspberryade. When they had drunk these, Uncle threw all the empty bottles at a great iron pillar in the corner. Then they turned on a few taps. It was very interesting. One of them sent out a great flood of greenish, evil-smelling liquid at such a rate that they began to think they would be washed out of the retort house. Then it stopped, and from the tap came a long groaning sound mixed with whistles, and a loud TAP, TAP, TAP.

"There's someone in that tank!" said Uncle. They went and examined it but could find nobody. It was very mysterious. Then, all at once, Uncle noticed that the cat Goodman, who had been absent during lunch, had now turned up, and his fur was streaked with the green stuff.

"You rascal!" shouted Uncle. "You've been rapping inside that tank and trying to fool us!"

The cat blushed.

"Sorry, sir. I came across that tank when I was chasing the rat, and all at once it began to empty. When the water had all gone I thought it would be a bit of fun to groan and whistle and rap inside a bit. I only did it for fun, sir,"

"Look here, Goodman," said Uncle, sharply, "this habit of joking is growing upon you; what you did wasn't funny at all! I thought for the moment that some unfortunate person had been put in that tank by Beaver Hateman. This sort of thing has got to stop!"

"I won't do it again, sir!" said Goodman meekly.

"You'd better not, and for a punishment you can go without lunch."

The cat looked hungrily at the remains of the feast but said nothing. However, the Old Monkey secretly gave him a meat pie, and he was soon rushing round again as full of beans as ever.

Then they walked over some slag heaps to a big

reservoir and had a good swim. It was very interesting swimming there because there are great big pipes and iron ladders in the reservoir, and a big iron thing in the middle like a buoy. They all climbed on this and then paddled it round the reservoir. After this they climbed to the top of a rusty iron tower by means of a spiral staircase, and had some singing in the open air. They sang several choruses, and then Uncle cleared his throat and said: "I've half a mind to give you a solo."

Everyone was deeply interested in this, for Uncle had never sung to them before.

"Please, sir, do sing!" begged the Old Monkey, his eyes shining. He loves singing, even by the Badfort crowd; and now, to hear his idol Uncle sing – this was rapture indeed.

"How I'd like to hear you!" said Goodman, running round in circles to show how pleased he was.

"I'm not much of a singer myself," said Cloutman in a heavy dogged voice, "but a bit of really good solo singing makes me feel fine."

"It would be a great pleasure to a humble acquaintance, sir, if you would favour us with a song," said the writing master in his polite refined voice.

In the end Uncle was persuaded.

"Don't expect anything very great," he said. "I'm badly out of practice, and shouting at Hateman hasn't done my voice any good. However, to please you, I'll try."

Uncle has a very small singing voice. Everybody was surprised. It sounded so strange coming from such a big creature, and he sings in rather a mincing way, very different from his usual thundering tones. They were all amazed.

This was the song:

> "Flowers in my garden grow
> Of which gardeners brag;
> But the sweetest flower I know
> Is a daisy on the slag.
>
> *"Honour to the daisies*
> *On the slag-heap high;*
> *Let us sing their praises*
> *Till they reach the sky!*
>
> "They say the loveliest flowers cling
> Beneath an Alpine crag;
> But the sweetest flower I sing
> Is the daisy on the slag.
>
> *"Honour to the daisies—"*

The Old Monkey broke down at this point and was led out weeping, but he soon came back so as not to miss anything.

To the great delight of the whole assembly Uncle

was persuaded to sing the four verses through three times more.

"Well," said Cloutman when, finally, he stopped, "I call that singing!"

"Singing," said Gubbins. "Sigismund Hateman is nothing to it!"

"Allow me to say," said the writing master, "that I have heard the greatest artists, but, without any flattery, I should put your singing by the side of that of Signor Maletti of Trieste, and I think the Signor would have to say that he was defeated!"

Uncle was very pleased at these comments, and he promised them presents when they got back.

"But where's Will Shudder?" he asked.

Shudder had not been well enough to join in the swimming or to climb the tower, but he had been lying on the top of a big slag heap near by and drawing the keen air into his lungs.

"I'm here, sir," he called down, "and I heard your singing; it sounded so faint and ethereal and fairy-like. It was really beautiful!"

Uncle glowed with pleasure and promised to give Shudder a wireless set when they got back. This seemed to make Shudder feel much better, and he was also delighted to hear that Uncle had invited the writing master to stay at Homeward for a few days.

By this time it was getting near sunset.

They were looking out from the top of the rusty

iron tower when they saw the seven hundred badgers arriving from the excursion train which, as it was such a long one, had had to stop a little way down the track.

They were striding out and singing their marching song:

"On we go, watching the setting sun;
Tomorrow we will do it, if today it can't be done!"

A big badger was marching in front giving them the first 'On we go' in a tremendous bass voice.

"The afternoon trip doesn't give them much time," said Uncle, "but I suppose they can manage a hasty look round the gasworks, and a quick dip in the tank before they roll up for the train."

When it was getting dark the seven hundred took some collecting from all the corners of the gasworks, but at last they were all found.

Also the cat Goodman had done something to make up for his tricks in the empty tank.

While running after the rat he had found ten sacks of dog biscuits in a boarded-up room behind a furnace. Uncle left a note to say he would pay the owner in full if he presented himself at Homeward, and he distributed the biscuits to the badgers on the return journey. They were immensely pleased, and the train resounded with song and merriment till they pulled up outside Homeward.

As he had promised, Uncle gave good presents to all the members of his party.

Will Shudder spent the rest of the evening trying out his new wireless set. The worst of it was that he could only get Badfort. There is a wretched little broadcasting station on the roof of Badfort which seldom works, but it was going that night and Shudder heard the following:

NEWS SUMMARY (Copyright).

Weather: Rotten.

Base accusations were levelled today against B. Hateman Esq., b.a., and a strong party of police from Badgertown have placed themselves outside the main entrance of his residence at Badfort. This unprovoked and grossly unfair action has made Mr Hateman seriously ill, and he is at present confined to his bed.

Public indignation runs high.

Mr Hateman asked us to state that, as he has heard that many sympathizers desire to send gifts, these should be sent

c/o J. Jellytussle Esq.,
The Bathing Lodge,
Nr Badfort.
Ham, vegetables, biscuits, Leper Jack of good
quality will be acceptable; in fact anything can be
sent, but not to the front door please, as the police
are still there.

THEY SET OUT FOR THE DWARFS' DRINKING FOUNTAINS

Next day all still seemed quiet. In the library Mr Benskin was executing designs with his golden pen, and Goodman and the One-Armed Badger were watching him. The One-Armed couldn't write at all, but he was a most painstaking creature and eager to learn.

"It's about time I went to see the drinking fountains," said Uncle, yawning. "I've heard they're not being kept in very good repair. An ungrateful lot, those dwarfs. Sometimes I wonder why I bother with them. As Badfort is more or less besieged by police I think this is a good day to go."

Uncle is very proud of the 144 drinking fountains he erected for the dwarfs in Lion Tower when he first became rich. They are mentioned on page 11,564 of Dr Lyre's History of Lion Tower, only three pages from the end, and you will remember that there is a large painting of Uncle opening them in his hall at Homeward.

"Please, sir, I don't want to miss my writing lesson," said Goodman anxiously. "I'm having one after the One-Armed."

"Very well, you can stay," said Uncle, but he was a bit surprised. The cat was certainly mad on writing at the moment.

"Can Mig come with us, sir?" asked the Old Monkey.

"Good idea," said Uncle. "He's been stuck in the kitchen a good deal lately. And Will Shudder had better come too. He still looks rather pale."

While they were getting ready Butterskin Mute arrived with a large pumpkin and a couple of splendid beetroot under his arm.

"What about you, Mute?" asked Uncle. "Would you like a look at the dwarfs' drinking fountains?"

"Oh yes, please, sir," said Mute, delighted. "Can I bring my rake?"

"By all means," said Uncle. "We might find it very useful. For instance, if the fountains are choked up, a rake would be the very thing for removing rubbish."

Mute was pleased, as he doesn't feel really at home without a rake.

Wizard Blenkinsop happened to call to see them that morning, and when he heard what expedition

was planned he suggested he might do some magic
and find them a shorter way.

"Splendid," said Uncle. "The drinking fountains
are a long way off, through Lion Tower. That's why I
haven't been able to keep a proper eye on them."

Blenkinsop got out his pocket spell–book and
turned to section 218.

How To Find A Short Cut to Any Given Place by Magic.

Tie a bundle of red leaves with ginkle-string.
Then mix with ashes from a fire lit by a
lunatic's aunt.
Salve.
Add wire from a green-eyed child's fish-hook.
Limmer.
Wash residue in tears of a broken-hearted goat,
then stir in a kangle-pot with scob liver.
Take residue and lay it on a flat warm
pavement. It will lie in the form of a rough
arrow and indicate route.

"That's all very well," said Uncle; "but these things
will take a good deal of getting together. 'Ashes from
a fire lit by a lunatic's aunt.' I don't know such a
person."

"Excuse me, sir," said Goodman. "Mrs Smallweed
might do. I was in her shop the other day buying
linseed. It was on a top shelf behind some rat-traps.
Well, we got it down, and—"

"Oh, buck up," said Uncle. "Is she a lunatic's aunt or not?"

"Well, she's got a nephew who comes to light her fire and I heard her say to him, 'You're nuts, Willie.'"

"I suppose that'll do," said Uncle. "Hurry up and get some."

"What about my writing lesson?" asked Goodman.

"Look," said Uncle, "you're here to help me first. Writing lessons come second. Get those ashes, and no rat-catching or foolery on the way."

Goodman streaked off to Mrs Smallweed's shop which is halfway between Homeward and Badfort.

"Now," said Uncle, "what else do we want?"

"We've got red leaves," said Blenkinsop; "there are some on that tree over there, but I haven't got a ginkle-string to tie them with."

"What is a ginkle-string?" asked Uncle testily.

"A ginkle-string is a long stretched-out piece of rag that's been used for cleaning pots and pans."

"Well, that one's easy. Bring one from the kitchen, Mig!"

The dwarf Mig was off like a shot.

"Now what's next on the list? – Wire from a green-eyed child's fish-hook? That'll take a bit of finding."

"No, it won't," replied Blenkinsop. "It's a wizard's standard ingredient, and I always carry at least one with me."

He opened his pocket book, and took out a short piece of wire.

"There you are," he said.

Uncle was now becoming interested. He had never done wizard work before, and it's very fascinating when you get into it.

"Salve! What's that?"

"Oh, that's a professional term," said Blenkinsop. "It means tie together loosely, roll in warm butter, and shake."

By this time Goodman had arrived back with the ashes, so they were able to *salve*, and then, with the addition of the wire from the green-eyed child's fish-hook, to *limmer*.

Limmering takes a bit of doing.

You take all the things for the spell and put them in a cardboard tube. You then blow them out three times while stamping on the ground. It sounds simple, but it's got to be done at the exact moment. However, it was done at last, and the residue, a shabby-looking bundle, was ready to be washed in the tears of a broken-hearted goat.

The difficulty was to find such a creature. There were lots of goats around, but none of them looked broken-hearted. Even Nailrod Hateman's goat, which had good reason for misery, only looked fierce.

They were quite at a loss, till the cat Goodman, who knows everybody, said he knew of a little tender-hearted goat who grazed secretly on the lawn outside Homeward. He went out, gave her a small pinch and told her to blub, promising to reward her with a bundle of choice hay if she did so. She was soon blubbering away, though her tears were hardly enough to wet the residue thoroughly. However they dampened the bundle, and Blenkinsop thought that would do.

Then they needed a kangle-pot. Blenkinsop had two or three at home, but it was too far to go and fetch them.

"I came across a pot in the library the other day, sir," said Will Shudder. "*It* looks to me remarkably like a kangle-pot."

"Please fetch it, Shudder," said Uncle.

A kangle-pot is a small red pot with leather

handles, and with curious figures engraved on it.

"Oh, that's a first-class kangle-pot," said Blenkinsop in a discontented voice when he saw it. He was rather jealous, for kangle-pots are extremely scarce, and yet absolutely necessary for wizard work, and this was a unique specimen.

The next stage of the spell was a hard one.

A scob is a savagely biting fish, eaten only by the Badfort crowd. To get scob's liver seemed very difficult.

"Won't the spell work without scob's liver?" asked Uncle.

Blenkinsop laughed bitterly.

"Really, sir, I'm surprised you should ask such a question. It shows how little you know about wizard work. We might manage at a pinch without ginkle-string or red leaves, but never, never, never without scob's liver."

"I think I can buy some," said Goodman. "I'm not certain, but I'm nearly sure."

"Here's sixpence," said Uncle, "and hurry."

Goodman ran so fast that you could hardly see him at all. He went once more to Mrs Smallweed's. She's a good friend of the cat and they often have a gossip together.

"I want a pound of best scob's liver," said Goodman, putting the sixpence on the counter.

Mrs Smallweed held up her hands in horror.

"Oh, Mr Goodman," she said, "you don't think I sell that, do you?"

"Yes, I do," said Goodman. "When I was here a few minutes ago I saw a parcel labelled 'Badfort' and smelling of fish. It was scob, now, wan't it?"

"Well, of all the cheeky cats! You are a bold-faced thing!" said Mrs Smallweed. "All right, I admit it. I do sell scob occasionally, but you mustn't tell anybody where you got it. It wouldn't do my business any good. Promise now."

"All right, I promise," said Goodman, and he seized the parcel of scob and rushed back to Homeward.

"Where d'you get it?" asked Uncle, curiously.

"Sorry, sir, I can't tell you. I promised not to. Hope you don't mind. It's proper scob's liver. I know about fish, and it's got a sort of bitter taste—"

"Stop talking," said Uncle, "and hand it over."

They were all ready now for the spell, but it had taken such a long time that they decided to have lunch first.

After a substantial meal, during which the wizard kept boasting of his skill, they went back to where Cowgill had already warmed the pavement with his oxy-acetylene blowpipe.

Blenkinsop was in his element. He stirred in the liver and threw the 'residue' on to the warm flat pavement. It lay in the form of a rough arrow. Suddenly it moved, became longer, and pointed directly at a massive stone wall.

"That's the place," said the wizard.

They tried to move some of the stones. Then they hammered and pushed, and even thrust knives into the crevices, but all to no purpose.

At last Uncle, who had been growing impatient, ran at the wall and gave it a great kick.

12

THEY REACH THE FOUNTAINS

Uncle's foot must have landed exactly on a secret spring for, all at once, with a rumbling sound, the wall slipped sideways on rollers, and before them stretched a short, well-lighted passage.

"There you are," said Blenkinsop. "I knew it would work!"

Uncle said nothing. He thought it had taken rather a long time to do the spell but he was pleased to have made the opening kick.

This really was a short way to the fountains, for when the party got to the end of the passage all they had to do was to lift a plain wooden handle. A door opened, and there, before them, were fourteen of the drinking fountains.

They were very fine. Made in marble, each one was carved with an elephant's head from the mouth of which water gushed. Uncle soon saw that some of the outlets must be choked up, for water was running over the marble rims of the basins. But that was not the worst thing. To his horror he saw that one of the marble mouths had been actually boarded up, and a shabby hut had been built in the dry reservoir beneath.

Over it was erected this sign:

YOUR SYD
Mends clocks, watches and windows, boils eggs and soup, does family washing (1/2d. per doz. pieces), knocks up workers at any given hour, frames pictures, wheels out invalids, trims hedges and hair, shaves beards.

YOUR SYD
Also sings at concerts, tans leather, teaches exhibition dancing, and washes dogs and cats

YOUR SYD
Has the best house for dwarfs' boots.
A special line in dwarfs' baby shoes. Difficult to get at most stores, but your syd has a large stock from Size 1 upwards.

P.S. *Something New*. High-heeled shoes for short dwarfs. Add at least an inch to your height.
Why be downhearted?

"Oh, sir," said the Old Monkey, "fancy setting up shop right in one of your fountains!"

Uncle motioned for silence and peeped into the hut. Inside was a thin man doing some washing in a small zinc bath. The clothes he was washing were so exceedingly small that they must have been dwarfs' baby clothes.

"Hardly bigger than postage stamps, this lot!" he was sighing. "I'm sick of this job!"

He looked up, saw Uncle looming outside the doorway, and jumped violently.

"I am Uncle, the owner of this castle," said Uncle solemnly. "I must ask you why you have the effrontery to set up a trading store in the bowl of one of my fountains?"

"There wasn't anywhere else," said Syd, trembling. "I've got to make a living somehow. I . . . I . . . didn't stop the fountain up, sir. It was done before I got here!"

"A miscreant's work!" said Uncle. "However, I can see you are an enterprising man, willing to do anything. Have you got a telephone?"

Syd looked like crying, but he pointed, with a soapy hand, to a kiosk over by the wall.

Uncle rang up Cowgill and told him to come at once with men and materials.

"Come by the route through Lion Tower; don't try the wizard's short cut," said Uncle before he put down the receiver.

Then he went back to Syd and told him that he had sent for his engineer Cowgill, and that a good wooden hut would be put up for him near the fountains.

"In return for this," said Uncle, "I wish for some information about the drinking fountains. They are meant for the good of the dwarf community and I can see they are not being cared for, or even used. Why is this?"

"They run with poisoned vinegar, sir," said Syd.

"Poisoned vinegar!" trumpeted Uncle.

Everybody was shocked. Poisoned vinegar is used by the Badfort crowd to throw in people's faces and make their eyes smart. Although it doesn't actually poison people, one drop of it can make a whole tank of water bitter.

"The first taste is enough to stop you drinking any more," said Syd. "It's all right for washing, though."

"This must be looked into at once," said Uncle. "Whoever is doing this must be punished most severely. Let me see, the fountains are fed from a tank reservoir above. How can we get up there?"

"There's an iron ladder, but it's padlocked," said Syd, "to stop the dwarfs' children from getting up."

Uncle, fortunately, had brought the right bunch of keys and they were soon up on a marble platform above the fountains.

This platform had a battlemented parapet all round it, and in the middle a huge tank reservoir with channels running from it to each of the fountains.

"Look at those, sir!" said the Old Monkey, pointing to ten little kegs which lay inside the parapet, nine of them empty and thrown on their sides, the tenth full and standing upright.

On each keg was a label which read as follows:

SNIPEHAZER'S VINEGAR (CONCENTRATED)

THIS PREPARATION IS UNDOUBTEDLY THE BEST ON THE MARKET. IT IS MADE WITH SCRUPULOUS CARE IN OUR LABORATORY AND IS ABSOLUTELY PURE.

FOR MAKING DRINKING WATER BITTER BORE A SMALL HOLE IN KEG AND SET ON EDGE OF RESERVOIR.

USE ONLY SNIPHAZER'S VINEGAR. THE GENUINE ARTICLE IS MADE SOLELY BY T. SNIPEHAZER (WIZARD).

DO NOT ACCEPT IMITATIONS.

"Have you seen anybody up here?" asked Uncle, controlling his anger with difficulty.

"Only the man from the waterworks who comes every Thursday afternoon," said Syd. "He comes to check the washers. All you can see from below is his bowler hat."

"I should like to point out, sir," said Will Shudder, "that this is Thursday afternoon."

"Good, good," said Uncle ominously, "we will take a look at this man from the waterworks."

"That's the way he comes," said Syd, "through that lift."

They had not long to wait before they heard the clanking of the lift door and a short man in a thick overcoat and a bowler hat came out. He was carrying a large gimlet. One look at the large projecting ears was enough.

"Ha!" said Uncle to the Old Monkey. "It's Goatsby!"

"What a good thing we came, sir," whispered the Old Monkey. "No wonder we haven't been hearing the fountains praised lately!"

As soon as Goatsby saw Uncle and his friends he turned pale, but he pocketed the gimlet hastily, and made a ghastly attempt at politeness:

"Oh, good afternoon, sir," he said. "What a surprise to see you here!"

"I may say the same about you. What are you doing here?" asked Uncle, gravely.

"I like it here," said Goatsby. "I come here for peace and quiet. I sit down by the side of this bubbling pool and think."

"The reservoir of a drinking fountain is not exactly a public lounge, is it?" asked Uncle.

"It makes me happy to be here," said Goatsby, with an utterly false laugh.

He was playing for time.

If it had been possible he would have dashed into the lift and vanished, but Uncle, Will Shudder, the Old Monkey, and Mute, his rake held menacingly high, barred the way and advanced towards him.

Goatsby dared not take his eyes off them, but at last, in spite of his thick overcoat, he turned to make a run for it. As he did so he stumbled over one of the empty kegs. The others lay beyond it. He fell with arms outstretched across them, with such force that they ran forward like the wheels of a roller skate and tipped him head-first into the reservoir. He fell in with a mighty splash, sank and then came up spluttering.

"Let him flounder for a bit," said Uncle, "and then pull him to the side with your rake, Mute."

This was done, and the last they saw of Goatsby was a sodden figure with water dripping from his projecting ears crawling into the lift.

"That makes me feel better," said Uncle.

He gave instructions for the fountains to be properly cleaned, and for Syd to be moved into the new hut. This was to be rent free on condition that he sent Uncle an account of the state of the drinking fountains every month. This he promised to do, and Uncle went home in high spirits.

13

SKINNER'S HOTEL

When they got back from the drinking fountain Uncle made a new resolution. As he slowly drew up into his trunk a quart of hot coffee from the tub at his side, he said:

"I shall have to give more oversight to things, you know. The state of those drinking fountains was a disgrace, and look at this—"

He threw across the table a copy of the Badfort News.

"Oh dear," said the Old Monkey, "has that paper-boy made a mistake again bringing that awful paper here? I've told him again and again!"

"I will be forced to take some action about this vile rag before long," said Uncle. "That is quite clear."

The Old Monkey read:

Our readers will be saddened to hear of another outrage by the Dictator of Homeward.

One of our esteemed citizens, Mr Laurence Goatsby, having heard of the disgraceful state of certain drinking fountains in Homeward, recently made his way there carrying a small keg of disinfectant, with which he hoped to make the fountains usable again. When he arrived on his errand of mercy he found the Dictator waiting for him. The latter made some offensive remarks and Mr Goatsby quietly tried to leave.

He was at once surrounded by a menacing crowd, some of them bearing lethal weapons. In an effort to escape with his life, Mr Goatsby unfortunately tripped and fell into the fountain reservoir, and has been suffering since from shock and a severe cold.

We call on all citizens to rise and resist to the death – Uncle, the fierce fat fool of Gangster Castle, Liar County, Robber Country, Taken-in-and-done-for-World.

"Oh sir, I'm ashamed to read it!" said the Old Monkey, almost in tears.

Uncle threw the newspaper into the fire with a contemptuous gesture.

As it was blazing up, the cat Goodman skidded into the room. He was in such a hurry that he dashed himself against Uncle's legs.

"Look where you're going!" said Uncle, still rather

cross after reading the *Badfort News*.

"Sorry, sir," said Goodman, "but I was rather excited. What d'you think – a new hotel has just been opened, the Skinner's Arms!"

"Where?" asked Uncle.

"In Skinner's Lodge, that big old house between Badfort and Badgertown. You know all the doors and window frames have been torn off for firewood by the Badfort crowd."

"Yes, I do know. It was a good house, and lately it's been an eyesore," said Uncle. "To have it done up and made into a good hotel is a splendid move. Who's behind it?"

"A rich man called Battersby," said Goodman, who, as usual, knew everything. "Oh, sir, it's going to be wonderful! There's to be a palm court – and a silver ping-pong room and very cheap meals."

Uncle and the Old Monkey were deeply interested.

"I may as well go and stay there for a night or two," said Uncle, "to make sure it is being run on proper lines and is a benefit to the neighbourhood. I am determined to keep a general eye on this."

The Old Monkey was very pleased. A rest from housekeeping for a day or so would be a treat. He went off smiling to get lunch ready, but was soon back to say there was a visitor.

"He comes from the Skinner's Arms, sir," said the

Old Monkey, "He's very polite, I must say."

"Show him in," said Uncle.

A shabby leopard came in, bowing rather humbly. Across his breast he wore a flashy blue-and-gold streamer which read: 'Skinner's Arms. Help yourself from the Silver Soup Stream. Runs night and day.'

"Ah, a soup stream," said Uncle, who loves a novelty of any kind. "This seems promising."

"Oh it is, sir," said the leopard, "and I'd be most grateful if you could see your way to make a firm booking. I get commission on each one, and to tell the truth I need every penny. I've got rather a big family, sir."

"You can book a couple of rooms for tonight," said Uncle, "for myself and the Old Monkey."

"What about Goodman, sir?" asked the Old Monkey. "He told us about the Skinner's Arms first, you know."

"Very well, he can come as long as he sleeps in your room," said Uncle.

So it was settled, and the leopard departed looking much happier as Uncle had given him a keg of salt beef for his large family.

At six o'clock that evening Uncle mounted the traction engine. He left Cloutman and Gubbins in charge of Homeward, with Captain Walrus on call.

When they arrived at the Skinner's Arms they found hundreds of badgers, who had been attracted by the new spectacle, camped round the hotel. The old house had been much brightened up with new paint, and coloured lights, and flowers in tubs. The porter, a smart young bear, seized Uncle's luggage and led them into the lounge. This was rather fine. It was painted blue and decorated with gold circles.

"Where's the manager?" asked Uncle.

"There's Mr Battersby, sir," said the bear.

Mr Battersby came out of his office. He was a fairly tall man who wore dark glasses and what looked like a rather tight wig of red hair. Uncle felt he had seen him before somewhere, but where?

"Your appearance here, sir," said Battersby, making a sweeping gesture of welcome, "reminds me powerfully of an experience I had in a hotel in Tokyo. We were all in the lounge, bored and listless, when a whisper went round, 'Sir Thomas Tompkinson is here.' In a moment, all our dullness was gone, for Sir Thomas was noted as a good companion, a keen wit, a splendid sportsman, and, above all, for his utter absence of swank. One young man said to me, 'I could hardly bear to go on living, but now Tommy's back I'll try again!'"

This speech was listened to eagerly by a number of badgers who had managed to get into the lounge. Uncle couldn't help feeling rather gratified.

"Thanks, Mr Battersby," he said. "I'll try to live up to your description. May I see my rooms now?"

"This way, sir," said Battersby and called down the passage: "Moses, blow the trumpet of welcome!"

A lean fox began to blow into a small brass trumpet.

Mr Battersby clapped his hands and called:

"Agnes, unroll the Gold Carpet of Welcome!"

A small fat woman rapidly unrolled what looked like a yellow stair carpet, and Uncle tramped down it feeling a little embarrassed. Goodman scampered along behind, his white coat looking splendid against the yellow carpet.

Uncle's room was large and spacious, and on one wall

was a huge enlargement of a photograph taken years before of the opening of the dwarfs' drinking fountains.

"Very well chosen," said Uncle.

Soon they heard a loud smashing noise.

"Mr Battersby smashes a large jug every evening to show dinner is ready," said Goodman. "Isn't it splendid?"

"Remember we are here on a visit of inspection, Goodman," said Uncle. "Your admiration should be moderate in tone."

All the same there was a lavishness in this act which appealed to Uncle, and he made up his mind to try one day soon having an even larger jug broken to announce dinner at Homeward.

They went down to the dining-room eager to see the much-advertised silver soup stream. There it was, a silver channel running round the table filled with hot soup, which was kept moving by a number of small electric paddles. Everybody took as much as he wanted by dipping a serving mug into the stream.

The help-yourself method also applied to the gigantic cooked fish, which lay on a silver platter which stretched the full length of the table. You just reached forward and took what you wanted.

"This is splendid, sir," said the Old Monkey, dipping his mug into the soup stream for the third time. As for Goodman he was in raptures, having, for once, as much fish as he could eat.

Uncle's pleasure in these arrangements was rather spoiled by the sight of a mysterious person at the other end of the table. He had propelled himself to the table in a wheel-chair, and his head was swathed in bandages. But he seemed to have a good appetite. He drank mug after mug of soup with a gulping noise that was distinctly unpleasant.

"Who is that?" Uncle asked Battersby, who had come in to see if all was going well.

"That's Mr Bateman, our permanent guest," said Battersby. "He's an invalid, but very brave."

"He doesn't look much like an invalid to me," said Uncle, "and I don't like the way he keeps dipping that mug into the soup."

"It's running away from you, sir," said Battersby.

"Yes, I dare say," said Uncle, "but it comes round my way afterwards."

Because he found the manners of his fellow guest so unpleasant Uncle was glad when dinner was over.

Outside his door he found a group of musicians. One had a bassoon, one a flute, while a dwarfish creature, dressed in a kimono, was playing a zither. They all began to sing a song when Uncle appeared.

"We love to hear of Uncle's deeds,
He makes us feel so glad;
His bounty makes the poor man rich,
And fills with joy the sad.
"How vast his stores of ham and lard,
How huge his vats of oil ..."

It went on for about twenty verses, and still there
seemed no prospect of it coming to an end.

"Thank you, friends," said Uncle, "for your

339

singing. I'm going to bed now, but you can go on all night if you like."

He gave them some money and closed the door of his room.

"Now for bed," he said.

The Old Monkey was there to make everything comfortable, and he turned on the bedside lamp. The moment he did so it exploded with a loud report.

This made Uncle jump and he sat down rather hurriedly on the bed.

There was a cracking noise, and at once the bed legs began to go through the floor. The boards were flimsy and worm-eaten, and before Uncle could get up he had crashed, with the bed, through a jagged hole in the floor into the room below.

The bed took some of the force of the fall as its legs collapsed under it, but he fell with a nasty jar.

Sickening clouds of plaster and dust filled his nose and eyes.

Trumpeting loudly with rage, and half-blinded, he took some seconds to see that in falling he had bowled somebody over, and that a huge roll of bandage was looping and unrolling along the floor. It only needed one glance at the sack suit and huge feet to tell Uncle who the soup-drinking invalid had been.

"So it was you, Beaver Hateman!" shouted Uncle, hurling a bed-leg at him. "No wonder the food stuck in my throat!"

Hateman hopped on to the window-sill. "Thanks for falling on me, you fat old barrel of lard," he said. "You've given me a good idea which I shall use to bring about your downfall – and soon!"

Then he vanished, laughing hideously.

The Old Monkey and the cat Goodman were looking down anxiously through the hole in the ceiling.

"Oh, sir, are you hurt?" asked the Old Monkey, with tears in his eyes.

"Not severely," said Uncle, "but my suspicions about this place have now been fully confirmed. Go to the office, ring up for the traction engine and ask for my bill."

"I'll help you brush yourself clean, sir," said the cat Goodman, jumping through the hole on to the wreckage. "I'm good at that."

When Uncle and Goodman went into the lounge, Battersby came out of his office to meet them.

"I'm very sorry to hear you have had a slight mishap, sir," he said. "Another room is, however, being prepared."

"I am not staying. Your floors are unsafe," said Uncle.

"Not for persons of ordinary weight, if you will excuse my saying so," said Battersby, smiling odiously.

"If you run a hotel, a person of any weight must be safe on any floor," said Uncle. "My bill, please."

Battersby went into his office and brought out a long sheet of parchment, very neatly made out.

Uncle took it, frowning, and began to read; as his eye fell on one item after an other he felt his temper mounting.

Dr to Skinner's Arms Hotel

	£	s.	d.
Gesture of welcome	1	0	0
Relating complimentary anecdote	3	10	0
Trumpet of welcome	5	0	0
Putting down gold carpet	10	0	0
Obtaining and hanging photograph of dwarfs' drinking fountains	15	0	0
Dinner (for three persons)		3	6
Serenade outside bedroom	100	0	0
Two rooms for night (1 single, 1 double)		2	6
Repairs to bedstead.......................	105	0	0
" " bedroom lamp	10	0	0
" " .. floor	214	0	0
	463	16	0
Less discount for distinguished visitor			2
	£463	15	10

With a great effort Uncle kept control of himself. Then he tapped the parchment.

"Explain this monstrous bill!" he said, his trunk waving to and fro, in the way it did when he was really angry.

"It's quite moderate," said Battersby. "Dinner 3s. 6d., two rooms 2s. 6d. – for three people, mind."

"This bill," said Uncle, "is a ramp!"

"A ramp? What is a ramp?" asked Battersby.

"A ramp is an attempt to get money by false pretences," said Uncle. "I refuse to pay, of course."

"Indeed," said Battersby, with a rascally smile. "This will look well in the *Badfort News*."

Then Uncle noticed that the little creature in the kimono who had been playing the zither outside his room was sitting at a coffee-table writing on what looked suspiciously like a hating book.

"I see, you've got their reporter here!" said Uncle.

"Hitmouse!" hissed Goodman.

"I am not afraid of anything that may be said in that scurrilous rag," said Uncle. "And I will make sure a strong article warning people about this hotel goes into the *Homeward Gazette*."

"Oh nobody reads that boring old paper!" said Battersby.

"Meanwhile," said Uncle, "as I am unusually heavy I will send workmen to repair the bed and ceiling. For the rest I give you two pounds – and that's the lot."

Battersby now lost his temper completely.

"You'll go to prison for this!" he yelled.

As the sound of his rasping furious voice a terrible suspicion seized Uncle. Goodman must have felt the same, for he suddenly jumped on to Battersby's shoulder and pulled off the tight red wig. At once a pair of huge ears flopped out.

"Goatsby!" said Uncle, breathing hard. "So it was you, Goatsby, trying once more to defraud me!"

"You're defrauding me!" Goatsby was now nearly beside himself. "You'll get six months in prison for this! No, six years – *sixty*!"

"Perhaps you have forgotten," said Uncle in grave tones, "that I am the chief magistrate in this area. Can you see me sentencing myself?"

Seeing that he was likely to be involved in a vulgar struggle if he stayed longer, Uncle made his way to the traction engine and they rode home.

14

ON THE UNDERGROUND

It was a dim winter afternoon, and Uncle was feeling slightly depressed. The morning had been quite prosperous. He had had some large cheques for maize, and had been asked by the King of the Badgers to open a sale of bananas and coconuts in aid of distressed badgers. He likes opening sales because it gives him a chance of wearing his best purple dressing-gown and elephant's gold-studded boots.

These were cheering things, but on the other hand the Badfort News had printed an utterly false description of his visit to the Skinner's Arms.

It had been headed: A MEAN MAGNATE.

And this is what it had said in smudgy black type:

```
The Dictator of Homeward Castle has a new
line in crime. He stays at good hotels and
refuses to pay his bills. A fine example to
us all!
```

Yesterday he went to Mr Battersby's new
establishment, the Skinner's Arms, and when
presented with a modest bill, refused to
pay. In addition he conducted himself like
a surly, ill-bred madman, breaking a lamp
and bed and smashing through a floor.

When the long-suffering Mr Battersby told
him that the only alternative to non-payment
of bills was prison, he calmly remarked that
he was the local magistrate and he wasn't
going to sentence himself.

Now we know what injustice really means!
Rise in thousands! Surround Uncle's mouldy
castle and burn it to the ground!

It was irritating how many people had read this,
while hardly anybody seemed to have seen Uncle's
truthful account in the *Homeward Gazette.*

He was brooding on what steps he should next
take against the Badfort crowd when the Old
Monkey led in the little dwarf Rubgo who keeps a
small grocery shop on the top of a high tower called
Afghan Flats, near where Uncle's aunt, Miss Evelyn
Maidy, lives with her companion, Miss Wace.

This dwarf was gulping with rage so that he could
hardly speak.

At last he said:

"Sir, you must come and help us. We are being
robbed, *robbed*, ROBBED!"

"Wait a bit," said Uncle severely. "If I remember rightly, you put a frog in my aunt's milk jug when I was visiting her some time ago."

"I'm sorry about that," said Rugbo, "but Miss Maidy got her own back – and more, sir. I can feel her umbrella still."

"My aunt," said Uncle, with a steady look at the little man, "took strong and effective measures to deal with an abominable action. Still, I am always ready to help sufferers from injustice. You may state the nature of the outrage."

"Outrage is a good word. That's just what it is, sir. They've put up the fares on the Underground!"

"What Underground? I know of no underground railway in this castle."

"You don't know the Dwarfy-Dwarftown Line from Number 1 Tower to Number 10 Tower?" Rugbo was plainly astonished.

"I don't know every corner of this castle of mine," said Uncle, "but wherever there is wrong-doing I make it my business to be there. I will examine the rise in fares and see if I consider it just."

"Oh, sir," said Rugbo, calming down a little, "thank you. I know you'll take my side."

"We shall see," said Uncle, and turned to the Old Monkey.

"Tell the One-Armed Badger to get ready," he said.

"Here he is, sir," said the Old Monkey, eagerly.

There seemed to be a sort of bale in the doorway. It was the One-Armed bowed to the ground with necessities for an expedition.

"Tell Cloutman and Gubbins to come. That'll be enough, I think."

Just then the cat Goodman appeared wheeling a small trolley filled with stone clubs.

"Oh, sir, look," said the Old Monkey. "Goodman will have to come."

So Uncle let him come.

"A stone club might be very useful," he said. "At any rate let us go and see this railway. But, mind you," he added looking at Rugbo sternly, "you will suffer if I find you have led me on a false trail."

"What you see, sir," said Rugbo, earnestly, "will make your hair stand on end."

"Lead the way," said Uncle.

Rugbo led them along a stone passage they had never used before. This lead to a steel gallery, and at the end of this was a lift which seemed to go down, down, down a long way into the ground.

When the lift stopped and the door slid open they found themselves in the booking hall of the dwarfs' Underground Railway.

What a booking hall! The members of Uncle's party were amazed, for the place was as large as a football ground and the walls went up so high they

were lost in a blue mist. And it was packed with indignant dwarfs.

In front of the booking office, where the crowd was thickest, there appeared to be a single mass of flattened dwarfs. And the yell of rage that was going up from them was so loud that ordinary speech was impossible.

"You see what I mean, sir!" screamed Rugbo.

Uncle nodded gravely, and motioned to the Old Monkey to go and read the notice which was just being put up. There is nothing the Old Monkey enjoys more than running to and fro over the heads of a tightly packed crowd. He ran to the notice-board so quickly that he hardly seemed to touch their heads. He paused, read the notice, and was soon back to report.

"It says that the fare between each station has been increased from one to one and a half bananas, sir!" he shouted into Uncle's ear.

"Get some bananas out of the pack," Uncle told the One-Armed. "We will take a ride on this railway and see what it is really like."

A rather greasy old wolf was acting as banana collector and porter.

"Why has the fare been increased?" Uncle asked him.

"Wages has riz," he said, "or supposed to. Mine's the same *and* too small."

Rugbo had left them in the booking hall, for he had to get back to his shop which he had left in charge of a young errand boy who was very apt to help himself to biscuits and raspberryade, but the rest of them got into a first-class compartment. Almost at once the train started and ran through a tunnel to Number 2 Station. Here the platform was so packed with travellers it was a wonder they weren't pushed on to the line. As it was, the train seemed to pass within an inch or so of their stomachs.

Seeing Uncle, the dwarfs avoided his compartment, but the overcrowding in the rest of the train was terrible.

"There are twenty under each seat, and at least fifteen in the parcel rack next door, sir," the Old Monkey reported.

"This is shameful," said Uncle. "At least twice the number of coaches is needed for decent travelling."

The guard, a shifty, depressed-looking man, came edging along the footboard of the train. He couldn't possibly have walked along the edge of the platform like any normal guard, for the struggling passengers were too tightly packed for that.

"No stop till Number 10. No stop till terminus!"

A howl of rage came from those on the platform and in the train.

"What," Uncle asked the guard sternly, "about those who want to get off?"

The guard said nothing, but pointed to a notice on the station wall opposite the train. It read;

DWARFTOWN RAILWAY

If train becomes overcrowded between stations 1 – 10 no stops will be made till terminus is reached. Travellers may be set down at required stations on return journey by payment of 10 bananas per stop.

By order.

SIMON EGGMAN (Managing Director)

"This is shameful!" said Uncle, disgustedly.

"Them's my orders," said the guard. At that

moment the train started, and the unfortunate guard, still clinging to the outside of the train, was swept into such a narrow tunnel that he had to flatten himself against the carriage. In spite of this a hole was rubbed in the back of his shabby coat, and his skin was beginning to be grazed as the train came to the next station. He did not seem unduly distressed, and went on edging down the train and shouting dismally, but Uncle was horrified.

"This is a disgraceful state of affairs!" he said. "I shall go and see this so-called Managing Director, Eggman, and ask him why he allows such bad working conditions."

"I know where he lives," said Goodman, eagerly. "He's got a big house on Number 10 platform."

"You seem to know more about my castle than I do," said Uncle.

"Well, I get into all sorts of places while I'm looking for rats," said Goodman.

When they got to Number 10 Station they all got out and soon saw the head office, over the door of which was a sign:

> DWARFTOWN RAILWAY
> Simon Eggman,
> Managing Director.
> *Cheap bananas. Inquire within.*

Goodman had as usual darted in front of the party. Now he rushed back to Uncle.

"Oh, sir, if you really want to see what Eggman is like, look in that side window!"

Uncle glanced in the side window and saw a big flabby man sitting in an armchair. Round him were gathered ten fat children, all like him, and all with beady eyes and sharp little teeth. On the table in front of Eggman was a pile of money, and all round the walls were shelves crammed with bananas.

"Another good day!" Eggman was saying. "Trains more crowded than ever, and fares up!"

The children cheered and Eggman tossed them each a banana.

Uncle looked no more, but went round to the office and rang the bell loudly.

In a few moments Eggman appeared. He had put on a thin black silk dressing-gown, and looked very respectable.

"Oh sir," he said in a humble voice, "how good of you to patronize our little railway. Times are hard, and I'm having great difficulty in paying the staff."

Uncle struck the wooden counter a heavy blow with his trunk, a sure sign he was getting angry.

"Listen, Eggman," he said, "I have a number of serious charges to make."

"Charges?" said Eggman, looking shocked and

surprised at the same time. He must have been a very good actor.

"Yes, charges," said Uncle gravely. "First, you are running a railway in my castle without my permission. Second, you are running it inefficiently. Third, you are under-paying your employees. Fourth, you are defrauding the public. Answer these charges."

Uncle twisted a stone club in this trunk as he spoke.

Eggman suddenly took an egg out of the pocket of his dressing-gown and threw it at Uncle and then tried to rush out of the door, but in a moment Gubbins had him by the leg. He might as well have struggled with a travelling crane. He was lifted and placed before Uncle who was wiping the egg out of his eyes with a towel handed to him by the One-Armed.

By this time a large number of dwarfs had collected. It was a good moment to pronounce judgment on Eggman, here in front of so many of those who had suffered at his hands. Even Goodman looked grave.

"You are guilty, Eggman," said Uncle in slow and solemn tones. "If any proof were needed your abominable action in throwing that egg at me has stamped you as an enemy of society. This is the sentence."

He paused to let his words sink in.

"First I shall take all your money and bananas—"

At this moment he noticed Hitmouse bristling with skewers and writing busily in a hating book.

"There is a reporter from the *Badfort News* present," he said. "Catch him!"

But the little wretch was too quick. He vanished in the crowd. Uncle knew that he would make the most of the unfinished sentence about money and bananas.

"To continue," said Uncle. "I will take all your money and bananas, Eggman, and start a fund called the Dwarfs' Benevolent Fund."

There were deafening cheers from the crowd.

"And you, Eggman, will work as a porter for those you have so heartlessly robbed, and lastly the railway shall be called the Homeward Railway. I shall appoint a new manager, double the number of coaches, and the train will stop at every station on every journey."

The cheering that followed this announcement went on for more than a quarter of an hour.

Uncle made a fine picture as he stood there, his trunk gently waving to and fro and a benevolent, yet firm look on his face.

But that night a special edition of the *Badfort News* came out.

The Dictator's BIGGEST Steal

We have pointed out, again and again, that the Dictator of Homeward is a thief. This afternoon he publicly admitted this. Filled with envy at the success of Mr Simon Eggman who has managed the Dwarftown Railway so well that the trains are always full, he got one of his brutal followers to knock Mr Eggman down and then calmly said: "I shall take all your money and bananas."

When Uncle read this he said in a stern voice: "I shall call at the office of the *Badfort News* tomorrow."

15

OFFICE OF THE *BADFORT NEWS*

The next day Uncle got up still determined to go to the office of the *Badfort News*, and see what he could do to reform things. The paper was a disgrace. It was full of attacks against the people of Homeward, and against any sober, honest person or decent trader.

The advertisements were also very low. Burglar outfits were offered for sale, also knuckledusters and false money. Uncle felt it was high time it was stopped.

The Old Monkey knew it was very dangerous for his master to go to Badfort, but nothing would move Uncle from his purpose.

He only took one stone club with him, to use as a walking stick, but he did take Cloutman and Gubbins as companions. This was a great relief to the Old Monkey. Also he was glad to have the cat Goodman with them because he makes even the most dangerous expedition cheerful.

Strangely enough, nobody noticed Uncle and his party walk into Badfort. This must have been because the scob fish were coming up Black Treacle Creek that day.

It is quite an event when this happens, for the Badfort people get scob oil from this small savage fish for their lamps, and also some people eat them.

Now, over by the stream which runs though Badfort, people were fighting and shouting over one small scob fish.

"This place never changes," said Uncle; "it's always full of quarrelling and shouting."

All the same they kept their eyes keenly on the look-out for any attack as they walked across the open space, scattered with tin cans and litter of all sorts, towards a broken-down hut, over the door of which hung a crooked sign which read:

> OFFICE. *Badfort News*

It seemed to be a disused dance hall. There was no floor, for it had been torn up for firewood long ago. In the muddy earth were many impressions of a large pair of feet. Along one wall ran a daubed message:

THE BADFORT NEWS NOW SELLS THREE MILLION COPIES PER DAY

Underneath this was a counter, and behind the counter stood Beaver Hateman. He had his back to Uncle, and a man who looked like a commercial traveller was trying to sell him something.

Uncle walked up to the counter and smacked it loudly with his trunk. Hateman threw a can of cold soup over his shoulder on to Uncle's velvet jacket; otherwise he took no notice.

"Attend to me!" shouted Uncle in a voice of thunder.

Hateman still did not look round, but said: "I seem to hear somebody shouting who has a voice nearly as rotten as the Dictator's!"

Uncle was so overcome by this cool, vile behaviour that he stood speechless for a moment.

The salesman lifted a large pair of boots on to the counter.

"These are the Ben Bandit patent policeman's boots, Mr Hateman," he said. "The heels are normal heels as long as the policeman is just walking along, but the moment the copper starts to run after a thief they explode. That soon brings him to a standstill."

"How much?" asked Hateman.

"Fifty pounds. It would be a hundred to anybody else."

"All right," said Hateman. "My usual terms. One halfpenny at the end of the first six months, one penny at the end of the year, and so on. Then you've always got some money coming in."

"That's not good enough," said the salesman in a disappointed voice.

"Oh, isn't it?" said Hateman, and seized the boots and pushed them under the counter. "I'm tired of haggling. I'm confiscating the boots for your own good. If the police found you with them you'd be for it. I'm doing you a good turn by taking them."

"But what about paying?"

"Paying! I've confiscated them! Nobody pays for a thing that's confiscated, you moondog! And now get out!"

Hateman seized the salesman and flung him out of a side door into some bushes. Then he slammed the door and turned round, and for the first time looked at Uncle.

"Oh, it's you!" he said. "What d'you want?"

"I've come on serious business," said Uncle, watching him closely and leaning on this stone club.

"You mean you want to subscribe to the *Badfort News*!"

This cheeky remark made Uncle boil over.

"Your rag is vile!" he shouted, and then noticed that Hateman was trying to edge towards an open case of duck bombs. Duck bombs are missiles often used by the Badfort crowd. When they burst they cover the person they hit with a 'vile sticky juice which stops him moving.

"Hold him, boys!" he shouted.

Cloutman and Gubbins instantly pinned Hateman by the arms.

"Now," said Uncle, "I mean to see the place where you print your degraded rubbish!"

The cat Goodman, who had been prowling round finding out things, came back to Uncle.

"It's here, sir, down this staircase. I can hear the clicking of a printing machine."

"Lead the way," said Uncle. "Bring the scoundrel with you, boys," he added.

Cloutman and Gubbins forced Hateman down a narrow staircase, and Uncle, the Old Monkey and Goodman followed. In a damp dark room they found a small badger working a rickety old printing machine.

"Are you employed by this man?" asked Uncle, pointing at Hateman.

"Yes, sir," said the badger. "He pays me a saucer of beans a day, and he's going to pay me ten pounds a week when I can set type a bit better."

"*Going* to pay you!" said Uncle in bitter tones. "The old story!"

"Oh, sir," said the Old Monkey, "the poor little chap is actually chained to the machine!"

"Cloutman," said Uncle, "set this unfortunate creature free! Gubbins, hold hard on to your prisoner meanwhile."

It would have done you good to see Cloutman just take the chain and break it as if it were a thread.

"Am I to go, sir?" asked the badger in astonishment.

"Yes, and be quick!" said Uncle.

The small badger was off up the stairs so quickly they couldn't see him move. All they could see was the end of his chain as he whisked up the stairs.

"And now," said Uncle, turning to Hateman, "let us look at the news that unfortunate creature has been setting."

"Oh, shut up!" shouted Hateman, whose face was so full of rage it looked as if it had been roasted. "You've lost me my best printer! He was an apprentice too. His father paid good money for him to learn the printing trade."

"His father," said Uncle, "never thought of him being fastened with a chain!"

"And why not?" said Hateman. "Have you never heard of anyone being bound as an apprentice? I bound him a bit firmer than usual, that's all!"

But Uncle was hardly listening. His eye had been caught by the grimy piece of paper held by a skewer against the printing machine. It was the copy from which the badger had been working.

"Hitmouse!" hissed Goodman. "That's his writing, sir, I'd know it anywhere!"

"This abominable sheet," said Uncle, and breathed

heavily, "is the work of your degraded reporter, Hitmouse."

"'The Dictator Hit by Well-aimed Egg!'" read out the Old Monkey in a shocked voice. "Oh, sir!"

Hateman laughed a horrible bubbling laugh. It was too much.

"Gubbins," said Uncle, "is that a sliding door in the wall?"

"Yes, sir," said Gubbins, "it leads to the moat."

"Open it," said Uncle to the Old Monkey.

Helped by Goodman, the Old Monkey managed to slide the door open. Cloutman and Gubbins dared not let go of Hateman who would have been up the stairs in a flash. As it was he struggled and yelled, but could do nothing.

When the door slid back they could see, beyond a slope, the black waters of Badfort moat, thick with old cans and rubbish, a painful contrast to the clear beautiful stream round Uncle's house. Beyond the moat lay the oozy stretches of Gaby's Marsh.

"Very satisfactory," said Uncle, moving back for a run.

"Now look here," said Hateman, "if you kick me up all the things I've done to you so far will seem like rapture."

The Hateman crowd often kick each other, but they hate being kicked up by Uncle. It is ignominious and painful, and Uncle only does it when it is well-deserved.

"Your threats have no effect on me," said Uncle.

"I shall have such a revenge that people will go grey when they hear of it!" yelled Hateman.

"Let him go, boys!" shouted Uncle.

Hateman bounded forward in an effort to get clear away. In vain did he try to dive into some withered bushes. There was a thud, and the body of the odious editor of the *Badfort News* soared up, up, up into the clear blue sky.

Hateman let out a yell so furious that it frightened hundreds of herons who rose squawking and flapping with him.

"Oh, sir, what a beauty!" sighed the Old Monkey. "One of your very best!"

"He's coming down in Gaby's Marsh," said Gubbins, "where the crabs are!"

"And the barking conger eels," said Goodman, running round in circles.

Indeed, as they watched, muddy water rose in chocolate-coloured fountains away in the distance.

"I trust," said Uncle, turning away, "that we have seen the last of those evil writings in the *Badfort News*."

But the Old Monkey shook his head as they began to walk thoughtfully home.

16

THE SINKING PARADE

It was the Old Monkey's birthday and he had had a splendid lot of presents, gum boots (though he doesn't often wear them, as his legs are too thin), a squash racket, a couple of chestnut roasters and several other things. His bedroom gets fuller and fuller. For instance, his window is so surrounded by tins of corned beef that it's like looking through a tin tunnel.

Uncle wanted to arrange a little extra treat for him.

"Is there anywhere you would like to go for a trip?" he asked.

The Old Monkey's eyes shone. A trip to somewhere new in the castle is what he loves.

"Oh sir," he said, "d'you remember when we were on our way to the Fish-Frying Academy we saw a notice 'To the Sinking Parade'. I've often wondered what it could be."

"We'll go," said Uncle. "Tell the One-Armed to get ready."

The One-Armed was not ready for once. He had been away gathering chrysanthemums for the Old Monkey's birthday. He soon appeared, so surrounded by flowers that he looked like a

walking bouquet. The moment he heard of the plan he hurriedly presented his flowers to the Old Monkey and waddled off to get his pack.

"I seem to remember the notice was on the top of a battened-down hatchway," said Uncle. "We'd better take Cowgill as there may be some engineering work to be done."

They also took Goodman and Butterskin Mute who had come to see the Old Monkey on his birthday. Cloutman and Gubbins were left to keep guard.

They made their way to the summit of one of Homeward's lofty towers, and there they found, as they expected, a hatchway labelled 'Sinking Parade'.

Cowgill had brought a powerful wrench and they

soon had the cover loose. As the work was going on they thought they could hear a lot of shouting, and when, with a united effort, the hatch cover was pulled aside, they saw it had formed the roof of a room.

The members of an indignant family were staring up at them. An old man and woman, a young couple and a number of children.

"Who are you, you great fat bounder in a purple dressing-gown?" yelled the old man.

"Modify your language," said Uncle, sternly.

"Here we are having to double up with Grandpa and Grandma because of the housing shortage," shouted the young woman, shaking her fist, "and the moment we move in, the place is broken up by a lot of inquisitive, idle rubber-necks!"

Uncle had had enough of this, so he jumped down and put some money on the table.

"We have come to pay a visit to the Sinking Parade," he said. "If we have, unwittingly, done damage to your roof here is payment. All we want is to be shown the way to the Parade."

The whole family stopped being indignant and stared at the money. They seemed dazed by it. At last the old man, who said his name was Tom Fullglass, recovered sufficiently to insist that he should show them the way to the Parade.

He was the worst possible guide. He was very apt

to sneeze, and when he did he sneezed so violently that he turned a somersault. This made him quite uncertain about which way he was going.

However, he got them into a dark gallery where a lot of people were sleeping against the walls and said he was sure this was the right way.

"Who are all these people?" asked Uncle.

Tom Fullglass sneezed again. He turned upside down and staggered about, and seemed unsure which end of the gallery they were making for.

"Look here," said Uncle, "I'm losing patience. You are not to sneeze again. It is a very bad habit you've got into. I want a clear statement about these people. Haven't they got houses to sleep in?"

Tom Fullglass didn't speak for a bit. He went nearly black in the face, but managed not to sneeze. Everybody stood around waiting for him to speak.

"All the houses round here have been grabbed by the Pointer family. I thought everybody knew that," he said at last.

"I did not know it," said Uncle, "but it is pretty evident from the sight of these unfortunate people in this gallery that there has been some monkeying going on. No offence to you, my friend," he said, looking at the Old Monkey.

When they got out of the gallery they saw an amazing sight.

Before them was an attractive circular lake with vast

towers grouped round it. Round the lake ran a broad curved walk labelled Sinking Parade, and on the edge of this walk were a number of large roomy houses.

Tom Fullglass, now that Uncle's stern eye was not on him, was having an orgy of sneezing, but at last he recovered from this and hurried up to ask if he could guide them further.

Uncle thanked him for his services, paid him half a crown to go away, coupled with a threat of a fine of five shillings if he came back, and most reluctantly he went off, sneezing and turning somersaults, like a living catharine-wheel.

"Let's look at the first of these Pointer houses," said Uncle. It was a fine house, six storeys high. On the door-post was a sign:

> MR RICHARD POINTER
> *No rooms.*
> *No organs.*
> *No circulars.*

Mr Richard Pointer was sitting under a cherry tree in his garden dressed in a rather old-fashioned silk suit.

"No rooms!" he shouted as he saw Uncle's party.

Uncle did not reply. He wished to inspect more houses on the Parade before he entered into any discussion.

It was very pretty by the lake. Parties of excursionists kept arriving, and all seemed filled with delight
at the great expanse of clear blue water. Some
had brought lunch and were already having a meal,
sitting on the seats which were liberally scattered
around.

Uncle walked further along the Parade. All the
houses seemed to belong to the Pointers. One was
labelled:

> MR FRIENDSHIP POINTER
> *No rooms.*
> *No organs.*
> *No circulars.*
> *No sellers of eagle beak fish.*

Another read:

> T. SMIGGS POINTER ESQ.
> *No rooms.*
> *No organs.*
> *No circulars.*
> *No sellers of eagle beak fish.*
> *No sellers of snout eels.*

The largest house, near the middle of the Parade,
had a summer-house in front of it. On the gate in
gold letters was printed:

MISS JEZEBEL POINTER

No rooms.
No organs.
No circulars.
No sellers of eagle beak fish.
No sellers of snout eels.
No visitors at all unless in possession
of a card which must be examined
by Miss Pointer's personal attendant,
Mr Albert Snell.

"What is all this?" Uncle said irritably. Quite naturally he hates reading notices telling him not to do things when he is in his own house.

He was about to charge up to the summer-house in which Miss Pointer, a rather plain elderly lady, was sitting when something surprising and terrifying happened.

With a loud creaking, as of hidden machinery, a section of the Parade began to sink. It was soon covered with water. Luckily Uncle and his party were near the gravelled path which rose steeply as it led to Miss Jezebel Pointer's summer-house, but the others on the Parade were soon struggling in the water, and might even have been drowned if two boats with the words 'RESCUE. Price per head, 10s.' printed on their sides had not approached them

rapidly. Uncle was appalled to see that before they were admitted to the boat the money had to be handed over.

After this the holiday-makers, wet and frightened, and with their holiday money greatly diminished, were landed on the Parade again.

Before Uncle could get to Miss Pointer, a fat man with very short legs ran up to him and said sharply:

"Where's your card? You can't go up there without a card."

Uncle looked him over and then said in a terrifying voice:

"One word more and I'll spill you in the lake."

Snell seemed overpowered and Miss Pointer's face took on a purple hue.

"Who are you?" she asked in a bitter voice. "I

don't think I know you."

Uncle lashed himself with his trunk.

"I am Uncle, the owner of this castle, and I don't remember having received any rent from you or any other member of your family."

Uncle could see many wheels and levers in the summer-house, and it seemed clear that it was from here that the whole machinery of the Sinking Parade was controlled. But how?

"There's a small lever there, sir!" whispered Goodman. "I can read the words 'up' and 'down' printed on ivory tablets."

"Where?" asked Uncle.

As he followed Goodman's pointing paw and peered into the summer-house, Miss Pointer's hand moved on the lever, and the Sinking Parade began to wobble up and down. Renewed cries came from the holiday-makers who were just beginning to get dry.

"Take your hand from that lever!" roared Uncle, but the Parade went on sinking.

Goodman suddenly leapt through the little window of the summer-house and dashed Miss Pointer's hand from the lever. She screamed but could do nothing.

"Thanks, Goodman," said Uncle.

Then he turned to Miss Pointer.

"A woman as old as you," he said severely, "ought to behave with more dignity and kindness."

"I'm not old," shouted Miss Jezebel angrily. "You ought to see my mother!"

An invalid chair, in which sat a very old woman, was just being wheeled up the path and they all turned to look at it.

"Wheel me right up to the summer-house," the invalid was saying in a surprisingly strong voice. "Working the lever and hearing the waves sloshing and the people shouting is my little daily treat!"

"It's a treat you will have to give up, madam," said Uncle.

"Who is this person?" asked Miss Jezebel's mother, staring at Uncle in a haughty way.

"He says he is the owner of this castle," said Miss Jezebel, sarcastically.

"Nonsense! Snell, turn him out."

Snell twisted his small fat hands together agitatedly.

"I'm afraid, Mrs Pointer," he said, "that he is speaking the truth. I've seen pictures of him."

"Well, I haven't," said Mrs Pointer, "and I don't believe he's the owner of anything."

"You soon will, madam," said Uncle firmly. "From today you and your family will live in one house!"

"One house, impossible!" screamed old Mrs Pointer.

"Your other dwelling will be used to ease the housing shortage in this part of my castle," continued

Uncle firmly. "You've had things your own way on this remote tower for far too long. I blame myself for not coming on a tour of inspection before this."

These words so enraged Mrs Pointer that she jumped right out of her invalid chair, seized an iron dog that was used as a door-stop for the summer-house, and hurled it at Uncle.

It missed Uncle and struck a small marble statue of Miss Jezebel Pointer dressed as Mercy and holding two marble children by the hand. It cracked the statue from top to bottom.

"That display," said Uncle, "has quite destroyed your claim to be a helpless invalid. Any person who can sling an iron dog with such energy is not very ill."

"Hear, hear!" said the Old Monkey, his eyes shining with admiration as he gazed at Uncle.

Uncle instructed Cowgill to make the machinery in the summer-house temporarily unusable and went to tell the rest of the Pointers that their houses were about to be taken over for the use of the homeless people in the gallery.

Mr Friendship Pointer said he would rather die on his own threshold than allow one homeless person to cross it, so Uncle curled his trunk round him and skimmed him like a pebble along the surface of the lake. He bounced five times, and then sank. Then he rose to the surface and started swimming to shore.

When last seen he was climbing on to the Parade, a woebegone object.

Uncle made his way back home again in a high state of satisfaction, and the Old Monkey assured him that he had never before enjoyed a birthday so much.

The Sinking Parade is still used, and on many a fine summer afternoon happy bathers enjoy the thrill of being suddenly submerged while they are sitting on benches. This is only done when they are in bathing costumes, and the machinery is under the careful supervision of Cowgill and his engineers.

17

LITTLE LIZ

One evening when Uncle was going to bed, he heard
a sort of shuffling noise at the front door and went to
see what it was. Of course he was followed by the
Old Monkey who never goes to bed till his master is
safely stowed away.

When Uncle opened the door he saw a large
bundle hanging from the handle. The handle is about
the size of a small pumpkin, for the front door of
Homeward is, of course, an elephant's front door, and
therefore extremely large.

The bundle, about three feet long, was suspended
from the knob by a thick band of leather. Uncle took
it down and carried it into the hall. There, under the
glare of the golden lamp which burns all night, he
saw at once that the bundle contained a living
creature of some sort, for movement and muffled
sound came from it.

Uncle and the Old Monkey soon had the bundle

undone, and saw that it contained a very ugly little girl dressed in a cheap sack dress, and with a handkerchief tied tightly across her mouth. A blue card was pinned to her dress, and she pointed to it, rolling her eyes, while the Old Monkey untied the handkerchief.

This is what the note said:

Dear Kind Sir,

In despair I am leaving my daughter outside your door. A person called Beaver Hateman is trying to kidnap her. If he gets her you know the sort of ransom he will ask for. I could never pay it.

Please, sir, look after my daughter. We call her Little Liz and she is loved by all. She can wash plates and cups, and never breaks more than one at a time.

Will you please shelter her till the danger passes?

Yours in distress,

AMELIA CABLEY

"I'm hungry," said Little Liz in rather a rasping voice.

"Give her some milk and a bun," said Uncle.

"One bun is no good to me," said Little Liz. "I said I was hungry."

"I didn't hear the word 'please'," said Uncle

frowning. "It is late, and a heavy meal would not be good for you."

While the little girl was wolfing a plate of buns and a quart of milk Uncle took the Old Monkey aside.

"To tell you the truth, I don't much care for the look of this girl," he said. "She reminds me of somebody I don't like – I can't think who."

"Just what I was feeling," said the Old Monkey.

"Well, we can hardly turn her adrift at this time of night. Put her to sleep in one of those disused pantries off the kitchen where you and Mig can keep an eye on her."

Little Liz went to sleep the moment she lay down on her camp bed. The Old Monkey looked at her for a bit, and then put an extra rug over her and left her.

Whom did she remind him of? He went to bed much puzzled.

Next morning, when the Old Monkey was preparing Uncle's bucket of cocoa, Little Liz bounced into the kitchen shouting:

"Any loin of pork for breakfast, Jacko?"

The Old Monkey flushed. He had never been called Jacko before, and he didn't like it. The girl's manners were really extremely bad. However, he always tried to be kind to little girls, so he said:

"Did you have a good night, my dear?"

"Rotten," she shouted. "I was dreaming about lobsters. What's for breakfast?"

Somehow the Old Monkey controlled himself.

"No loin of pork, anyway," he said. "We have ham and cocoa."

He carried the cocoa-bucket into the hall and the irritating little girl ran after him.

"Ham, goody good!" she screamed. "Who's the cook in this place?"

"Never you mind," said the Old Monkey.

As they got to the hall Uncle came majestically down the stairs, and Goodman folded the morning paper neatly and ran to him with it.

"Oh, what a horrid cat!" said Little Liz. "Keep him away from me."

Uncle put on his great horn-rimmed spectacles, and gave her a look before, which even she seemed to wilt a little.

"Take her into her room, lock her in and give her a plain breakfast, and let her stay there till she

becomes more polite," he told the Old Monkey. "Gubbins, remove her."

Gubbins had turned up to get his orders for the day, and at the sight of him Little Liz seemed to realize it was useless to rebel. She looked sulky, but she walked meekly with Gubbins to the kitchen.

"Very disagreeable girl, sir," said the Old Monkey. He seldom allows himself to say anything as severe as this.

"I call her detestable," said Uncle.

Goodman, who had run after Little Liz to make sure she wasn't up to anything, now came rushing back.

"Oh, sir," he said, "that's not a proper little girl. I've seen little girls before and they don't look like Little Liz. Don't keep her, sir. Turn her out, sir. There are lots of young rats I like better than her, sir."

Uncle looked at Goodman sternly.

"Now, Goodman," he said, "you mustn't let your worst feeling overcome you. This little girl is in danger from Beaver Hateman. We don't know where Mrs Cabley — that's her mother — lives, and until we do she must stay here."

"I don't believe she's got a mother at all!" said Goodman.

"Goodman," said Uncle even more sternly, "be merciful to the young and helpless. Remember you were once in a similar position and I—"

"I wasn't a fraud!" interrupted Goodman beside

himself. I didn't try to take you in! You're just being stupid about this girl!"

"Oh, Goodman," said the Old Monkey very shocked, "how can you speak like that?"

"You'd better go and wrap up some parcels," said Uncle, "and cool down."

Goodman went off looking upset and muttering to himself.

Uncle was busy most of the morning with cheques for maize and other correspondence, but towards the end of it the Old Monkey appeared with a twisted-up piece of paper in his hand.

"It's from Little Liz, sir," he said. "She pushed it under her door."

"Let's hope she has taken a turn for the better," said Uncle.

Little Liz had written:

REVERED and honourable UNCLE.

I am afraid I upset you a little. The word UNCLE is like music to my mother and me, and we often speak about you at dark times. Dear good sir, forgive me and let me ask you one favour. Do take me to your museum, and the dear good monkey as well. I have a feeling you don't want me in your castle much, but if you take me to the museum you'll learn where I live and I can go home.

Yours,

LITTLE LIZ

Uncle frowned as he read this.

"I don't much like the tone of this letter," he said. "It's humble enough, and yet there's a kind of cheek running through it. 'You'll learn where I live,' it says. Perhaps her mother works there! But I tell you what, I've never been to the museum. I told Blenkinsop to stock it when I bought the castle, and it's time we went to see it. I must say I look forward to the prospect of getting rid of this girl. She's nothing but a nuisance."

The Old Monkey jumped for joy. Two good things together, an interesting expedition and the hope of saying goodbye to Little Liz.

"Oh, sir, could Goodman come?" he asked. "I'm sure he's sorry for being rude."

"You can ask him," said Uncle. "To tell you the truth, I well understand how he feels, but he went too far."

The Old Monkey returned in a few minutes looking surprised.

"Goodman says thank you, sir, but if Little Liz is going he would rather stay at home."

"What is wrong with the cat?" roared Uncle. "So much fuss about a bad-mannered girl! We'll start after an early lunch – without him!"

"Very good, sir," said the Old Monkey sadly.

Little Liz behaved very well during lunch and while they were getting ready. She had a notebook in her pocket and said she was going to put down as much as she could about the specimens in the museum.

"I see by the plan that there is a tea-room at the museum," said Uncle, "so we need not take any provisions."

They started off by going into a boot-cupboard just outside the dining-room door. All they had to do was to pull one of the shelves to one side, but it was important to do that with the main door of the cupboard shut. If you left it open the shelf wouldn't move. It was crowded in the boot-cupboard with the door shut, but after a bit of shoving the shelf moved, and in front of them was a small railway siding with a very small train labelled museum.

They managed to squeeze into the carriage, though Uncle found it a tight fit, and they were wondering how to start it up when, to their surprise, Noddy Ninety appeared, wearing a train-driver's cap.

"Hello, Ninety," said Uncle. "I haven't seen you since the visit to the treasury. Is Oldeboy still going to Dr Lyre's school as I told him to?"

"Yes," said Ninety, "he goes on Tuesdays and Fridays, and he's dyed his hair grey now, silly chap."

"What are you doing here? I thought you worked on the line between Biscuit Tower and Watercress Tower?"

"I go where there's passengers, and the Museum Railway's busy today," said Ninety. "The fare's sixpence, except for you, of course, sir."

Uncle doesn't pay fares in his own castle, so Ninety had nothing to collect. He soon got the engine started.

At the first stop, which was called Rhino Halt, a thin but very happy-looking man came running to the side of the train.

"Got my museum money at last, Ninety!" he said joyfully.

"Sorry, Needler," said Ninety. "We can't take you today. Full up."

Needler burst into loud sobbing.

"After all I've done to save up! Done without lunch for nineteen days, and all to get into the museum!"

"Let him in," said Uncle; "we'll make room."

Needler's no-lunch habit had made him so thin that he slipped into a very small corner of Uncle's carriage.

Little Liz put out her tongue at him, but Uncle saw her and said sternly:

"If you do that again you will be put off at the next station!"

"I'm sorry," said Little Liz very quickly.

"Also, Needler," said Uncle, "I will pay your fare."

He handed sixpence to Ninety

Needler burst into tears of joy. It really seemed unnatural for a man to cry so much. His tears overflowed his handkerchief and fell on to the floor in a stream.

"Thank you abundantly, sir," he said. "I never thought I would see this day. The cost of living keeps going up so much. But now what joy I've got in front of me! A long lovely walk through all the museum rooms, tea – they do you well at the tea-room for a halfpenny – and then I'll buy some picture postcards and take the rest of the money home, and live like a prince for a week!"

"I'm only glad you've cheered up," said Uncle, who hates crying of any sort.

The next station was Museum Park. As soon as they got out of the train they saw a gigantic sign printed in gold:

Visitors to the Museum and Park are warned that the sight of so many marvels can be overwhelming.
We recommend, in case of faintness, *Gleamhound's Smelling Salts* for Attacks by Burglars. *2s. 6d. per bottle.*

"Luckily," said Needler, "I have a bottle of the salts with me. I knew I'd need them as I'm so excited before I start. I'll take a sniff right away."

"Wait!" said Uncle, but he was too late.

Needler had taken out a small green bottle, taken a sniff, and immediately fallen down on the platform.

"Oh dear, Mr Needler's been taken ill!" said the Old Monkey, very distressed.

"Nonsense," said Uncle. "Can't you keep it fixed in your mind that Gleamhound's remedies work backwards. Luckily I have with me some Gleamhound's Paralysing Snuff for Bandits. 'Sprinkle a little in the Bandit's face and he falls flat.' It's a first-class tonic."

Uncle sprinkled a little powder from the box on Needler's face. The effect was immediate. He sat up and said:

"What happened?"

Uncle told him.

"Have the sign altered," he said to Ninety. "It's most misleading."

"I don't think it was there yesterday," said Ninety, "but I'll see to it."

Outside the station was a motor-coach filling up with visitors to the museum. It was rather shabby and blotched with mud, and was labelled:

Roundabout Joyous Route to the Museum.
Visit Mud Ghost, Ezra Lake
and Snowstorm Volcano.

The Old Monkey said he would love to see these things, but Uncle was rather suspicious about the motor-coach as he saw in very small letters: *Manager* B..... H.T...N B...F..T underneath the direction notice.

"Who runs this coach?" he asked Ninety.

"I don't know," said Ninety, puzzled. "It wasn't here yesterday. Things seem different today. I can't make it out."

"It does look as though the Hateman crowd are somewhere about, sir," said the Old Monkey.

"I certainly don't like the look of that coach," said Uncle.

"Oh, let's go in the motor-coach!" shouted Little Liz, jumping up and down.

"We'll walk," said Uncle.

18

UNCLE'S MUSEUM

When they got outside the station, Museum Avenue stretched before them. It was called an avenue, though it was actually lined not with trees but with colossal elephants. Each was far bigger than Uncle and stood with trunk upraised.

At first it was rather impressive, but Uncle soon got tired of the long double line of elephants. One huge statue of yourself is all right, but to walk along an avenue of more than life-sized figures of yourself makes you feel small and tired.

Also Needler was counting the elephants in a dull tired voice which got on Uncle's nerves.

"Four hundred and sixty-two, four hundred and sixty—"

"What's all that counting for?" asked Uncle crossly.

"To see how many elephants."

"There are five hundred," said Uncle. "It said so on

a small notice at the beginning of the avenue. So will you please stop gargling numbers."

At last they came to a man who was sitting at a table by the side of an elephant statue. Over his head was a board with this inscription:

> WISDOM SAGE
>
> *Counsellor and General Adviser.*
> *Terms moderate if right, and*
> *immoderate if wrong.*
>
> (*N.B. Any terms are immoderate if wrong.*)

Wisdom Sage was finishing off a good lunch of roast goose and sage-and-onion stuffing.

"Hallo," he shouted as they approached. "You see here goose stuffed with sage" (pointing at his plate), "and you see here" (pointing to himself) ". . . Sage stuffed with goose!"

He burst into a peal of laughter.

Uncle hardly smiled. He was tired and wanted to get on.

"That's an old joke, Sage," he said, "but I'd like to sample your boasted wisdom. How far is it to the end of this everlasting row of elephants?"

"Three hundred yards," said Sage promptly.

Uncle was getting angry.

"If that was true," he said, "we could see the

Museum from here, and there's no sign of it!"

"Ha, ha!" said Sage. "It took Blenkinsop a long time to think out this illusion scheme. It's one of his best.

"We'll go on," said Uncle. "I suppose you want to be paid for this piece of wisdom."

"Only two-and-sixpence," said Sage. "If I had been wrong I should have charged you five shillings as wrong advice is always expensive."

Uncle tossed Sage half-a-crown which he pocketed before going on with his lunch.

They pushed forward, and after half-a-dozen more elephants there appeared to be a change in the air. There was a pearly grey mist ahead of them. Suddenly this lifted, and there, just across a large green lawn, stood the museum.

They stood still, lost in wonder.

"Blenkinsop has excelled himself," said Uncle at last.

The building was eight-sided, and made of some sort of pink stone. There were blue arches and high green pinnacles, and the front doorway was stupendous, being built of three pink rocks each as big as a house, and shining with silver stars. In spite of being so very solid, it appeared to change as you looked at it. Sometimes the pink stone turned almost green; sometimes the towers became round instead of square.

As they stood watching a tall red tower that seemed to be turning into a colossal palm-tree, Wisdom Sage came up behind them.

"I forgot to give you one opinion," he said, "but I'll give it to you now. That girl with you, d'you know what she is? She's not a girl but a snake, and that's such a very right opinion that I'll charge you nothing for it."

And he vanished into some flowering bushes.

"I don't like that man," said Little Liz, "and I'll go after him and tell him so."

"If you go back you stay back," said Uncle.

When they got to the museum entrance they found in the hall a large statue of Uncle playing the bass viol.

Underneath it were these words:

OUR FOUNDER — PATRON OF THE ARTS

Uncle was rather gratified by this, and began to hum one of the tunes he played.

"I must ring up the Maestro," he said to the Old Monkey. "It's time I had another music lesson. I've been rather pressed for time recently."

"Oh yes do, sir," said the Old Monkey, who loves going to Watercress Tower where Uncle's music master lives with his friend the Little Lion.

Little Liz giggled behind them.

Uncle turned sharply for he hates being laughed at, but the horrid girl seemed to be looking at a stuffed swordfish hanging on the wall.

"Look at that fish!" she said. "Isn't it lovely? Oh, how I'd like to see that sharp sword go right into Wisdom Sage!"

"You are a very cruel girl!" said Uncle, and determined to get rid of Little Liz the moment they got home. Meanwhile the thing to do was to forget her as much as possible. He bought a Museum Guide, and then, seeing Needler's eager look, bought another for him.

"For me, sir?" said Needler, his eyes filling with tears.

"Yes, and don't cry!" said Uncle.

"Just let me say this—" began Needler.

"Now, look, we haven't time for all that," said Uncle.

"Magnificent – lavish – noble – astonishing – glorious – gift!" said Needler. He spoke so fast it sounded like one long word. This was clearly the day of his life.

Now they all started to look at the exhibits. It was clear that they were in a very fine museum.

Besides having a Natural History section with stuffed animals in it, there was a zoo with living animals.

Here again Blenkinsop had shown great skill. The

animals were always near, and always awake. Uncle had a few cakes in his pocket, and he handed them to his party to give to the animals. Little Liz, of course, ate her portion herself.

In the Museum Guide was written:

To do honour to the Founder's well-known kindness to animals, no living creatures are kept in this zoo for more than one day. They are then dismissed to their haunts with three days' ration of choice food. Places in the Museum Zoo are much coveted and there is always a long waiting list of animals ranging from bison to wombats.

"Very gratifying, very gratifying indeed," said Uncle.

Needler had already got his handkerchief out, but seeing Uncle looking at him hastily put it away again.

They then came to a set of rooms devoted to tableaux of the Founder's Life. The first of these showed Uncle as a young, hard-up elephant. Then came his first stroke of fortune and rise to wealth and power. No hint of the regrettable bicycle-stealing incident of his youth.

It was very touching. Uncle forgave Needler's sobs of admiration.

After this they came to a room labelled:

PUBLIC ENEMIES

They were about to go in when Wisdom Sage appeared from the tea-room.

"Just another bit of *free* advice," he said. "Note, I say free. Be careful when you go in there. There is no charge for this, so take good heed of what I say. Keep your eyes open!"

"Oh do be careful, sir!" begged the Old Monkey.

On the door was a tablet.

> WE GIVE HERE A REPRESENTATION OF A HORDE OF REPULSIVE BEINGS WHO HAVE LONG INFESTED THIS NEIGHBOURHOOD. BY THE ILLUSTRIOUS EFFORTS OF THE FOUNDER THEIR EVIL DOINGS HAVE GENERALLY BEEN FOILED, AND THE PEOPLE AND ANIMALS IN THIS AREA LIVE IN PEACE AND PROSPERITY.

Uncle flung the door open.

Inside, on a low platform, stood a waxwork group showing Beaver Hateman and some of his allies. Filljug and Nailrod were a bit shadowy at the back but Hateman, well to the front, dressed in his worst sack suit and holding a duck bomb ready to throw, really looked very life-like.

With Sage's warning still in his ears, Uncle only took one look and then dropped to the ground.

It was lucky he did so, for the waxwork figure came to life and Beaver Hateman cast the duck

bomb at Uncle, using immense force. At the same moment Uncle felt a sharp pain in his leg as Little Liz stuck a skewer into it.

Now the hideous plot was clear. Little Liz had used Uncle's well-known kindness of heart to lure him to the museum.

"Oh, sir, Little Liz is Hitmouse!" shouted the Old Monkey. "Look out, sir! Look out!"

"Oh, infamy!" sobbed Needler, tears spouting from his eyes.

Trumpeting with rage Uncle charged forward, but the danger was over. Seeing that his duck bomb had missed, and had only splashed harmlessly against the passage wall, Beaver Hateman gave an appalling shriek of baffled fury and disappeared down a trapdoor in the floor of the case, and Hitmouse, well, the last they saw of that detestable so-called little girl was the hem of a sack dress vanishing down a ventilator.

Fortunately Uncle was hardly hurt at all. He had a few skewer stabs, but some Magic Ointment, skilfully applied by the Old Monkey, soon put them right.

Needler hung his handkerchief to dry out of a near-by open window. He had been crying so much that his eyes had nearly disappeared.

"Is the danger really past, sir?" he asked. "I've hardly any tears left."

"Good, you won't need any. All is well," said Uncle, once more erect and masterful as he turned to Sage.

"Well, Sage," he said, "your wisdom has saved us from great harm."

He pulled a bag of gold out of his pocket, for although he usually doesn't carry much money he had brought some that day to pay for teas, etc.

"Oh, I don't want anything," said Sage. "I was so very right I can't make any charge."

"Then," said Uncle, "you will please accept this as a token of our great gratitude."

"Very well," replied Sage, "if you put it that way. Goose is dear, and my income is not large. I'm so frequently right."

"And now," said Uncle, "let's go to the tea-room, and have the very best tea they've got."

They soon found the tea-room, an excellent place partly below the museum and looking out on a sunken garden.

The garden kept changing. Some of the roses

changed slowly from red to yellow, and some of the bigger flowers actually seemed to come forward and look through the window. In the middle of the lawn was a fountain which sent up a great column of water that curved into a beautiful water-arch. This was big enough to walk under. Now and then pale blue-and-white clouds floated through the garden.

Nine black bears brought in the tea. There were some cakes that almost overpowered you, they were so rich and scented.

While they ate they looked at the postcards Needler had bought. There were two of the outside of the museum and a very good one of the statue of Uncle playing the bass viol.

"Get a couple of those on the way out," said Uncle to the Old Monkey. "I'd like to send one to my aunt, Miss Maidy, and also one to the Maestro."

"Shall I bring you some Blenkinsop Buns?" asked one of the bears when they had been eating for a time. "They're the best of all."

"By all means," said Uncle. "Let's try them."

Blenkinsop Buns looked like ordinary currant buns, but their taste kept changing. One moment they tasted like raspberry jam, the next like honey, and then like banana ice-cream.

"Oh, sir, can I take a Blenkinsop Bun home to Goodman?" asked the Old Monkey. "He's missed so much by not coming to the museum."

"Take one certainly," said Uncle. "In a way we owe the cat an apology. He was quite right to be so suspicious. To think we were giving shelter to the detestable Hitmouse."

"The disguise was very cunning sir," said the Old Monkey, "but we must be more careful in future."

19

THE GREAT SALE

The sale of bananas and coconuts in aid of aged and distressed badgers which, you'll remember, Uncle had been asked to open, was about to take place.

The King of the Badgers was organizing it, and it looked as if everybody was giving something, and thousands of people were coming.

Truckloads of bananas and coconuts came in every day. Great traction engines pulling trailers loaded with Whang Eggs, a sort of preserved egg painted red specially loved by aged badgers, arrived almost hourly.

Six motor-coaches had been ordered for the day to bring people from Wolftown. Ivan Koff had postponed a meeting of the Dog-Washers' League, so that he might give a vote of thanks to Uncle.

Even doubtful characters like Sir Ben Bandit, the financier, Abdullah the Clothes-Peg Merchant and Mother Jones (from Jones's siding) had sent gifts and promised to come.

The day before the sale, the King of the Badgers came to see Uncle to make final arrangements.

"A surprising letter in the post this morning," he said. "Beaver Hateman and all his supporters have written to say they intend to come to the sale, and whatever you, my dear sir, decide to give, they will give more."

"A good statement," said Uncle, "if we can believe it."

"I know you have not yet said what your gift will be, but if you do now perhaps sheer pride will drive this somewhat shifty character to make a great effort to exceed it."

"I warn you," said Uncle, "that Beaver Hateman will think nothing of promising a million crates of bananas and then declaring himself bankrupt."

"Too true, I'm afraid," said the King sadly.

"Therefore," said Uncle, "I see no reason to alter my original plan, and that is to declare what I am going to give on the day. It will be a great surprise, I assure you."

"Oh, I'm certain of that," said the King. "We must just try to be patient."

The sale was to be held in the Badgertown Stadium. A great field had been walled in and thousands of seats had been built round it in tiers. The platform for the opening had been built out a little way into the amphitheatre, and raised so that all

who were on it were in full view. There was a table
in front of Uncle's chair with a microphone on it.
Uncle does not need a microphone of course, his
voice of thunder can reach the limit of any building.

The working committee, under the supervision of
the King himself, had piled round the platform a
positive mountain of bananas, coconuts and Whang
Eggs.

When the great day came, Uncle put on his best
purple dressing-gown, his elephant boots with
diamond tips, and a gold hat embroidered with
rubies. He also carried his festival watch, a great
time-piece almost like a small clock and so covered
with jewels that it was hard to see the hands. A special
gold-plated traction engine had also been brought
out to take him to the stadium.

What a day it promised to be! The sky was blue,
the air soft and mild, and as the morning went on
files of creatures could be seen crossing the plain on
their way to the sale. Even grizzly bears were coming
from the mountains, and carrying coconuts too.

After lunch a big crowd of Uncle's followers
gathered for the ride to the stadium. There was no
need to leave a strong party behind to guard
Homeward as Beaver Hateman and his party were
actually seen setting out for the sale in old carts,
sledges and on broken-down motor-bikes.

Goodman, looking through the field-glasses,

reported that he thought they were all there, Beaver Hateman, Hitmouse, Jellytussle, Nailrod, and Filljug, to name only a few.

"And Beaver Hateman's got on what looks like a better suit than usual," said Goodman.

"Good," said Uncle. "Let us hope that for once their black hearts have been touched!"

They had a good ride to the stadium. The traction engine was burning sandalwood, and made the air fragrant as they rode along.

Bells rang and trumpets sounded a loud fanfare as Uncle entered the stadium. The King of the Badgers led the way to the platform where a huge chair had been provided for Uncle, and a small gilded throne for himself.

A number of aged and worthy badgers were placed on either side of Uncle, and the Old Monkey and Goodman were given seats near him to represent the many inhabitants of Homeward.

As the procession of dignitaries mounted the platform, the Badfort crowd entered to take seats near it. They looked almost respectable for once. Beaver Hateman was wearing a new sack suit made out of a potato-bag. There was not a skewer to be seen about Hitmouse, Jellytussle was shaking quietly but far less objectionably than usual, and the ghost Hootman slid in a polite shadowy way into a seat.

Before the ceremony began a hundred young badgers sang a melody: "Hail to Glorious Uncle."

It went well, too, though Beaver Hateman was seen to stop his ears, and Nailrod Hateman sneezed all the time.

The King of the Badgers then spoke:

"Ladies and Gentlemen," he said, "it does me good to see such a vast gathering. Friends from near at hand, and wolves, tigers and bears from remote forests. I am particularly glad, too, to see our hardy adventurous neighbours from Badfort."

At this moment Beaver Hateman's followers broke into their tribal cheer, a deafening yell of "Stinggoon! Stinggoon!"

When he could make himself heard again the King continued:

"But I am sure I voice all your feelings when I say that the most glorious feature of this assembly today is the presence of the much-loved owner of the Homeward Castle—"

There was tremendous cheering. To Uncle's surprise Beaver Hateman kept quiet, only stopping up his ears and squinting.

When Uncle rose to speak there was deafening applause that lasted for nearly ten minutes.

"Your Majesty, friends and neighbours," he began. "I think I can say that I am always in sympathy with those who are less fortunate than myself."

Uncle was so sure that Hateman would object that he stopped and looked at him, but Hateman merely sniffed loudly.

"I'm glad this great effort is being made," Uncle went on. "Many need this help. Great quantities of bananas, coconuts and Whang Eggs have been given, and now, my friends, buy and give all you can. I now come to my own personal contribution."

There was a dead silence in the stadium. Even the Badfort crowd stopped shuffling, sneezing and sniffing.

Uncle put his hand in his pocket and took out one banana, one coconut and one Whang Egg.

"These are what I mean to give," he said.

There was a moment of shocked silence, and then Hateman yelled:

"A rotten beggarly gift and from the richest man here! I was going to give a million bananas myself, but now I'll give nothing, and I'll show what I think by clearing out now! Give them a joberry, boys!"

Hateman's followers all filed out, singing a hideous song, rattling sticks, and snatching bananas from the pile at the base of the platform.

When they had gone Uncle continued:

"I will now finish the sentence I began before I was interrupted. At all times I wish to avoid the appearance of display, so I began my speech very quietly. I repeat: my gift will be one banana, one coconut, and one Whang Egg—" he paused impressively – "for every minute of the next five years. Some of you who are good at arithmetic can work out what that means!"

The badgers are not good at arithmetic, but they knew this meant a vast number, and their applause was deafening.

While the cheering was going on the King of the Badgers motioned to his court mathematician, Professor Badgerinstein, and had a whispered exchange with him.

As soon as the cheering stopped the King said:

"Professor Badgerinstein has gone to feed the figures into the court computer. We now await the results of the calculations. Meanwhile, I can safely say that all sick and aged badgers will be splendidly looked after for years to come. Now one more cheer for our benefactor—"

Uncle gave one smile round, waved his trunk, and took his seat, perhaps a trifle heavily, in the huge chair provided for him.

Then tragedy struck.

There was a sudden appalling crash and Uncle, his chair, and his table disappeared together into the hollow place beneath the platform. For a moment everybody was struck dumb. Then a great cloud of dust rose and obscured the platform. This was no ordinary dust. It seemed to have pepper in it, and everybody was taken with violent sneezing.

Even while sneezing, the Old Monkey and Goodman managed to crawl to the edge of the jagged hole and peer into it.

But there was nothing to see – even when the dust subsided. Uncle had disappeared. So had his table and chair, and the piece of platform on which he had stood. All that was left of this splendid presence was the great jewelled festival watch which must have had fallen from him as the platform gave way. The Old Monkey gathered it up, weeping.

"It was sawn through. The platform was sawn nearly through!" said Goodman. "Look, look!"

Goodman and the Old Monkey examined the broken edge of wood, and while they were doing so Badgertown police arrived and confirmed their suspicions. The whole square of platform on which Uncle's chair had been placed needed only the extra pressure given by Uncle as he sat down after his speech to collapse entirely.

Loud wailing arose, and everywhere groups of

melancholy badgers began searching for their benefactor.

Darkness was coming on, and the Old Monkey was distracted. There seemed no clue, no hope.

All at once there was a clatter of hooves, and a lean man wearing a cowboy hat rode up on a sweating horse. He was called Wolfskin Webber and lived near Badfort on the Wolftown side.

"You lookin' fer der big guy?" he shouted.

"Yes, yes," came from a thousand anxious voices.

"Wal, I jest cam' ridin' pas' Badfort, and I see a lot o' dem Hateman guys with a big furniture van. They was laffin' fit ter split."

"Go on, go on," gasped the Old Monkey. "Did you see inside the van?"

"Nope, I never," said Wolfskin Webber, "I don't hang aroun' dem guys no more n' I kin help, but I hear a sorter trumpetin' and buttin'—"

This was it. The terrible secret was out. A council of war was held at once with the Old Monkey acting as chairman. It was clear now that a furniture van with a sliding open top had been backed in below the platform, and that when the floor had given way Uncle had been dropped neatly in, and had at once been motored off to Badfort. And while this was being done, the rest of the Badfort crowd had thrown pepper in the air to confuse his friends and make a quick getaway possible.

The position was indeed grave.

"Back to Homeward," said Captain Walrus, "to collect stone clubs and other fighting materials – and then make a united attack on Badfort."

The meeting agreed that this was the best thing to do.

"But it will take time!" said the Old Monkey. "I can't wait. He may be very stunned and tortured. I must go and do what I can!"

"I'll come with you," said Goodman.

Captain Walrus and Cowgill promised to get things quickly organized at Homeward, and the Old Monkey and Goodman started for Badfort. They knew they were going into terrible danger but they had to do it.

"Luckily I've got my savings in a money-bag under my shirt," said the Old Monkey. "I often carry it with me in case of need."

"That gives me an idea," said Goodman. "Today's Tuesday, and Blenkinsop has a branch at Sable Gulf that is open from six to six-thirty. We might just catch him. Let's see if he can think of anything."

"He'll take too long," said the Old Monkey miserably. "You remember the short cut to the dwarfs' drinking fountains!"

"You never know," said Goodman. "As it's urgent he might hurry for once!"

They were pleased to see a light still burning in

Blenkinsop's small wooden hut in Sable Gulf. Not far beyond towered the vast, black bulk of Badfort.

Luckily the wizard had stayed late, for people had been so occupied with the sale that he knew that any customers needing spells would only come after it was over.

"Wizard," panted the Old Monkey, desperately, "I need your help – now, quickly!"

The Old Monkey was so out of breath – he isn't as used to running as Goodman is – that Goodman had to tell the tale of the kidnapping.

"I'll help, of course," said Blenkinsop. "Wait a minute while I get a kangle-pot and a bit of moon-misty flamingo, and—"

"Please, please, Mr Blenkinsop," pleaded the Old Monkey. "I can't wait while you do a spell, I can't!"

"I can't promise results without a spell," said Blenkinsop.

"What about Clutchclamp?" said Goodman.

"What d'you know about Clutchclamp?" said Blenkinsop crossly.

"I signed for the registered parcel at Wizard Glen when you bought some," said Goodman. "I remember what a fuss you made about it being so valuable and putting it in the safe at once. And I—"

"What is Clutchclamp?" interrupted the Old Monkey. "Do hurry!"

"Clutchclamp! That's a good idea," said

Blenkinsop, "and I have a small quantity here. But it won't do. It costs too much!"

"*Give* it to us," said Goodman. "Surely you can do that for once! For Uncle. Come on, give it to us – free!"

"If you knew anything about wizard work," said Blenkinsop, "you'd know Clutchclamp won't work unless paid for *in cash*!"

"Prove it!" cried Goodman excitedly. "Prove it! Go on. Can't you see the situation's desperate? Give it us now! I always remember how mean you were over saucers of milk and the way you—"

"*I* can pay for Clutchclamp, whatever it is – now," said the Old Monkey.

"I doubt it," said Blenkinsop. "It is a rare pill which makes the person who swallows it invisible. It also opens locked doors. And – it costs exactly one hundred pounds!"

"I have a hundred pounds four shillings and sixpence," almost shouted the Old Monkey, fumbling for his well-worn wallet, "all my savings – here."

"Who'd have thought it!" said Blenkinsop.

"*You'd* never give all your savings to help *any*body – that I do know!" cried Goodman.

"You'd better be more polite or I'll put a spell on

413

you!" Blenkinsop warned him.

Blenkinsop went to a small safe and brought out a round green box in which lay one bright pink pill.

"Swallow that," Blenkinsop told the Old Monkey. "It will last for twenty-four hours."

The Old Monkey swallowed the pill, and sent Goodman to Homeward to say what he had done, and to urge them to hurry with preparations for the attack.

The Old Monkey, feeling very frightened, for he was still not sure if the pill would work, walked up to the front gate of Badfort. A sentry was there, sitting on a barrel with a crossbow by his side, but as the Old Monkey went past him he only moved slightly to take another banana from a pile in front of him.

The Old Monkey felt better. He really was invisible.

In the big front hall of Badfort a monster meeting was being held, presided over by Beaver Hateman. The Old Monkey paused by the open door to listen.

Sigismund Hateman was singing a song with a chorus of "Stinggoon" which everybody yelled.

"See that pompous humbug Unc
On the platform raise his trunk,"

sang Sigismund, and the rest all shouted: "Stinggoon!
Stinggoon! STINGGOON!"

"Watch him spouting like a pump,
Watch him *sit*, the oily lump:
That's the moment –
  CRUMP!
    CRUMP!
      CRUMP!"

At every 'CRUMP' they stamped their feet; then
they burst again into the chorus:

"Stinggoon! Stinggoon! STINGGOON!"

The Old Monkey felt shaken. Although he was
invisible the loud singing and rhythmic stamping
frightened him.

"We'll have a million out of the old
dog at the lowest ransom!"
bellowed Beaver
Hateman. He
threw a Black
Tom   bottle
out   of   the

door, just missing the Old Monkey. It struck the sentry, and stunned him.

"So much the better for us when the attack begins!" thought the Old Monkey, shuddering as he hurried on.

He did not know where to go in the rickety galleries of Badfort. There were hundreds of rooms, many with the roofs falling in, and all the passages were piled with rubble and broken glass. The only light was an occasional gleam from a scob-oil lamp.

He dared not call Uncle's name for fear the party below might hear. What could he do?

He was just standing at the door of a miserable room labelled 'Burglar's Outfits' and feeling hopeless, when he remembered what Blenkinsop had said about Clutchclamp.

"It will make you invisible and open doors."

"I'll trust to the magic," thought the Old Monkey, and felt a sudden urge to turn round and go back. He returned nearly to the entrance. In the corner there was a big stone staircase he had not noticed before, and his feet seemed to go up the broken dirty steps without any effort.

At the top of the steps there was a huge door fastened with a chain and a big lock, and before he could even use his magic power and go through it he heard a firm voice beyond it saying:

"I'll never pay that scoundrel a ransom of a million

pounds! No, I will not, even if I stay here all my life!"

The Old Monkey's heart was filled with delight. He had found Uncle.

20

THE RESCUE

As he looked at the massive iron-bound door, the Old Monkey repeated to himself as bravely as he could: "That door will open."

To his unspeakable joy the door began to open slowly and softly. No rattling of chains.

Uncle did not see it move for he was peering out of a small barred window.

"Sir!" whispered the Old Monkey.

Uncle turned and saw the open door. Nobody was there. Nobody. Was this a trick?

He stood there watchful, wondering.

"I'm here to help you, sir," whispered the Old Monkey.

"Where are you?" asked Uncle, looking in the air, everywhere. "I can't see you!"

"Shush, sir! Don't speak so loudly. I'm invisible because of Blenkinsop's spell! I am here, really, sir, right here in the doorway—" The story poured out

419

of him. He was so excited he could hardly keep his voice in a whisper.

When Uncle had heard him through, the old ring came back into his voice, his eyes flashed. He was feeling himself again.

"You have done magnificently," he said, "and I shan't forget it! Now let's take a look at these gentry downstairs. You say a strong party is on the way from Homeward?"

"Yes, sir."

"If only I had a stone club or two!"

They crept down the stairs. At the bottom was a recess.

"Look, sir!" whispered the Old Monkey.

There were two weighty objects fastened to the wall, and written underneath them were the words:

These stone clubs were captured from the Dictator of Homeward by B. Hateman Esq., m.a., and are placed here as trophies of his skill.

"That's better!" said Uncle, pulling them from the wall.

"Excuse me, sir," said the Old Monkey, "I've still got the power of the spell in me, and we're passing over a trapdoor. I can see through it and directly below are two great underground vats filled with Black Tan and Leper Jack."

"Open the trapdoor," said Uncle, "and prop it open with stones."

It was easy enough to do this as there are always lots of stones scattered about in Badfort. The singing and shouting were loud now, and soon they stood in the doorway of the celebration room.

Beaver Hateman, at the head of the long stone table, had just risen, smiling hideously, to speak.

"Well, lads," he said. "This is the best day's work we've ever done. We've got the Dictator safe at last – twenty rescue parties can't get him out of that upstairs room! Let's visit him and tell him the ransom terms. That'll make him suffer!"

"Can I stick a skewer into him, sir?" said Hitmouse. "I've made a big one!"

"Of course, of course, and see a strong article about the meanness of millionaires goes into the *Badfort News* tomorrow. Come on, boys!"

"Stinggoon!" came the harsh, sonorous chorus as everybody rose.

At that moment Beaver Hateman saw Uncle. He seemed, hardened as he was, to turn to stone.

As he stood staring at the massive figure, holding the two clubs there was a clatter of many feet outside, and above that sound the voice of Captain Walrus could be heard raised in true sea-dog thunder.

"Steady! Keep your eyes lifted for the swabs. Marlinspikes ready!"

Beaver Hateman dived under the table and slithered past Uncle's legs like a maddened snake.

But Uncle turned just in time. Beaver Hateman made straight for the open space in the centre of Badfort. Uncle knew well that he planned to get lost in the maze of rooms which surrounded it. This he was determined to prevent.

Uncle thundered after him, and caught him just as he was getting near the office of the Badfort News on the other side of the square.

Even for Uncle it was a great kick-up.

Beaver Hateman was holding a huge lighted cigar in his hand, and the wind made it glow so that everybody could see in the sky what looked like a slowly soaring red light.

Then it came down, down, down, towards Gaby's Marsh.

In the meantime Captain Walrus and his party were driving the rest of the Badfort crowd before them with blow after blow. Some managed to escape into the rickety galleries, but most were forced into the same marsh, filled with barking conger eels and biting crabs, in which their leader lay engulfed.

And Uncle had not finished yet. He seized a scob-oil lamp and flung it through the open trapdoor into the underground tank filled with Leper Jack.

"Everybody get out!" shouted Uncle to his party.

At once, in the entrance to Badfort, a great eruption took place. The liquids stored in the vats were fearfully inflammable, and one set fire to the other. The flames mounted into a ghastly fountain of purple fire. This lit the countryside for many miles, and all Badfort seemed turned into a leaping mass of sinister flame.

Uncle and his party stood for a minute or two watching, and then Uncle said:

"We will now quietly and joyfully march home, our pathway lit by the destruction of the vilest castle of infamy ever constructed."

In the hall of Homeward Uncle suggested they had a short festive supper and then went to bed. It seemed funny to see a flagon of hot cocoa apparently approaching Uncle by itself, for the Old Monkey was still invisible, of course. He played a very good trick on Goodman, going into a corner and squeaking like a rat. You should have seen the way Goodman dashed to catch a rat that wasn't there! Everybody laughed very much, and so did Goodman.

"As for tomorrow," said Uncle, "we will have a quiet day of festive congratulation by ourselves, when the Old Monkey, and all of you, will be suitably rewarded."

"But everybody will want to come, sir," said Captain Walrus.

"If they like to come we can't stop; them," said Uncle, "but no public festival is to be arranged."

But they all knew nothing could stop the next day being observed as a day of revelling.

Uncle was soon in bed and snoring happily, but Cowgill said to Captain Walrus:

"I say, old chap, don't you think we'd better have a few illuminations and flags for tomorrow night? It won't take long to arrange."

I agree with you," said the Captain, "and I've got a special electric star in my lighthouse that I've been wanting to try out for months."

So they all went to bed, after a last glance out of the window to see if Badfort was still burning. It was, though not as violently as it had been.

Next morning, when Uncle awoke, the Old Monkey was already by his bedside. The spell had now worn off and Uncle smiled when he saw him.

"Ah, nice to see you again, my friend," he said. "You look none the worse for your terrible experiences, I'm glad to say."

"Neither do you, sir," said the Old Monkey. "The King of the Badgers is already here with an illuminated address for you."

"I said no public rejoicing," said Uncle, "but it's well meant. Show him in."

The King of the Badgers had already had breakfast, but he joined Uncle in a golden flagon of cocoa.

He told Uncle it would be impossible to prevent crowds of people from coming to congratulate him personally.

"Well," said Uncle, "I shall see they are well provisioned, but my chief purpose today is to make a presentation to the Old Monkey."

After the king had gone Uncle and the Old Monkey had a look through the telescope at Badfort. The volcano of flame had pretty well burnt itself out, but Badfort, although even more battered than before, was still standing. The fact is it's not very inflammable, as nearly all the doors and windows have been used for firewood.

"It can't be helped," said Uncle. "At any rate they have had a terrific lesson."

By the evening many thousands of visitors had arrived and it seemed impossible to avoid some sort of public ceremony.

Uncle and the Old Monkey sat side by side on a marble bench supported by six stone lions, and after a few words of congratulation from the King, Uncle spoke.

"Friends," he said, "it is always encouraging when skilfully laid schemes of crime come to nothing, and you have all been rejoicing with me in a mighty and glorious victory. I greatly value the many unexpected gifts that have been sent to me. It is hard to single out any when all have been so good, but I was greatly touched when your revered monarch brought from his private art gallery a hitherto unknown picture of myself opening the dwarfs' drinking fountains. It is by the great artist Waldovenison Smeare, and, as you know, his works are practically priceless.

"I thank you all for your kind thoughts. Most of all I thank all my supporters for their prompt and brave support last night. Under the leadership of Captain Walrus, you all, Cowgill, Cloutman and Gubbins, Mig, Butterskin Mute, and Whitebeard, formed a strong attacking party. Goodman the cat used his knowledge of spells to get Wizard Blenkinsop to act swiftly. Mr Will Shudder and Mr Benskin held the fort here. All behaved nobly, and I thank you, but my chief desire today is to give special honour to my faithful friend, the Old Monkey. Last night he outdid all his previous achievements. Alone he made his way to Badfort, after spending the whole of his life savings in the purchase of one powerful spell with which he succeeded in liberating me!"

Here the applause became deafening.

"He put down one hundred pounds to save me. All he had. I now take this bag containing one thousand gold pieces and hand it to him."

Screams of delight greeted this.

"All I have left to say," continued Uncle, "is that I would give my friend far more, but he has scarcely room to stow it. I will merely say he can always count on me to the full resources of my fortune."

Uncle seized the Old Monkey in his trunk, and, holding him high above the crowd, said:

"Three cheers for the most faithful friend in the world!"

As Uncle put the Old Monkey gently down again the King of the Badgers came forward with a glittering medal attached to a broad golden ribbon.

"The King of the Badgers," Uncle announced, "wishes to bestow on the Old Monkey the highest honour in his kingdom. Our friend now becomes a Knight of Bustard Land!"

The order was bestowed, and the cheering began again. As it was at last dying down, Uncle held up his trunk for silence.

"And now, my friends," he said, "I want you to spend the rest of the evening in rejoicing. Cowgill, please turn on the illuminations."

Uncle had hardly stopped speaking before everywhere shone out in blue, red, silver, green and yellow light, and high, high, above Lion Tower, on the edge of which Walrus Tower stands like a pencil, shone Captain Walrus's tremendous new star.

The revelry was in full swing when a young badger brought Uncle a letter that had just been handed in at the gate.

It was from Beaver Hateman and read as follows:

To the Dictator and Swindler

So you got away last night did you, you oily bounder? Just like you to set our noble mansion on fire, but I'll tell you, you firebug, that you did us a good turn. All the money-lenders' offices have been burnt out. We owed a lot to these gentry, but now all the books and I.O.U.s are burnt and we are free of debt!

I said we would get a lot out of you and we have.

We are at once starting a revenge so fearful that anyone who speaks of it will develop lockjaw.

B.H.

"That fellow takes some putting down, I must say," said Uncle. "He'd get out of anything."

The Old Monkey was looking through the telescope at Badfort.

"They've got out some broken chairs and made a little fire. I think I can hear faint singing, sir. They seem to be having some sort of party."

"Party!" said Uncle in disgust. "Come, let's forget them and have a good sleep and then a few days of congratulation and comfort."

RED FOX STORY COLLECTIONS

Do you enjoy getting into the spirit
of things? Step into the supernatural with the
assortment of unearthly tales in SPOOKY
STORIES. Experience the weird and wonderful
worlds discovered in FREAKY STORIES and
marvel at the amazing stories collected in
MAGICAL MYSTERY STORIES.

MAGICAL MYSTERY STORIES
The Conjuror's Game by Catherine Fisher
The Thirteenth Owl by Nick Warburton
Words of Stone by Kevin Henks
0 09 940262 9 £4.99

FREAKY STORIES
The Runton Werewolf by Richie Perry
Henry Hollis and the Dinosaur by Willis Hall
Tom's Amazing Machine by Gordon Snell
0 09 940174 6 £4.99

SPOOKY STORIES
Seven Strange and Ghostly
Tales by Brian Jacques
The Creepy Tale by
Pichie Perry
A Legacy of Ghosts by
Colin Dann
0 09 940184 3 £4.99

RED FOX STORY COLLECTIONS

This series of value-for-money paperbacks each comprise several of your favourite stories in a single volume! Whether you want to follow the action-packed adventures of Hal and Roger Hunt in THE ADVENTURE COLLECTION or discover the myths surrounding Arthur and his Knights of the Round Table in KING ARTHUR STORIES these bumper reads are full of epic adventures and magical mystery.

THE ADVENTURE COLLECTION
by Willard Price
Whale Adventure and African Adventure
0 09 926592 3 £4.99

BIGGLES STORY COLLECTION
by Captain W. E. Johns
Biggles in France
Biggles Defend the Desert
Biggles: Foreign Legionnaire
0 09 940154 1 £4.99

KING ARTHUR STORIES
by Rosemary Sutcliff
The Sword and the Circle
The Light Beyond the Forest
The Road to Camlann
0 09 940164 9 £4.99

RED FOX STORY COLLECTIONS

If you are looking for a little animal magic then these brilliant bind-ups bring you stories of every creature, great and small. There are the fantastic creatures that Doctor Dolittle lives and works with in DOCTOR DOLITTLE STORIES, the bold and brave animals described in ANIMAL STORIES and there are three memorable tales of horse riding and friendship in PONY STORIES.

DOCTOR DOLITTLE STORIES
by Hugh Lofting
Selected stories from the Doctor Dolittle Books
0 09 926593 1 £4.99

ANIMAL STORIES
The Winged Colt of Casa Mia by Betsy Byars
Stories from Firefly Island by Benedict Blathwayt
Farthing Wood, The Adventure Begins
by Colin Dann
0 09 926583 4 £4.99

PONY STORIES
A Summer of Horses by
Carol Fenner
Fly-by-Night by K. M. Peyton
Three to Ride by Christine
Pullein-Thompson
0 09 940003 0 £4.99